JUDGE NOT

A Sam Tate Mystery

by
Nikki Stern

**Ruthenia
Press**

445 Sayre Drive
Princeton, NJ 08540

ISBN: 978-0-9995487-9-0 (print book)
      978-0-9995487-8-3 (ebook)
LCCN: 978-0-9995487-9-0

Library of Congress Cataloging-in-Publication Data is on file with the Library of Congress.

Acknowledgments

This one's for the super fans, loyal readers who pushed me out of a tough time and back into the world of Sam Tate. I don't know what I'd do without you.

Steve Axelrod, author of the Henry Kennis mystery series for Poison Pen Press, performed his usual insightful structural editing wizardry. Lisa Romeo, a widely published essayist and memoir author, offered much needed copy editing. And thank goodness for the invaluable services of proofreader Jeanette DeMain.

Diana Ani Stokely of GRAFIX to go has once again applied her talent to the cover design and her patience to the arduous task of typesetting. Special hugs to Barry and Eve Doyle, who helped me set the scene for the last part of the book and whose lifestyle remains an inspiration to me.

Judge not, that ye be not judged. For with what judgment ye judge, ye shall be judged: and with what measure ye mete, it shall be measured to you again.

— Matthew 7:1-2

Chapter 1

His name was John, aka Jack Frost. He would become the first victim in a multi-state killing spree that put law enforcement on high alert, involved multiple agencies, and placed Sam Tate in the center of the most dangerous case of her career.

Frost never had a clue.

On his last day on earth, the Sacramento homicide detective reported to his precinct as usual. It was a beautiful April morning. He had little on his plate, just one open case. Six months from retirement, he wasn't choosing to rest on his laurels, but if work slowed from time to time, he wasn't about to argue.

Spring fever had taken hold of most of the officers on duty and no wonder. People were finally rid of their pandemic masks and only the surliest naysayers grumbled, "until the next one." Sacramento had a lot going for it—the mountains on one side, the ocean on the other, plenty of entertainment, strong sports teams, and a growing economy. The weeks between late March and mid-June, though, were in a class by themselves, with mild temperatures, plenty of sunshine, and wildflowers in abundance.

Frost stood outside the precinct at midday, indulging in a cigarette and considering his good fortune. He felt content, a state of grace he never expected to reach. Yes, he missed his Ellen. They'd been married twenty years and she'd been gone ten. Memories consoled him, as did the presence in his life of his daughter and her husband, a good man, and their two well-adjusted children.

His professional life had been likewise satisfactory. He loved his work. Fairly routine, except for one case twenty-two years earlier that had briefly made him a statewide celebrity. A perp (Frost still thought of assailants that way) who the media dubbed the Back-To-School Killer had murdered five teachers, two in September, two in January after the winter break, and another following spring break. The women were stabbed in the eye and left in front of three different middle schools, along with black and white notebooks. Some of the bodies were discovered by students arriving early. The community was afraid and outraged.

After the first death, Frost and his partner, Lonnie DeMarco, looked for a connection between the victim and the killer. Maybe he was an ex-boyfriend or husband. Maybe he'd been her student, someone who felt unfairly singled out or ignored in class. Maybe she'd expelled his son.

When the second body dropped ten days later, Frost began to consider the bigger picture. The murderer had a problem with teachers in general. Was he a serial killer? Bodies three and four confirmed it. The California Bureau of Investigation came on to help. Still, no break in the case.

By that time, most of the state knew about the Back-To-School Killer. Officials considered canceling the annual state educators conference, scheduled for downtown. When CBI and local police promised both visible and undercover protection, they relented.

Frost posed as an elementary-school history teacher. He made friends, attended a few lectures, and kept an eye out for anyone out of place.

The second day, he noticed a small man with a large briefcase skulking through the crowded hallways. When the man reached inside to retrieve a piece of paper, Frost contrived to bump into him.

As he'd expected, the contents of the briefcase spilled onto the carpet: a dozen notebooks, a small bottle of chloroform, and a lethal-looking stiletto. The piece of paper contained the names of twelve attendees, all women.

The suspect turned out to be a long-ago student traumatized by a grade-school teacher. He kept his phobia repressed until his daughter became engaged to a professor. The killer confessed on the spot and pleaded guilty in a packed courthouse some months later.

Frost and DeMarco were feted and offered promotions. Each declined, but they agreed to represent the department (along with the chief, naturally) to the media. There was a trip to the Governor's Mansion, a couple of national interviews, and a ceremony where the mayor gave them keys to the city as Frost's proud family looked on.

Nothing remotely as exciting ever happened again. Cancer took both his partner and his wife. His daughter married and moved to Los Angeles. He spent the holidays with his grandkids and tried to imagine a life of retirement. The daughter had it on good authority that security jobs in LA were plentiful, especially for a one-time cop with a headline-making case on his resume.

Frost clocked out at five, picked up Chinese, and headed to his one-story, three-bedroom house. It had always felt a little cramped. Now he rattled around in it. If he sold while the market was hot, he might be able to afford a tiny condo in Los Angeles.

At the edge of nightfall, he heard a knock. He opened the door to a smiling face. "Hi," the visitor said, handing him a black and white notebook.

Frost looked down. Rookie mistake. He jerked his head up in time to see the sharp object pierce his cornea and make its way into his brain.

Chapter 2

Lieutenant Sam Tate spun in her new chair, a gift from the department, according to Sheriff Tanner. He'd also granted her a more flexible work week, which gave her a half-day off on Fridays. A raise would have been preferable, but Sam wasn't about to quibble.

The half-days off meant she could spend time in D.C. with FBI Assistant Director Terry Sloan. Their work kept them seventy miles apart. The arrangement wasn't going to be long-term, not that she knew what lay next. For now, she was content with a steady man who loved her, a new house, and a rescued mixed-breed named Jax.

She still longed to put to bed her nagging questions over the wedding shooting that destroyed her family. At least the nightmares that had plagued her since childhood appeared less frequently.

Her professional life was something else. Seven months after she apprehended the Dry Ice Killer in New York during a two-week vacation in Manhattan, she went back to her job as Criminal Commander for the Talbot County Sheriff's Office on Maryland's Eastern Shore.

Being second in command gave her some power. She loved her team, respected her boss, appreciated the opportunity. But she was relegated to staying in place.

Sam hated the idea that she'd reached her peak at thirty-eight years old. She wasn't about to find another position, not when she'd held four jobs in eleven years. She missed being a detective. Her therapist told her she was on her way to a new life, one that might put the bad dreams behind her for good. She just needed to be patient.

"Ha!" she said aloud. Jax raised his head to look at her, prompting an affectionate smile. "All okay, good boy," she said. Satisfied, he let out a sigh of contentment and returned to his nap, only to be startled by a knock on the door.

"Got a minute, Lieutenant?" The lanky young man who popped his head in always made Sam smile. His quick thinking on a serial case last year earned him a promotion from patrol deputy to detective. His colleagues also learned Pat McCready could get off a great shot if required.

"Always for you, Detective McCready," she responded. "What's up?"

Jax bounded over in search of a head scratch. McCready complied, his mind elsewhere.

"I came across some information while I was compiling notes from the domestic complaint last night," he said.

"If it pertains to that case, you should take it up with Sergeant Gordy. I'll review everything at our next meeting."

McCready bounced on his toes, trying to keep his natural enthusiasm in check.

"Lieutenant, it's not about any of our current cases. It's more something that relates to your, uh, experience. I mean, it's probably nothing, but ..."

Sam felt a momentary flutter. "Okay, Detective. Tell me what you've found."

"This all started with my uncle's brother-in-law, Roy," McCready began. "He's from Sacramento, okay? Well, he was, but he's moved back East to be closer to the family after his divorce. Okay, that may not be relevant," he added when Sam frowned.

"What is important is that he told a story about some killer that was active right when he lived there. The guy murdered five teachers over seven months. Stabbed them through the eye and left their bodies right in front of the schools. Pretty grisly. Two Sacramento detectives caught him. California has the death penalty and back then, they used it on this guy, although it took seven years."

"How is this relevant to me, or rather, to this department?"

McCready put his tablet in front of her. He brought up the website for the Sacramento Bee.

"I decided to research the case on my own time, Lieutenant. Just curious to see how crime-solving was covered in the days before everyone used social media. Then I found this recent obit for one of the lead detectives, name of Jack Frost if you can believe it."

Sam scanned the article. "Says here he was killed outside his home two months ago," she summarized. "An ice pick to the eye and a black and white notebook at the scene. Creepy, even perversely clever but not a shock. The man was a homicide detective. He likely investigated plenty of violent crimes during his career. Someone with a grudge decided to take him out using the same method as the serialist."

"Hold on, Lieutenant, there's something else I need to show you." McCready turned the tablet around, brought up a second screen, and turned it back. All the while, he was shaking his foot fast enough that Sam felt her desk vibrate.

Another news site. This one belonged to the Billings Gazette. Curious, she read:

Rosebud Undersheriff Found Dead at Tubb Ranch

by Cameron Doyle

Forsyth, MT, June 14th. Rosebud County Sheriff's Office has announced the death of Undersheriff Mackenzie "Mac" Scott, 38. His body was found on Anika Vista Ranch, north of Lockwood, nearly a week after he went missing. The ranch belongs to the Tubb family.

Dillon Tubb, son of owner Carter Tubb, found the body around 6 pm yesterday near one of the cattle pens. The family has disavowed any knowledge of the incident before the discovery.

The death is considered suspicious. "It's been cool at night, which may have preserved some of the biological evidence," said a representative from the coroner's office in Billings. "We hope that will aid in our investigation."

Mac Scott achieved some notoriety when he caught Deke Garrity, aka the Cattleman Killer, eight years ago. Garrity was accused of murdering three prominent cattle ranchers by breaking their necks and then branding them because he believed they practiced animal cruelty. Garrity was sentenced to death and executed last year after his last appeal failed.

"This is a heinous crime," declared Rosebud County Sheriff Jarrod Greene. "Mac was a dedicated law officer, a loving family man, and a good friend of mine." He asked that anyone with any information call the department hotline.

We will continue to update this story as further information becomes available.

Sam reread the article, aware of McCready's intense gaze. He wanted a reaction. She wanted to keep a lid on her emotions until she had a chance to examine them.

"The article is dated a few days ago," she observed.

"Yes, ma'am."

"These two homicides have elements in common, I'll grant you that. A dead investigator. A duplication of the MO used by a serial killer brought down by the very men who are now victims of someone else. On the other hand, this Montana case isn't nearly as specific. People's necks are broken, either by accident or on purpose. As far as branding a victim, that may not be unusual out in Montana. Let me ask you: Have you located any more such incidents?"

"Not as of yet," McCready admitted.

"Pat, you can do anything you want on your own time, and that includes researching unusual cases. But if you're in here to ask me if I think there's cause for further action, I'm afraid I don't. Nor do I think in any event we'd have any jurisdiction. Do you?"

"No, ma'am, I guess not officially." McCready reached for his laptop. He looked like a puppy who'd been sent to his crate.

"Look, the similarities between these two homicides could be a fluke, but you keep track. If another detective known for chasing serial killers goes down, let me know. I'll pass it along to the FBI. Okay? And let's keep this between us."

"Yes, ma'am. Thank you." He rose.

"Shut the door on your way out, please."

As soon as he left, Sam pulled up a copy of Police Chief on her screen and started scrolling through the magazine for a statistic she'd seen. There it was. Fewer than fifty active-duty officers die annually from all causes. Halfway through this year, the magazine listed twenty-three deaths, eleven dead from disease or accident and twelve killed by suspects in traffic stops or domestics. One robbery, one drive-by.

Then there was the dead detective stabbed with an icepick and now, a dead undersheriff with a broken neck. Different methods, different months, different states, different settings. Nothing that suggested a pattern and certainly nothing that made the cases remotely her concern. Or so she reminded herself as she reached for her phone.

Chapter 3

Jax's gentle woof brought Sam awake. The dog had his nose atop the tangled mess of sheets on her bed. In the dark, she could feel rather than see his concern.

She pulled herself up to scratch behind his ears, then kissed his head. "It's okay, boy," she whispered. "Your nutty human just had another bad dream."

She swung herself over the side of the mattress and tapped her watch: 2 am. Par for the course and utterly frustrating. She had a new bed with a comfortable mattress. New furnace. Windows that kept out the chill, the dampness, the heat, and the humidity. She'd cut her drinking and her caffeine consumption in half. Hell, she was still seeing a therapist every three weeks or so. Okay, her skin looked better but the nightmares persisted.

Sam grabbed a pen and wrote down what she remembered of the dream before it slipped away. White dresses with red stains, burning buildings, poison potions, a knife, a gun, a syringe, an enemy with eyes of emerald. As always, she arrived too late, or too unprepared, to be of much use to anyone.

Might as well let the dog out, she thought. She allowed herself a moment of gratitude for the new house with the pocket-sized backyard. Then she gathered her long, thick mahogany curls into a clip and whispered, "Let's go, boy."

Jax, thrilled with the break in his routine, tore down the stairs and waited at the door while Sam grabbed a lantern and disabled the alarm. No sense in disturbing the neighbors by turning on the backyard light.

She stepped into the humid blanket of air that was June and listened to the tree frogs. Easton was a busy town, even at the ever-expanding edges, but the night belonged to the creatures that clung to the river.

While Jax did his business and some bonus exploring, Sam considered her conversations with the police chief in Sacramento and the Montana sheriff. She'd ignored the practical voice that told her not to succumb to her curiosity. She'd reminded herself about limits and boundaries. She'd cautioned herself against confusing instinct with impulse.

She'd called the sheriff anyway.

Earlier in the day, she put in her first call to Sacramento PD to speak to the police chief, Lindsay Block. She explained she'd promised a curious nephew with an overactive imagination that she'd follow up on his theories about the murders.

"I don't know anything about a murder in Montana, Lieutenant Tate," Block said, her voice heavy with fatigue. "My responsibility is to the people of Sacramento. Yours is to—where did you say you worked?"

"Talbot County, Maryland, Chief. And I'm not trying to interfere in any way. I promised I'd pass along this information, period."

"From a kid who was surfing the web. Does your nephew expect you to fly out to the West Coast and solve this for us?"

"I have no idea what he expects," Sam answered, "which is why I don't have children."

Block chuckled. "I hear you. I admit this Montana case is interesting, but we're focused on Sacramento. We've got plenty of suspects. Frost was well known to his fellow officers and to the criminals he arrested over a long career. He was an exemplary officer, and we will find the person who ended his life."

Sam ended the call and placed another to Sheriff Greene. She left a voicemail.

He called an hour later, using Facetime. The man she saw was in his mid-forties, bulky but not fat. Short black hair with a touch of gray, brown eyes, and a nose that might have been broken when he played high school football. His big grin stretched across his broad face.

"I can't lie, Sheriff Tate," he began. "I'm excited to meet you. You're a little bit of a celebrity, at least among county sheriffs. We're gonna have to make this short, though. I'm in the middle of an investigation."

"Please, call me Sam." She didn't bother to correct him on the "sheriff" part.

"Sam it is, and you can call me Jarrod or JJ since my middle name is John. So, what can I do for you?"

"I wonder if I could ask a few questions about Undersheriff Scott's death."

His face tightened. "What's your interest in all this?" All business now, his tone noticeably sharper.

Sam thought she'd play it straight. "Someone in my office noticed your homicide bore some resemblance to a case in Sacramento from two months ago."

"They got a dead law officer with a broken neck and a brand?"

"Not exactly, but their deceased detective worked on a serial-killer case just like your undersheriff did."

"Where's the California serial killer now?"

"He's dead."

"So is Deke Garrity, the serial murderer Mac hunted down and sent to the electric chair. That's the only connection I see."

"The MO in each instance matched those of the original serial killers."

"Again, I need to ask why you're so interested. You work for the FBI?"

Sam laughed. "God, no. I just thought you might be interested in hearing about a similar case."

"Lots of people are killed when someone breaks their neck. Did you know cartels often brand their victims post-mortem?"

"I do know that, JJ. I promised my detective I'd share the information."

Greene sighed as if she'd disappointed him. "Sheriff Tate, I don't know what's going on back East. Maybe it's a slow workday. Maybe you're trying to help here, although believe me, if the FBI has something to tell me, they wouldn't hesitate to call over to Helena. I hope they don't. I don't need complicated. Murders out here are often personal. Mac was an up-and-up cop, but he tangled with plenty of bad people who were primed to hold a grudge. We're working up a list right now, and we have more than enough assistance."

"Good to know. Appreciate your time, Sheriff Greene."

"So long," he said and disconnected.

In hindsight, she regretted her calls. Neither department head had an interest in any case but the one in front of them. The MO for Mac Scott wasn't really that unusual. Two deaths did not make a pattern. Criminal cases tended to be depressingly similar. Copycats showed up from time to time. She employed a deputy turned detective whose powers of observation could occasionally shade over into obsession, a trait she recognized in herself.

Time to let it go.

She whistled the dog back inside, wiped off his feet, and led him into the bedroom. They made themselves comfortable and eventually fell asleep.

Chapter 4

McCready's concerns about a copycat killer held Sam's attention for the rest of June. Then other misdeeds took precedence. Talbot Country experienced an influx of summer visitors. A parallel rise in crime kept her unit busy. She handled several suspect interviews and found herself back in the field.

As August appeared, she got a chance to look more closely at the incident reports from the website Police 1 for the last three months. She kept an eye out for articles about officer deaths that mentioned serial killers. Unfortunately, the wire service didn't allow the kind of detailed search she needed. Not that she knew exactly what she was looking for.

Sam flagged a couple of cases and promised herself she'd run them by Terry when she saw him on Friday before their four-day vacation in the Shenandoah Mountains.

She found him in his office mid-Friday afternoon staring at his computer. Not at budgets or crime scene photos but rather at floor plans, along with pictures of lamps, office furniture, and carpet samples, along with a palette of color combinations, along with the words "FBI HQ/finishes" and "furnishings/senior management."

"Are we decorating already?" she asked with a light laugh.

"How am I supposed to decide?" Terry grumbled. "I honestly don't give a damn if the new office walls are eggshell white or robin's-egg-blue."

"I thought you had at least six months before the Bureau moves to the suburbs."

"That's not long in practical terms," Terry replied. "We have a lot of people and technology to accommodate." He gave her a pleading look. "Any ideas?"

"This is not my area of expertise, Assistant Director," she joked. "Unless you want me to shoot the decorator for putting it on you." She looked over his shoulder.

"Let's see. Go for off-white on the walls. Gives you more options. Don't get a leather couch, it's sticky in the heat and chilly in the cold. That beige tweed is a safe bet. Get a lamp with simple lines. How about this one?" She pointed at the screen.

"As for the desk and bookcase, stay black. Your chair should offer maximum comfort for those late nights when you find yourself stuck at your desk. The desk, by the way, should have at least one drawer that locks. That's all I got."

"You are a marvel, Tate," Terry said. He stood and pulled her into him for a lingering kiss.

"Can I expect more of the same in the mountains?"

"You can. I just have one more message to answer."

"Can't whoever it is wait?" she teased.

"Senator Sean Parker isn't known for his patience."

Sam struggled to keep her expression neutral. "What does he want with you?" she asked.

"Parker sits on two committees that each have a say as to how the Bureau operates and how the funding is allocated. The Criminal Investigative Division has always grabbed most of the spotlight."

"You do all the glamorous work," Sam replied. ""Interstate bank robberies, mass shootings, organized crime, serial killers." She mentally snapped her fingers, reminding herself to talk with Terry about the cases she'd been tracking. Although she hated to bring business on vacation, she didn't want to wait.

"It's more than that," Terry was saying. "These days, counter-terrorism and counter-intelligence units are more critical than ever. Fine by me, they do important work. However, the increased interest translates to more constituent pressure on representatives and more concern by legislators. Funding priorities could shift away from my division."

"That would be too bad."

"Sean Parker agrees."

Parker was the freshman senator from Maryland who'd somehow managed to secure a seat on the powerful Homeland Security and Governmental Affairs Committee. He was believed to have influential friends, although no one could say who they were. Old money, new money, individual donors both visible and less so— all had combined to land him in the Senate. Nothing untoward about any of it.

What was unusual was that, although Parker never mentioned organized crime during his campaign, he became an ardent supporter of the FBI's efforts to quash the mob, particularly on the East Coast. His zeal struck his colleagues as misplaced and out of touch with the reality of modern crime.

"Of course, he doesn't want the focus to shift away from your unit." Sam couldn't keep the bitter note out of her voice. "You've been investigating a group of East

Coast mob families for several years. He's determined to eradicate any trace of the people who probably helped put him where he is now."

"We don't know—"

"Don't know what? That Sean Parker was adopted by a family in Rhode Island with mob connections? I thought that was an open secret."

"You don't like him."

"I don't trust him, Terry. His resemblance to me is uncanny, right down to our unusual green eyes. The only other person in my family with these eyes was my grandmother. Who had an illegitimate child she gave away right around the time Parker was born."

"Which makes him your half-uncle," Terry said. "He admitted as much to you last year."

"And never spoke of it again. Yes, he offered me a job with the Secret Service, which I declined. Not because I was worried about nepotism, but because I was never going to work for the Secret Service. I can't figure him out. Is he really my half-uncle? Were his parents connected to the mob? Was he the man I'm sure I saw at my brother's wedding twenty-nine years ago?" She rubbed her forehead, trying to fight off the impending headache.

Terry took her hands. "You want to know if he's a bad guy or a good guy. DNA won't answer that question, but it can tell you some things. I don't know if his is on file. Let me see what I can do. We can put at least part of the mystery of the green-eyed man to rest, okay?"

Sam looked up at the man, grateful beyond measure to have him in her life. "Okay," she said. "Now, are you ready to get out of this polluted city and into some clean mountain air?"

Terry pushed a few papers into a briefcase and wrapped an arm around her. "You have no idea how ready I am to get out of here. At least it's been a relatively quiet summer. The criminals slow down in August."

Not all criminals, Sam thought.

Chapter 5

Althea Taft pulled up at the four-mile mark and checked her pulse. Not bad, considering the heat. Coming up on Labor Day weekend, the temperatures remained well above eighty, the humidity even higher.

Sweat soaked through her UGA t-shirt and dripped into her eyes. Her leg ached where she'd been kicked last month by a suspect with steel-toed boots. Nasty bruise but no broken bones. At least she'd caught the SOB.

Her watch chimed. A new message from QT, short for Quidley Tara Jones, a special agent with the Georgia Bureau of Investigation. Colleague, partner on one memorable case, and now a good friend.

Go for five or call her friend back? She opted for the latter.

"QT Jones," the voice answered. Smooth, concise, authoritative. Like the woman herself.

"Hey, girl. How are things in Decatur?"

"Detective Taft! Things are good. How about Marietta? How's the leg? Has the department let you off the leash yet?"

"Back to chasing bad guys."

"Not literally, I hope," Jones replied. They both laughed.

"Soon enough, QT.

"Okay, go-getter. Speaking of business, did you get a text about one of our old cases?"

"Yeah, same as you probably did." Taft sighed into the phone. "Anonymous sender with new information that will upend the Headhunter case. Seemed a little off."

"Right? I mean, what new information? Our guy is sitting in a cell in Butts County while his lawyer busts his ass trying to appeal the death sentence."

"Won't happen, QT."

Taft and Jones had teamed up five years earlier on the case of the serial killer who posed as a headhunter. The man killed six young women over six weeks, luring them with a phony website promising career advancement. He then set up "candidate interviews" at an unfinished building at an office park in Marietta. There, he disabled his victims before removing their heads. He left behind a taunting note printed on orange paper that read: "Now you're the headhunter."

After an unfortunate contractor discovered the headless bodies, Taft's boss suggested she and her partner team with the GBI, which assigned Agent QT Jones. Together, the three women caught the assailant, but not before two more victims turned up along with the orange note, sending Atlantans into an uproar.

The team attracted a great deal of attention for a short time. Taft's partner was killed a year later while investigating a domestic dispute. The remaining two investigators collected fan mail and marriage proposals, then these dwindled. Taft received a promotion, Jones a raise. Each moved on to new cases. They stayed in touch.

Now some jackass was claiming they'd missed something.

"Let's see where our helpful citizen wants to meet," Taft suggested. "Probably an abandoned warehouse at midnight."

"Girl, you read too many mysteries."

It turned out the informant asked to meet at noon at the children's playground at the Grand Park Zoo on Labor Day, four days away. Whoever it was had chosen a time and a location that complicated plans. An isolated building at midnight might prove dangerous for the law officers. A crowded venue would pose a logistics nightmare, what with large crowds expected for the holiday weekend.

Pulling together a team was easier than negotiating with zoo officials unwilling to shut down the facility and shut down a major revenue stream. Jones advised against changing the venue. No one wanted to spook the mysterious texter.

In the end, both sides reached a compromise. Visitors would be directed away from the playground area for two hours on the pretext that a prescheduled private event was taking place.

Labor Day dawned hot and muggy. The sun rose as a muted orange ball in the mist, then clawed its way up to hang in a hazy sky. With the humidity in the eighties and the temperature forecast to reach the mid-nineties, the weather promised to be as sticky as the logistics.

Jones, Taft, and their people arrived hours before the park opened to set up the meet area. Lifelike mannequins would be used alongside undercover cops to fill the playground. Although zoo employees had been pre-vetted, they were again searched as they arrived.

For the next few hours, the police kept a close watch on all the entrances and exits as well as the perimeter.

"I hate this," Taft said to her friend.

"Hate what?" Jones asked.

"The fact that we're setting up to meet someone who is either an informant or a psycho, and we don't know which. At the zoo, of all places. I used to come here as a kid, QT. Same slides, same merry-go-round. Mostly the same exhibits. I grew up with a single mom who worked two jobs. A trip here was the highlight of our month, our little two-person holiday. The zoo is supposed to be fun, safe, maybe a little educational. Not a place for serial killers."

"I know, Althea. Don't worry. We'll get what we came for one way or another, and we'll do it while the rest of these folks enjoy the day none the wiser."

A few minutes before noon, panicked voices arose originating in the section called the African Forest on the opposite side of the zoo from the playground. Curious, the crowd pushed toward the disturbance. The noise level rose. Team members struggled to hear each other. Taft caught a few words here and there, something about a missing child or an escaped big cat.

The announcement system came to life. An official-sounding voice requested visitors to make their way slowly and calmly toward the exit. Instead, the crowd began to behave as crowds do, which meant pushing and yelling. A few brave souls continued to push towards the exhibit instead of away from it, their phones out and held above their heads.

"Attention, team," Jones yelled. "We have a potential mass panic situation. Zoo officials are handling it along with local police. Do not interfere and do not draw your weapons unless confronted with a direct threat to your life. I repeat, do not draw down!"

"Do you think he'll show?" Taft asked.

"Unless the motherfucker started this madness so he could sit back and laugh at us," Jones replied as a swell of people stampeded through the playground, knocking over human and inanimate figures alike.

Jones slapped the back of her neck. Damn mosquito, she thought. She faltered and fell to the ground.

"QT!" Taft rushed over. The pinprick surprised her. She fought against the darkness, but a strong arm kept her from tumbling even as her vision failed.

"Ladies, nice to meet you. I know the situation is a little confusing right now. Come, let me help clear your heads."

Chapter 6

"What the ever-loving hell, Sloan? Why aren't we all over this?"

Terry absorbed Lena Small's heated opening salvo, which arrived without preamble. In the eighteen years he'd known her, from their days in Quantico through their parallel rise through the FBI ranks, to her appointment as the Atlanta bureau's special agent in charge, he'd never known her to lose her cool. In this instance, he couldn't blame her.

"Lena, I am so sorry."

"I knew these women," she went on, no less heated. "There aren't as many Black female investigators as you might think. They were damn good at their jobs, Terry. Neither of them had reached forty years old. They deserved a long and successful career. They did not deserve to be beheaded and their bodies left in a shed for a zookeeper to find."

"I know, and I'm truly sorry. I assume GBI is—"

"Handling the case? Yes, they are, and they're damn good at what they do. But the mayor is pushing them to hold a press conference tomorrow so they can reassure the public. It might help if they had a little more information from the FBI. Which, I might add, should be all over this case."

"Lena, we can't just barge in."

"Yes, we can. This goes way beyond a state investigation, Terry Sloan. I've recently been made aware of several cases with similar patterns in California, Montana, and most recently, in Illinois. Do you know how? Someone who works for me is in a chat forum that studies serial cases. Strange little hobby he shares with an enthusiastic young detective in Maryland who in turn owes his interest to his well-known boss. She, by the way, happens to be a cracker-jack detective with some experience hunting serial killers and an FBI assistant director for a boyfriend."

"Lena—"

"I'm going to guess Sam Tate has been tracking the similarities between these killings. When the number climbed to three, she let you know."

"She did."

"Then why the hell haven't you brought in the FBI, Assistant Director?"

"This horrible turn of events has happened within the last week with a three-day holiday in between, Lena. The death of the state trooper in Illinois was brought to my attention three weeks earlier. I'm not making excuses, but we need time to strategize before we act."

"Strategize? With five officers in four states dead? Goddammit, you're in charge of criminal investigation for the Bureau. This has FBI written all over it and you know it."

"Stop right there," Terry barked. "I mean it. Stop chewing me out and listen. First, the FBI doesn't charge in and take over without an invitation, and you know it. Second, I'm in charge of this division, yes. The position comes with a little bit of leeway and a lot of responsibility. You're part of the bureaucracy; you should know how it works. That doesn't mean I'm sitting still."

He lowered his voice. "Yesterday, I met with my boss and his boss, who happens to be the Bureau's second guy. I spent the rest of the day reaching out to state DOJs to inform them we believe these cases are connected and to strongly urge the relevant leads to accept our assistance. As far as I know, they've done that. Still waiting on Montana."

Small snorted. "Guess they want to go it alone. Rugged individualism and all that."

"They'll come around. This morning I'm calling the SACs in the local field offices closest to where the murders occurred. You were first on my list, but you beat me to it. No surprise there."

"The Bureau doesn't have a field office in Montana."

"We don't need Montana right now," Terry replied. "I've already asked our profilers to work up a personality composite. If we're looking at a serial killer, he's breaking all the rules. Or she or they, depending on who we're looking for. So, for the love of God, step it back, SAC Small."

Small exhaled. "I'm sorry I went off on you, Terry. These latest deaths feel personal somehow. Don't misunderstand me; I realize all the victims are important."

"I get it. We're putting our best people on this, Lena, I promise you. You will be kept in the loop. We need to know who the killer may go after down the line."

"Another cop with a history of chasing serial killers," she replied. "Could be you, Terry. Could be Sam Tate. Hope you realize that."

"I do, Lena."

Chapter 7

"Thank you all for coming together on such short notice. I'm Assistant Director Terry Sloan, and I head the FBI's Criminal Investigative Division, or CID."

Sam looked around as Terry called the meeting to order. She was seated at a long table in a room that seemed a little large for the six people physically present. The rest of the group appeared as faces contained inside small squares on a wall-mounted screen at one end of the room and duplicated on the tablets in front of them. Sam counted eight squares in all.

"This is a closed meeting to discuss a series of brutal murders that have impacted several police departments across several states," Terry said. "The FBI has detected a pattern that indicates these murders may be the work of a serial killer. You're all here because you concur. For simplicity's sake, we'll designate this as a joint task force made up of representatives of the affected jurisdictions and agents from the Bureau."

"Onscreen," he continued, "we have police chiefs from Sacramento, California, and Marietta, Georgia; a senior detective with the Georgia Bureau of Investigation or GBI; and a senior officer from the Illinois State Police headquarters in Springfield. Agents from the Bureau's Sacramento, Springfield, and Atlanta offices are also represented."

"At the table, we have Special Agent Molly Kinney, a lead investigator with BAU-4, the behavior analysis unit that deals with violent crimes against adults. Next to her is Special Agent Rob Stein, a senior analyst from the Bureau's Violent Crimes Apprehension Program or ViCAP. They are specialists in collecting and analyzing information, and they'll be available to your departments upon request."

Sam nodded at the slim, copper-haired Kinney. She was always interested in women who worked in law enforcement. Kinney might be a good person to get to know.

Stein, a lanky man with a hipster goatee, gave a thumbs up. He caught Sam looking at him and blushed.

Terry introduced his two special agents next. Mike Fuentes was a senior agent, a veteran in his early forties with a buzz cut and lively brown eyes. Dakota Williams was ten years younger, a stunner with almond eyes and shimmering raven hair pulled back.

Sam was next. She'd asked Terry to keep things short and sweet. She was something of an outsider, although she suspected her reputation preceded her. Additionally, she had a relationship to the Assistant Director none of the guests needed to know about.

"I've also asked Lieutenant Sam Tate to join us," Terry said. "Her day job is with Talbot County Sheriff's Office in Maryland. However, she's also worked on and solved several serial investigations. Her insights will be helpful."

"A killer-catching superhero," Stein exclaimed, then put his hand over his mouth. "Sorry, Lieutenant. I'm a big fan."

Sam laughed. "No offense taken, Agent Stein. But I left my cape at home." Her little joke landed lightly, and she caught the twinkle in Terry's eyes.

"Excuse me?" One of the screen attendees spoke. "Casey Wong, Sacramento Bureau. Aren't we missing Montana? The branding case."

"We tried to contact the Rosebud County sheriff," Terry replied. "Still waiting to hear back. Other state agencies want a go-ahead from him first. Autonomy tilts in the direction of local departments, it seems."

"No surprise," Wong replied.

"We've got enough to work with," Terry continued, "especially with your much-appreciated cooperation. All these deaths are significant, but this latest gruesome and public execution in Atlanta has made national headlines. We need to get ahead of this."

"Amen to that," someone muttered.

"Let's keep moving," Terry said. "Several murders have occurred over the last six months that have significant commonalities. One, all the victims are law officers. Two, the victims each led investigations into previous serial killings in their locale. Three, all of them were murdered using the same method that was used in their separate serial cases. And four, in all of the original cases, the offenders were caught and jailed. Two of them have been executed and two remain locked up, except one who killed himself rather than surrender."

Terry took a breath. "I'll take a few questions now. Major Timothy Powell, Illinois State Police, go ahead."

Powell was a stocky man with thinning hair and a khaki mustache that complemented his uniform. "How did ViCAP figure out our cases were connected?"

Stein appeared uncomfortable. "To be honest, we didn't."

Sam volunteered, "A young detective who works for me picked up on the Sacramento and Montana homicides back in June. I told him he could look into anything he wanted on his own time. He connected with an agent within the Atlanta FBI office tracking the same cases."

"Lieutenant Tate is minimizing her own detective work connecting these cases," Terry said. "We have another question. Go ahead."

"Chief Lindsay Block, Sacramento PD. Yes, I had a conversation with the lieutenant back in July, as I recall." Sam put the familiar voice with the face of the woman with salt-and-pepper hair falling to her shoulders. "So, what's the order of these homicides? I assume ours was first."

"Sacramento in April, Montana in the middle of June. The Illinois state trooper went missing around July 4th, although his body was just discovered. Georgia was last Sunday. Yes?"

A red-faced man with spiky gray hair coughed to get attention. "Chief Morgan Paulson, Marietta PD," he said. "We're looking at one murder almost every month. That's a pretty ambitious schedule considering we're seeing a different setup for each victim. Plus, he's on the move. Do we think he's acting alone?"

"GBI Agent Charley Grisby here," a light-skinned Black man with thick glasses cut in. "I want to know why this person moves around. That's not what serial killers usually do. Is it related to the selection of victims? If so, why those particular people? Why now?"

Terry held up a hand. "These are just a few of the questions that need to be answered. Here's where you come in. The original case files that belonged to each of your detectives-turned-victims contain crime scene photos, autopsy reports, background on the victims and the killers, and interviews with friends, relatives, and colleagues. Go through it, organize it, and get it to Agent Stein."

"Anything else?" Powell asked with a trace of sarcasm.

"Yes," Kinney volunteered. "We're here to help you. Get us the old files and anything you have about the current murders, no matter how far along you are. Rob will cross-reference the names you give us with our database. BAU-4 will work up a profile to see what lines up. We're not going to stop while we wait for you, but we're hoping you won't make us wait too long."

"We need your input," Terry added. "If there's one killer on the move, chances are you won't see a repeat of this horrific crime in your jurisdictions. But someone else will. We need to put a stop to that and see justice served for the men and women who died for doing right by their jobs. Do you agree?"

Everyone assented.

"Great. Then we'll meet again in a week. Please ask your people to pull together as much as you can digitally. Our agents are going to have a lot to go through. If you have any concerns before that time, please contact me directly. Thank you."

The screen went blank. As Sam rose with the others to leave, Terry signaled them to keep their seats.

"Hold up," he told them. "There's more."

Chapter 8

"Thanks for hanging back, people," Terry told them. "I want to continue the discussion with this smaller internal group. Not trying to hide anything. On one hand, I don't want to get anyone's hopes up. On the other, I don't need anyone going solo based on something they hear. That includes the people at this table as well."

Sam busied herself with her notebook. Even though Terry hadn't mentioned her by name, she felt slightly guilty. She'd gone rogue once or twice herself, especially when she felt a situation called for action. She believed in teamwork, but sometimes she got ahead of the team.

She noticed Fuentes fidgeting and wondered if he had the same inclinations. But it was Williams who gave her a wink. Sam covered her mouth with her hand to hide her amused expression.

"We have to work cooperatively and quickly," Terry went on. "Rob, you will need to be your diplomatic self. You may have to press the locals to get you that information. I've already spoken with your director about the urgency of this project."

"You're talking about at least a hundred people to cross-reference," Stein pointed out.

"The local and state agencies will have done a lot of the leg work. And I know you have some sort of algorithm in place to help you find and analyze patterns." Terry's smile was broad enough to placate the skittish Stein.

"What do you want us to do about Montana?" Fuentes asked.

"I'm not sure," Terry replied. "It's possible Undersheriff Mac Scott's death was unrelated to our investigation. A broken neck isn't a signature move and neither is branding, believe it or not. I'm going to start by contacting the AG's office in Montana. Depending on what he contributes, I might send you and Williams to Big Sky Country. Ever been out that way?"

"Nothing west of Texas, sir," Fuentes said.

Williams raised a hand. "I have family out there I was planning to visit."

"That's convenient," Terry said. "Let me talk to you after we break."

Williams smiled.

Stein raised his hand. "Any chance we're looking at a group killing effort, all with roughly the same motives, like a Justice League?"

"Rob, have you ever run across anything like that before?" Sam asked.

"Well, no, at least not among the violent crimes subjects we deal with. Still, it's not hard to imagine. I mean, there's a club for everything and everyone nowadays. Gives people a sense of camaraderie and a sense of purpose. Grief feels isolating. Maybe a few folks got together to form a bereavement group for people impacted by a serial killer. Maybe a few of them took it further and decided on revenge."

"Against the detectives?" Fuentes asked.

"What about a serial killer fanboys and fangirls club?" Williams asked. "Possibly including true crime junkies who think their tortured heroes have gotten a raw deal." She turned to Sam. "Lieutenant, didn't you run into those types when you were investigating the Dry Ice Killer?"

"I did," Sam admitted. "Most were fixated on crime-solving. Some were obsessed with the murderers. Admiring psycho killers may be weird, but it's still a far cry from killing for them."

Molly Kinney put up a hand.

"First of all, while the majority of victim-adjacent people might have vengeful thoughts, they'd be unlikely to act on them. And as Agent Fuentes said, why turn those feelings on the investigators who caught the killers? As for serial killer admirers, they exist mostly to share information and discuss methodology. We all know copycat killers exist. But these new murders share one key difference from the originals."

"Victimology," Sam suggested. "Our victims aren't middle-school teachers or ranchers or female jobseekers between twenty-three and thirty."

"No," Terry said. "They're cops who collared killers."

Fuentes drummed his fingers on the table, then stopped, struck by a thought. "Could our killer be jealous of the attention the detectives got? The whole hero treatment, right?" He looked at Sam, who ducked her head. "Articles, interviews, maybe a key to the city, or cities, who knows what else?"

"Netflix specials," quipped Stein.

Light laughter rippled through the room.

"Believe me, people remember the killers, not the case detectives," Sam remarked.

"Special Agent Fuentes raises an interesting point," Kinney said. "Envy can inspire a homicide or a series of them. So can the need for attention. I don't know that jealousy is the driver in this instance."

"You don't think these are rage killings?" Williams asked.

"Oh, I do, Agent Williams. I'm merely suggesting this killer has a plan, one that makes him or her the opposite of impulsive."

"Doesn't mean the guy isn't jealous," Fuentes huffed.

"How does he pick his victims?" Williams asked.

"He pulls them from the news," Sam ventured. "He does a quick search for a list of serial killers in the last twenty-five years. Maybe he picks the ones with the catchy names. Maybe he then searches for articles on the lead investigators in each case and chooses the ones who got a lot of attention." She looked up from her notes to see the group staring at her.

"You got a lot of attention, Lieutenant," Williams noted.

Terry jumped in. "Okay, people. Your points are valid. We'll give Molly a chance to create a working profile and go from there."

Stein's phone buzzed. He glanced at it once, then swore.

"What's up?" Terry asked.

"I set up a program that scans wire services like Police 1 and alerts me to any articles containing keywords specific to what I'm working on. So, for this case, I developed an algorithm that uses keywords and other parameters I can explain to you."

"What's the bottom line?"

Stein gulped. "We've got another body."

Chapter 9

"The victim had been discovered in a small campsite near the Frio River in Uvalde County, Texas. Or rather, his charred remains had been noted by the park ranger who'd investigated evidence of an illegal campfire. She reported to the Department of Public Safety." Stein looked up. "Those are the Texas Rangers."

"We know, Stein," Fuentes said.

"Right. Anyway, the headline here is that forensic collection and DNA testing confirmed the victim was Mateo Pérez, age thirty-three, a detective with the Uvalde Police Department. Been missing since Memorial Day."

"Memorial Day?" Sam asked. She made a note in her ever-present notebook. "Do you have any more information?"

"Pérez solved a cold case involving prostitutes who'd been burned alive over the previous decade. His interest was personal. One of the missing women was the daughter of one of his mother's friends. He worked the case in his spare time and finally caught the guy, some lowlife they'd all dubbed the Frio Killer."

"What happened to him?" Sam asked.

"He's at a supermax, sitting on death row."

"Looks like we've got another one," Williams noted.

"Fuentes, reach out to the San Antonio office and connect with the lead agent. Molly and Rob, anything you can add to the profile will be helpful. Offer our services," Terry said. "Even if this murder goes back to the end of May, we've got a lot of bodies falling in a

38

relatively short time. Lieutenant Tate, see me in my office in ten or so." He rose. "I'll need more from each of you, I'm sure. But for now, keep this on the DL. In time, we might have to contact every department in the country. But not yet. The last thing we need is a stampede of cops looking to protect their own."

On the way out, Sam got a text from her administrative assistant.

you have flowers.

She called the office.

"Melanie, hi, it's Lieutenant Tate. Flowers? Is there some occasion I'm forgetting?"

"I don't know, Lieutenant, but the bouquet is beautiful. I just worry they won't last the weekend. I mean, I can send a picture so you can see them fresh."

"Is there a card?"

"Hold on." The young woman cleared her throat. "It says, 'Welcome to the team. I look forward to working with you. 'No signature."

"Odd. Okay, well, look, why don't you keep them on your desk or take them home if you think that's best."

"For real? I mean, I can bring them back Monday."

"Whatever makes you happy, Melanie. Just leave the card on my desk."

She disconnected, then headed to Terry's office. In the corridor, a slender woman in a gray suit barreled headlong into Sam, who staggered back. "Oh, my goodness," the woman exclaimed. "I am so sorry. Are you alright?"

"I'm fine," Sam replied. "Are you okay?"

"I'm embarrassed," the woman replied with a rueful smile. "This was my doing. I'm usually far more careful." The accent was American but with a vaguely British inflection. "We believe anything of consequence is confined to the screen in our hands. I'm always scolding my son about keeping his head up."

"I'm guilty of inattention myself," Sam admitted. "No harm, no foul."

"Excellent. Well, nice to run into you, Lieutenant." She walked off before Sam had a chance to ask the woman if they'd met before.

Outside Terry's office, the ever-cheerful Millie Jefferson greeted Sam. "I'm afraid Deputy Sloan is tied up right now. Do you want to wait?"

"Thanks, Millie. Would you tell him I'll see him this evening? By the way, do you know the name of that woman who just crashed into me?"

Terry opened the door to his office. He ushered Agents Fuentes and Williams out and signaled Sam to enter. "I know, I know," he called to his secretary. "I have a call in five minutes. I only need two."

Terry closed the door and the blinds and gave Sam a brief but fierce kiss. "Thanks," he said as they broke apart. "I needed that."

"Me, too. Seems we've got a situation."

Terry flopped into his chair. "It's a mess. And why now?"

"An anniversary maybe. Or an event that caused him to put his scheme in motion."

"You don't think we're dealing with a basement dweller who pulled an idea from a graphic comic book one day?"

"It's not that random; quite the opposite. He's been knocking off victims every month since April. I agree with Molly Kinney that this is triggered. These murders took some planning over a period of time. Not sure why he's launched his murder spree this year."

"I wonder if that's deliberate or not." Terry frowned. "Damn, I need to check in with state brass in Montana. We have no jurisdiction, but I feel as if their case is similar enough to these others that we have to check it out."

"You need an invitation. That'll be a tough sell."

"True. I wish I could send you, Sam. You have a feel for these kinds of investigations."

"I didn't realize you were a fan of my less-than-subtle approach," she teased.

"Your approach is fine, except for the go-it-alone part."

She gave him a friendly arm punch. "Come on, Terry. I'm a great team player."

"Sure," he said with a grin. "When you remember you have a team."

"Point taken. And I promise I understand boundaries, especially when it comes to FBI work. Speaking of which, thanks for the flowers. That's a lovely welcoming gift. I don't suppose you sent them to all the team members?"

Terry shook his head. "I didn't send any flowers, Sam. Maybe I should have. It seems you have a secret admirer. What about a card?"

"Unsigned and innocuous. Someone looks forward to working with me."

"Someone in our group?"

"How, Terry? These are people I met maybe an hour or two ago."

He kissed the top of her head. "The flowers might represent a thoughtful gesture or a bad joke. We'll get to the bottom of it. Right now, our priority is to catch this guy before—"

"He catches us," Sam said.

Chapter 10

When Sam left, Terry sat as far back as his unreliable old chair would let him and looked around the office. Nothing wrong with it, just old and tired. Like his chair. Like the building. Like he felt some days.

He had to admit he appreciated Sam's suggestions about putting comfort above all else. More space and a more user-friendly chair might not be so bad. Neither would a place to live outside D.C. A place he hoped to share with Sam.

He directed his thoughts back to the matter of the murder in Montana. Sam had shared with Terry her conversation with Rosebud County Sheriff Jarrod Greene. "He seemed to be a fan of mine," she admitted. "But when I asked about the undersheriff, he shut down. This was back when we had two bodies instead of six. And I was a small-town cop from back East with no business in his business. Maybe he'll open up to you."

Terry had his doubts. The wider open the space, the more space locals preferred. Outsiders weren't always welcome. Exceptions might be made for people with jobs to offer or cash to pay. Anything related to the federal government was suspect. Besides, he'd left a message at the sheriff's office. His call was never returned.

Montana's Division of Criminal Investigation was under the state's DOJ. According to its website, which Terry carefully perused, the division maintained a statewide database. Agents and staff assisted on a panoply of crimes, "at the request of city, county, state, and federal law enforcement agencies." DOJ was careful not to tread on any toes.

Sam mentioned that Sheriff Greene indicated he might use the state agency for help identifying the culprit.

Let's see if he did, Terry thought.

He began by contacting the Denver office SAC. He'd met John Schultz at a crime conference years earlier. Both men hailed from Colorado and had other interests in common. They'd kept in contact. Schultz might be able to hook him up with someone from Montana DOJ.

The conversation was pleasant, though brief. Schultz's eldest was entering college, which made Terry feel simultaneously old and incomplete. His son would have been in junior high school, had he lived.

He finished the call and stared at the wall.

The therapist he saw following the deaths of his wife and unborn son warned him to expect grief to revisit him at unexpected moments. The best approach was not to fight it but to give it air, then lock it away again.

He let the tidal wave of pain wash over him, carry him out to sea, and wash him back to shore. He tried the deep breathing he'd seen Sam practice. The agony faded to a dull ache and then receded altogether.

Schultz had given Terry two names, one an assistant AG, the other the chief of the Investigations Bureau. Terry chose to call the latter, one criminal investigative head to another. While Terry's group was many times the size and scope of any agency in Montana, he assumed state officials wouldn't be particularly impressed by that fact.

He was put through to Ned Blackwolf.

"Chief Blackwolf," he began and stopped.

"Call me Ned," the man said with a chuckle. "The tribal leaders of the Crow Nation aren't all thrilled with my designation as it is. They've taken pains to remind me the white man's title has no currency on the rez."

"Appreciate the input, Ned. Please call me Terry."

"Good. 'Assistant Director 'is pretty formal." Blackwolf had a deep voice, warm with a hint of steel beneath.

An excellent voice for a leader, Terry thought.

"John Schultz just shot me a text," Blackwolf went on. "You're inquiring about a murder in Rosebud County? Why not call the sheriff over there?"

"He's been hard to reach. I assume you know about the murder in Rosebud County."

"I do."

"It shares disturbing similarities with four other murders over the last five months. The victims are all law officers who once solved a serial murder in their districts. The individual MOs duplicated those used by the original killers our victims investigated and arrested."

"I heard about the Atlanta case. Grisly business."

"We've communicated with the various agencies where these murders took place, starting with local departments. Everyone expressed an interest in teaming up. Sheriff Greene is the exception. We've already held a meeting with the other officials to discuss how we might all work together. Meanwhile, the remains of a detective have been discovered in southwest Texas under similar circumstances. They've also reached out to us."

The last was an exaggeration for which Terry offered up a silent mea culpa. "I had an agent place a call to Sheriff Greene in Rosebud County," he continued. "When we didn't hear back, I followed up personally. Didn't hear a thing. I don't need his input, Ned, but I'd appreciate his cooperation to at least rule out his murder."

Terry heard Blackwolf typing into his computer. "The undersheriff's neck was broken. He was branded postmortem near a cattle ranch. Same MO as the killer he previously arrested. Scott was seen as a hero."

"And now he's a dead one, possibly by the hand of someone who's moving across the country."

"And you haven't heard from Greene or any other Rosebud County official? Hang on."

More typing. "Okay, a report was filed with the Forsyth Medical Examiner. The death has been ruled a homicide. The sheriff's office released a statement that suggested they were speaking to several 'persons of interest. 'Nothing about which other agencies, if any, are working with the sheriff's department. Doesn't mean he hasn't availed himself of their resources."

He paused. "In theory, we folks in law enforcement are the good guys. In real life, some are saints, some are sinners, and some are assholes. Greene operates just outside the rez I used to call home. Genial sort of fella at first, but his department is quick to zero in on certain ethnic groups for minor infractions and major crimes alike. The ranchers love him, though."

Blackwolf took a beat. "How about this? The Investigations Bureau has several field offices, kind of like the FBI does in places other than Montana. The office closest to Forsyth is in Billings. I can send a message down there asking if they've reached Sheriff Greene over this killing. It's more'n likely, as Rosebud County would need some forensic assistance at the very least."

"That'd be helpful, Ned."

"Sure, and if you're ever in the area, stop by."

"My mother lives in Colorado Springs. I may head up north from there."

Blackwolf laughed. "Great. Just keep in mind Montana ain't Colorado."

Chapter 11

"Do you have any friends?"

Sam yanked herself back to the present. She'd been trying to recall her dreams. Wasn't that something therapists always asked their patients? In her case, the dreams were usually nightmares filled with horrific images or nonspecific terrors. Paths led nowhere, walls suddenly appeared. People she cared about begged for help and dissolved before she could reach them. She'd seen flashes of white-hot light and felt cold, so cold.

"I'm sorry, I don't understand," she said to her therapist.

"I asked you if you had any friends, Sam."

Dr. Putnam folded her hands in her lap. Today she'd traded her usual slacks and white blouse for a periwinkle dress that appeared tailored to her petite figure. A few silver strands mixed with the highlighted brown hair she wore pulled back.

I hope I didn't give those to her, Sam worried. She doubted she was Dr. Putnam's most difficult patient. She'd resumed in-person sessions just after she returned from New York last year. She tried not to miss appointments. She had trouble opening up. Who didn't? Sometimes she had to force herself to talk about the traumatic past that invaded her dreams and the uncertain future that disrupted her waking hours.

"You seem to be elsewhere, Samantha," Putnam observed. "Are the melatonin tablets I recommended helping you to sleep? What about the meditation exercises I gave you?"

"They just need time to work," Sam replied, although the truth of the matter was, she hadn't tried either. She suspected Putnam knew. "I'm sorry about drifting. Terry's division is launching an investigation and I've been invited to consult."

"That understandably occupies your attention. Does it excite you?"

"It interests me."

"More than your day job?" Putnam queried.

"I mean, there are individual cases that get the heart racing and then there's the reality of a job that involves primarily paperwork. That's as true in the FBI as in Talbot County Sheriff's Office."

"Okay, that makes sense. I imagine it's fun to share work experiences with Terry."

"Well, sure."

"Let's get back to my original question," Putnam continued. "Do you have friends?"

Sam squirmed. "Sure, I do. Terry, for one. People at work, like Bruce Gordy. I'm still in touch with Abdi Issen, my former deputy, now sheriff of Pickett County, Tennessee. Same with Larry Zielinski, my former partner at Metro Nashville PD."

"Except for your significant other, you're naming current and former work colleagues. It's good to stay in touch, but what about female friends? Anyone with whom you regularly share confidences."

"I...uh." Sam's mind went blank. "I worked with some terrific ladies up in New York on the Dry Ice Killer cases last fall. There's Paula Norris who works for the FBI and, oh, Carol Davidson, my CIS. We've gone shopping..." she trailed off.

"And do you keep up with any of them outside work and the occasional event?" Putnam persisted. "Do you regularly make plans with these people? Celebrate birthdays and holidays? Travel together? Help each other out? Chat or text about personal matters?"

"Everyone's pretty busy these days, Dr. Putnam."

"Good friends make time for each other."

"I guess so."

"Look, Sam. I think you've coped remarkably well given the high-profile cases you've handled over the past few years, cases that have thrust you repeatedly into the media spotlight. I've never seen you so engaged as when you're investigating, solving puzzles, tracking the bad guys, and generally getting out there. Yet you seem to believe that retreating is the best way for you to cope with your unresolved issues about the past."

"I go where the work is, Doc."

"I'm trying to understand how you are with retreating so thoroughly from that kind of adventure."

"Nature of the job, Doc," Sam replied, trying not to sound testy.

"I'm aware that you've faced challenges in establishing a career path, Sam. Meanwhile, Terry's journey is more of a straight shot. Does that frustrate you?"

"Maybe some, but it hasn't affected our relationship."

Putnam raised an eyebrow. "We'll save that topic for next time. As for your career, I wouldn't presume to advise you on specifics. I sense you're unfulfilled, though. I have no doubt you're a wonderful lieutenant." Sam winced. "But you have no place to go within that department. You need to consider how you can find an opportunity that makes use of your impressive mental and physical skills."

"Am I hearing you say I'm stuck?"

"Are you?"

When Sam didn't answer, she continued.

"I believe you'll find your path. You already know your strengths as well as your weaknesses. You take risks, but you consider the consequences. You know how to lead, and you know how to delegate. Let me get back to your personal life. You seem to be extraordinarily self-aware and that can negatively impact your personal life."

"Classic introvert," Sam jested.

"Introverts can have friends, Sam. Oftentimes they form deep and long-lasting relationships, connections that are vital to emotional health. Terry provides a solid foundation, but I'd like you to think about how you can connect with other people, particularly other women. Start by joining a professional organization. The Mid-Atlantic Association of Women in Law Enforcement might prove useful both from a professional and personal standpoint."

"Good idea."

"You still exercise regularly, I assume."

"Running with Jax in the morning and getting in several yoga sessions a week. I also use weights at home."

Putnam nodded. "I'm glad you have a dog," she said. "They make wonderful companions. I would consider taking a yoga class or joining a gym. Another way to meet people."

"I'll look into that." Sam felt an undercurrent of resistance move through her core and pushed back against it. "These are very positive ideas. Thank you."

Putnam peered at her patient over the rim of her half-glasses. "You're carrying around quite a bit, Sam," she said. "Your childhood losses, your somewhat peripatetic adult life. I worry that you might get impatient and convince yourself you've used up your luck or goodwill or whatever keeps you in one place. You need to build a community that goes beyond work colleagues and a man you see once a week if that."

Putnam leaned over and tapped Sam, who sat with her arms folded across her chest.

"Hey," Putnam said. "I can understand where you're coming from. I think a part of you wants to put down roots. A bigger part, though, can't imagine a foundation that doesn't crumble and disappear."

"Not surprising, given my past," Sam pointed out.

"The past doesn't have to write the future, Sam. Trust yourself, trust the people around you, trust that your life can be full, meaningful, even joyous at times. Can you do that?"

"I hope so," Sam replied.

At the end of the session, Sam made her way out to the street and, on impulse, sent a text. The response—absolutely—made her smile.

"See, Doctor Putnam?" she heard herself say. "I'm taking your advice."

Chapter 12

Dakota Williams was by any objective measure a stunning woman, with her high cheekbones, smooth chestnut skin, hazel eyes, and glossy hair that fell past her shoulders on those rare occasions when she let it down.

Ever since she could recall, she'd attracted attention, even when she didn't want it. The product of a union between a Cheyenne woman and a half-Black, half-Vietnamese war veteran, she and her parents lived as outliers on a Montana reservation until her father packed them up and moved them to Washington, D.C.

In slightly more cosmopolitan circumstances, she still found herself an object of fascination among her classmates. When her mother died and her father abandoned her to his sister to raise, she became the focus of pity mixed with envy. Some of her peers in high school sought to make friends, while others decided they needed to bring the beautiful girl down a notch or two.

In Sam Tate she saw a kindred spirit, someone who'd lost her parents and gained unwanted notoriety. A good-looking woman whose wavy hair, perfect teeth, and bright-green eyes might have caused others to doubt her abilities—until she proved them wrong. A woman who found her true calling in law enforcement.

Terry Sloan was an equitable boss who believed in mentoring his agents. He may not have been blind to her appearance, but he took great interest in her academic record, the praise of her academy instructors, and her superlative reputation at DCPD. She felt as if she'd found her calling.

Her partner Fuentes, after an awkward period of one-sided attraction, stowed his machismo and became the perfect cohort—older, more experienced, funny, and loyal. "You got my six, Williams," he told her. "And I got yours."

Now they were split up, with Fuentes headed to Uvalde, where the FBI had been invited after some hesitation to work with the Texas Department of Public Safety's Criminal Investigations Division. At least the Bureau had a toehold there. Montana would be a more difficult sell, as the assistant director made clear.

"Agent Williams, keep in mind you're making what amounts to a courtesy call on your vacation time. You will stop in Helena to update Ned Blackwolf and if he clears you, head to Billings to share information with the MBI regional office and listen to what they have to say. That's it. Listen and share. Take a few days to visit your aunt and come back. You're testing the waters. Keep your credentials in your pocket and your FBI jacket at home. Are we clear?"

"Yes, sir."

Later, she wondered if he'd ever used those words with Sam.

Montana's state capitol was small by most measures, with the Rockies providing a stunning backdrop, especially in early September. A quick ride from the airport took her past several Victorian mansions dating back to the days after Helena's gold rush glory. She drove with the windows open, breathing in the crisp, fresh air that seemed in short supply in Washington and thinking about what she hoped to accomplish.

Ned Blackwolf turned out to be a genial, knowledgeable, and good-looking Montana native. Williams couldn't help but notice his chiseled face, silver-flecked black hair, and bare ring finger. Blackwolf, a Crow, had moved off the reservation after high school. Williams had no experience of the life. Her mother's sister, Catori Two Moons, still lived there.

When talk turned to the murder of Undersheriff Mackenzie Scott, the discussion became serious. "You should be made aware that Sheriff Greene made an arrest just yesterday. He used analysts attached to our Major Case Billings office and gathered the appropriate evidence needed. The man is Cheyenne. He lives on the reservation." Blackwolf looked for a reaction. Williams remained outwardly impassive.

"Scott was killed at the Tubb ranch," he continued, "which means off tribal land. That puts the case in the hands of the county police."

"And effectively eliminates a path to FBI involvement," Williams noted. "No other suspects? Maybe someone who worked or lived at the ranch?"

"None that I heard about. The accused, Townson One Bear, had a couple of run-ins with the undersheriff. Mostly minor stuff, like public fighting, maybe a speeding ticket. He was briefly a suspect in a string of robberies, even though he had alibis for every one of them."

"Was One Bear singled out?"

Blackwolf sat back, his arms folded across his chest. "Can't say."

Or won't say, Williams thought.

"One more thing," she said. "You mentioned the Major Case forensic team's involvement. What about experienced investigators? Rosebud County Sheriff's Department has fewer than half a dozen deputies. No one is listed as a detective, at least not on their website. Seems they might have used the help on a homicide investigation."

Blackwolf stared at her for a long couple of seconds. "I assume you would like to stop by our Billings office. Let me see if I can get you in to see the field supervisor. If anyone has any insight into how the investigation has been conducted, it would be him."

"Happy to share what information I have," Williams replied. "Maybe he can give me some insight into Sheriff Greene. I could meet him, fill him in."

Blackwolf placed his elbows on the table and put his hands together as if in prayer. The look he gave her was unreadable.

"A word of advice, Special Agent Williams, and I suspect your supervisor already told you this. Tread very carefully."

Chapter 13

Fewer people attended Friday's update on the killer. Among those absent was Special Agent Dakota Williams, who remained in Montana.

Sam experienced a twinge of disappointment. She and Williams had gone for drinks the week before, a last-minute meetup instigated by Sam as she left her therapy session. She'd pegged the younger agent as potential friend material and she wasn't wrong.

To begin with, Special Agent Williams showed she had some serious Washington clout by getting them into an exclusive "cocktail lab" attached to a world-class restaurant, both of which were usually booked months in advance.

"Did you badge them?" Sam asked, "Or did you just show your face, and they fell all over themselves?"

"Look in a mirror, Lieutenant Tate. Those green eyes of yours probably function like a free pass."

Over exotic drinks, the two of them traded workplace stories along with frank assessments about the challenges of being strong, smart women. They ignored the gawkers and laughed when the bartender explained that power brokers were a dime a dozen but gorgeous women who could be mistaken for movie stars were more unusual.

They parted company with promises of another get-together the following week. That wasn't going to happen.

Sam turned her attention to her laptop. Every one of the participants received two reports last night, one from BAU and one from ViCAP. Sam perused hers before work this morning in place of her run.

Terry cleared his throat.

"If I can have your attention. As you all know by now, the charred remains of a detective from Uvalde, Texas, Mateo Pérez, were found at a campsite where the serial killer Pérez had captured had once burned his victims. In light of that development, we've invited Ranger Bodie Steel, from Texas DPS's Criminal Investigative Division, and Manny Rivera, Uvalde's new police chief to this meeting. Gentlemen, I imagine Special Agent Fuentes brought you up to speed."

"More or less," Steel said. His twang was strong. "Have y'all decided our murder fits the pattern the FBI has identified? And can we expect any further murders in our county?"

"As to the first, we hope your investigation yields usable DNA," Terry replied. "The killer is very careful, but no one's perfect. That leads me to the one bit of good news we have."

The Zoom callers leaned into their screens.

"Forensics investigators in Sacramento and Springfield managed to recover trace amounts of skin on the wire-bound notebook in the first instance and a partial palm print on the trunk of the car in the second. Those samples match each other. However—" he held up a hand as if to forestall a question, "neither matches anything in CODIS. We're still waiting on Atlanta and Uvalde, of course."

"CODIS is missing information, I've been told," Steel said.

"To a certain extent," Stein countered. "Our databases depend on input. A lot of local jurisdictions don't fill out the paperwork on violent offenders."

"We have an opportunity here to coordinate the information we do have," Terry pointed out. "We've got two samples. Let's see if all four match."

"Or five, if Rosebud County decides to get with the program," Fuentes remarked.

"Do we have any information on that subject from Agent Williams?" Kinney asked.

"She's still on the trail, am I right?" Fuentes asked, glancing at Terry.

"We expect to hear from her later on," Terry said. "For today, we're going to see what Agent Stein has to report. And Agent Kinney has worked up a profile. Some of you may not see the value in these sketches, but the Bureau has used them in the past to help solve murders. Let's begin with Agent Stein."

The young man pulled himself out of his slouched position.

"Ok. We received lists from Sacramento, Springfield, and Atlanta. Nearly 200 names in all. These included not only friends and relatives of the original victims but also the criminals who crossed paths which each of our law officers. Our first victim, John Frost, had the longest list because, I'd guess, he had the longest career. We took these names and looked to see if any of them showed up on the NCAVC database."

"Any matches?" Chief Block quizzed.

"In Frost's case, just one. Two more popped up, one tied to each of the Georgia investigators. All of them are currently in prison. None of them have anything to do with serial killings. And none of them could or would tell us whether a vengeful relative has taken up their cause."

"I doubt it." Molly Kinney spoke up. She was dressed all in black, which highlighted her red hair but also the seriousness of her work.

"Molly, please summarize your report."

"You're all professionals, so I shouldn't need to cover the basics, except to say that the categories of serial killer types are considered more fluid than they once were. Killers might be motivated by a combination of factors: lust, greed, envy, rejection, or the desire for attention. They are often triggered by a traumatic event. Some use the act of murder to make a statement, right a wrong, commemorate an event, or address a need. Ritual is an element of each murder. Serialists differ from assassins, whose work is purely transactional. There is an emotional component to their actions."

Kinney glanced at her tablet. "Our guy—and yes, I think it's a man—has staged a series of complicated scenes. Maybe he had help, but I don't believe he's working with a partner. He's fit enough to meet the physical requirements needed to, say, put a body in the trunk of a car or behead two women."

"He's scrupulous in his research and his execution. His approach takes control and a degree of maturity or experience. I'm going to put him into his mid-thirties, give or take a few years on either side. His attention to detail might indicate a thorough man with, for lack of a better way to put this, a dead conscience. That's probably how he appears to the outside world, even if his actions are driven by rage. He may hold a job that requires an analytical mind but not an overabundance of interaction. Possibly a researcher, computer coder, electrician. He's probably a conscientious employee. His job allows him to travel or at least control his own schedule. He earns a decent living. He's single, which allows him to spend his income on travel and incidentals."

"Like a chainsaw," Grisby, the GBI agent, said.

"I agree with Lieutenant Tate that he is finding his targets by researching them. It does seem as if he has inside knowledge. Some of the details he includes in his restaging of the original murders were never released to the public."

"I knew it," Fuentes exclaimed. "Our killer is a cop. Or an ex-cop."

"Or an analyst," Stein volunteered, then added, "but not from my department."

"Or he's an anonymous member of an online group which might include someone else with insider knowledge," Block suggested. "I'm amazed at what people feel is fine to share as long as no one uses real names."

"Maybe he has a relative in law enforcement."

"A prosecutor or a public defender," Powell, the Illinois State Police major, suggested.

"The point is," Kinney interjected, "we don't know how he gets his information or whether what he knows has any bearing on his activities. He'd likely be killing anyway."

"Any insights into his timing, Molly?" Fuentes asked.

"You mean, why now? First, we have to determine if the murder in April was his first or if there were earlier incidents."

"What about motive?" Chief Rivera asked.

"I still think it's envy," Fuentes said. "Maybe he got passed over for a promotion. Maybe he didn't get credit on a case he closed. Maybe his work wasn't appreciated."

"Anyone connected to my detective's case would be well into his fifties, if not older," Block said. "Not to mention Frost and his partner, who's since died, pretty much handled the case on their own. Besides, resentment is part of any stressful workplace. It doesn't send people across the country on a killing spree."

"It's not envy or resentment that motivates our killer," Kinney said. "It's—"

"Judgment," Sam cut in. "Our suspect targets the investigators because he judges them to be failures, not successes."

"He thinks he can do better?" Rivera asked.

"He thinks we can do better," Sam replied.

"That doesn't make any sense," Powell protested.

"I think what Sam means," Kinney replied, "is the killer feels justified in bringing down the harshest punishment possible on the people who have worked on serial killer cases."

"So our person—the Judge –"

"You're giving the killer a name?" Stein asked.

"Someone's bound to sooner or later," Fuentes replied. "Anyway, why does the Judge go after these cops? What are they guilty of? They did their jobs their jobs. They all caught the bad guys."

"Not quickly enough," Sam replied. "Not before the murderers claimed a couple of victims."

"That's just messed up," Steel said.

"Maybe not," Kinney said. "If the killer's anger is rooted in a single incident tied to a serial killing, these executions are how he directs his rage."

"Why doesn't this Judge person go after other serial killers?" Block asked. "Do us all a favor."

"Maybe," Sam suggested, "our unsub sees the cops as more responsible than the killers."

"Are we back to looking at relatives of the original victims?" Powell asked.

"We did that as soon as Agent Kinney shared the profile with us," Stein offered. "Unfortunately, none of the dozen or so thirty-something people we highlighted had profiles in our database, and all of them have alibis, according to information your agencies shared with us. We'll have to expand our parameters."

"Which means we're now looking for a needle in a much larger haystack," Terry said.

Chapter 14

"Fuentes, Tate, my office," Terry ordered as the small group left the conference room.

He shut the door and moved behind his desk. "Have either of you heard from Agent Williams?" he asked.

"Not since Tuesday evening," Fuentes said. "Her text said she'd met with your state contact in Helena, sir, and driven to Billings for a second meeting. She said it went well. When I asked if it looked like one of our serial-killer cases, she replied, 'maybe not but it's something.' I told her to leave it alone."

"And she was due back last night?"

"Yes, sir. She was supposed to see her aunt Wednesday and fly home yesterday. She didn't."

"The highway from Billings to the reservation runs through Rosebud County," Terry said. "Do you suppose she took an extra day and decided to drop in on Sheriff Greene?" His expression indicated he thought it was a terrible idea.

"Not necessarily," Sam said. She almost added, "She's not like me," but realized she didn't know if Williams had an impulsive side.

"She would have told me," Fuentes said of his partner. "She's conscientious about keeping me in the loop. Besides, I did more searching. Agent Williams never checked in for any return flights from either Billings or Denver. I'd call the aunt, but I forgot her name."

"Two Moons," Sam said. "First name Cat, short for Catori. Williams mentioned it last week when we went out for drinks."

"Fuentes, get a number for the woman and call her," Terry told the agent. "Don't alarm her, just ask when she expects her niece."

He placed his hands on the table and lowered his voice. "I don't need to tell you how serious this is. Not only because I have an agent in Montana who might have crossed the line from observer to investigator, but because in doing so, she may have put herself in harm's way."

"Do you want me to go out there?" Fuentes asked. "I can hop a flight, be in Billings late tonight their time."

"You just got back from Texas, Mike, and I was hoping you could get to Atlanta next."

"I can go," Sam said. The two men stared at her as though she'd grown a second head.

"Under whose authority?" Fuentes blurted out.

"I don't need anyone's authority to visit Montana," Sam retorted.

"No offense, Lieutenant, but we've already misplaced one team member, and she's an actual FBI agent."

"Mike," Terry cautioned.

"I can go as myself," Sam said. "I can make it into a mini-vacation, see an old friend from college, Lori Spielman."

She pushed ahead. "Lori has been asking me to visit for years. She's in Big Horn County, right next to Rosebud. Now's as good a time as any. I have a couple of days coming. It's the weekend, but maybe the head of the Billings field office can carve out an hour for me. I could visit Sheriff Greene. I met him on Zoom. He seemed to be a fan of mine. I can also talk with the aunt."

"All this in between your visit with Lori Spielman?" Terry asked, his skepticism on full display.

"I'm good at multitasking. As far as meeting Greene, he probably lives close to where he works. Honestly, my lack of connection to any federal agency is a positive."

"This is not a good idea," Fuentes protested.

Terry thought a moment. "Mike, get the aunt on the phone. Let's see what she has to say. Then I'll decide."

He looked at the door. Fuentes took the hint and left the room.

"Terry, I—"

"Look, Sam—"

They talked over one another, a common occurrence that in this instance broke the tension. In the quiet that followed, he fixed her with a stare.

"I know you're trying to help," he said at last. "What else is going on?"

"What? Nothing. Like you said, I just want to be of assistance."

"You want to get back out there, don't you?"

She looked at the floor like a child caught out for lying.

"It's hard to go from field work to administrative work, Sam. Fulfilling in some ways but a lot less action."

"That's not what's going on here, Terry. I'm not going on official business. I wouldn't go as Criminal Commander for Talbot County Sheriff's Department, either. Law officers take vacations, don't they? Besides, I have a feeling about this. I know gut instincts are supposed to be guides, not directives. But something about Sheriff Greene ..."

"You mean your admirer? How do you plan to get to him on a weekend, Sam? You were in the area and thought you'd drop by for a visit, see if he happened to run into an FBI agent, also in from Washington?"

"Not exactly," Sam said. "I'd use a more subtle approach."

Terry walked over to the window. He was weighing the pluses and minuses of her proposal and calculating the risk to his department but mostly to her.

He turned back to her. "Give me five minutes or so. I want to talk to Mike, see what he learned from the aunt. It's his partner who's missing, and he needs to feel comfortable. Oh, and don't you need to contact your friend, Lori?"

"I'll do that while you talk with Fuentes. Or maybe I'll go track down the elegant blond woman I ran into last week. She probably doesn't work here, though. Too classy for government work, present company excepted."

"Sam, what the hell are you talking about?"

She recalled her brief encounter with the woman in the gray suit the other day. "She knew my name. I suppose I have something of a reputation, but it felt odd."

Terry interrupted, "Good-looking woman, slim, medium tall, ash blond hair, blue eyes, impossible to guess her age or origin for that matter?"

"That sounds like her. I thought she might be British, but she could be from anywhere."

"You bumped into Suzanne. I'm surprised you two didn't spontaneously combust upon impact." Terry snickered. "She doesn't work for us or any other branch of any government except as a consultant."

"Really? And what is her field of expertise?"

"Ah, that's a story for another time. And so is yours. For now, wait here while I go get Mike. Then we'll all sit down and make a plan."

He walked out before she could respond.

Chapter 15

Early Saturday morning, Sam flew to Billings. She sat in economy like the tourist she was supposed to be. Her badge was tucked away in her purse, her firearm left behind. If she needed a gun, she would find one in Montana.

During the flight, she reviewed the previous day's meeting with Terry and Mike Fuentes. The call to Catori Two Moons yielded little information, only that the woman had expected her niece Wednesday evening. She assumed FBI business had kept the younger woman busy. Fuentes tried to ease her concerns. He wasn't sure he'd succeeded.

The men had reluctantly agreed to Sam's unofficial visit. Terry never asked for details about her friend Lori from Montana. Sam had gone to school with someone who married a Montana rancher. Lori or Lisa, she couldn't remember. The rest was what she deemed a necessary fiction, not that she felt comfortable with it.

She left a message with Sheriff Tanner and another with Bruce Gordy about needing a few days off to see a friend in need. Given the precarious position she was in, she reserved the right to provide as few details as possible.

During the two-hour layover, she spent a few minutes gazing at the majestic Rocky Mountains. Her phone interrupted her reverie. She connected to the sound of barking.

"Either you're at the dog park or Jax is calling," she laughed.

"I'm hoping to tire him out. Maybe he won't notice how much he misses you," Terry said.

"Does that work for humans as well?"

"I'll let you know after my run, provided our fur baby gives me an opportunity."

"I'm sorry I'm not there. It's challenging to have a dog in the city, especially a young, active one."

"It's even more challenging to have a weekend without you, Sam. Take care, okay? Ah, here's Jax now. Seems he has a friend he wants me to meet. Gotta go. Love you."

"Love you, too," she replied. As usual, she waited too long and spoke into dead air.

A hearty breakfast improved her mood and sharpened her resolve. Over a Denver omelet, she reviewed her notes and contemplated her next moves. She didn't know what happened to Williams between Tuesday and Friday, but she couldn't afford to imagine the worst. She needed to be level-headed and strategic about her approach.

She'd contacted a senior detective with the Montana Investigations Bureau's Major Case field office in Billings. Ethan Puhl was a veteran officer, originally from Pennsylvania, who'd been living in the area for more than twenty years. He'd served as a sheriff's deputy in neighboring Yellowstone County, honing his skills as a detective before he joined the state DCI. His bio listed him as a certified crime scene investigator who specialized in shooting reconstruction and blood stain pattern analysis. Nothing about branding, although Sam presumed such attacks weren't unknown in Montana.

Puhl showed interest in her abbreviated pitch. Her name recognition didn't hurt. People were fascinated with her story, an annoying truth but also a way to get a foot in the door.

They agreed to meet at 2 pm at Ebon Coffee Collective, not far from the airport and just a few blocks from the hotel Sam had booked for the night.

Cool, dry air enveloped her as she walked to her rental car. High clouds skittered across an open sky, helped by a thin wind. She stayed in the moment as long as she could.

Ethan Puhl wore his salt-and-pepper hair high and tight, mostly white at the sides with a generous amount of black on top. The style either reflected a military background or accommodated a receding hairline. His face was wide, his slate eyes shrewd. His facial hair stopped short of a full mustache and beard but well ahead of a goatee. Jeans, boots, and a chambray shirt completed the look. Montana man personified, minus the hat.

His smile appeared genuine, as if he was delighted to spend a free Saturday with her.

"Sam Tate, good to meet you. I'm Ethan Puhl. Welcome to Billings." They shook hands. "Was the flight okay?"

"Just fine. Thanks for meeting on your day off, Agent Puhl."

"Not at all. Since I'm off-duty, though, call me Push."

"Push Puhl?" Sam chuckled. "Did a so-called friend stick you with that nickname?"

"Army buddy. He claimed it described my approach to life, although I prefer to think of myself as more of a give and take kind of guy. You want coffee? I promise it'll be some of the best java you ever tasted. Not much in the way of food here, just burritos, waffles, and toast. And an apple pie I'm partial to." He patted his stomach.

"I'm good with coffee, thanks."

They ordered coffee and Puhl asked for the pie with two forks "just in case."

The coffee arrived hot and black, along with a small container of cream and another with oat milk. The pie showed up shortly after. The aroma of apples and sugar filled the air.

Puhl forked a piece and sighed with contentment.

"This pie is worth making the trip into town," he said. "That and a chance to meet the infamous Sheriff Sam Tate. Wait, are you still a sheriff?"

"Not quite. I head the Criminal Command Division for Talbot County Sheriff's Office in Maryland. My rank is lieutenant. Kind of like an undersheriff," she added and watched his gray eyes spark.

"And you're in Montana on a case?"

"I'm visiting a friend," she said. She'd already decided not to mention the missing FBI agent. "But since I'm here, I thought I'd collect background on an incident out near Forsyth here that resembles a homicide we're working on back East."

"You're talking about Mac Scott's murder." A statement, not a question, paired with an assessing gaze. Sam felt like a clue pinned to a murder board. "Surprised you'd know about that. How's it the same if you don't mind me asking?"

"I can't go into details, but our vic was in law enforcement. The method of death was set up to look like the work of someone he arrested years earlier for murder, someone who's still in jail."

Puhl sipped his coffee, his movements slow and deliberate. She had to keep herself from squirming.

"Sounds like a case I read about in Sacramento," he said at last. "Or maybe I'm thinking about Atlanta. That one made the nightly news, as I recall."

Sam folded her arms and let out an audible puff of air. "There's a little more to the story."

"I figured as much. You here on behalf of the FBI?"

She put up her hands. "Absolutely not. I work in Talbot County. I'm on vacation. The FBI asks for my opinion on occasion with regard to certain cases." She lifted her shoulders as if to say, "What can you do?"

"I see. So, someone in the FBI sees a pattern and since you're already out here on vacation, you volunteered to check around, see if the homicide over in Rosebud fits the pattern."

Sam ignored his disbelief. "Yes. Unfortunately, the sheriff doesn't seem inclined to speak to any of my colleagues. I hoped maybe he'd feel more comfortable talking with a fellow sheriff."

"You do know an arrest has been made. Arraignment's the end of this week."

"I heard. Do you think he's got the right person behind bars?"

Another flash behind the eyes. "You think he doesn't?"

"I'm not here to criticize, Push. I just want to find out if he has all the information he needs. I assume you were brought in to go over the crime scene, seeing as the sheriff's department doesn't have any experienced detectives."

Puhl sighed. "We serve at the behest of the local authorities, Lieutenant. In other words, we usually need an invitation. Jarrod's not real fond of letting anyone into his sandbox. Doesn't mean he failed to do everything by the book. The county coroner was out there. Evidence was collected and sent to the State Crime Lab. No one from Major Cases was called to assist in the investigation. Townson One Bear is Cheyenne, but the tribal police don't have any jurisdiction outside the rez. Was anything screwed up? I can't say. That's for a court to decide."

Sam considered everything Puhl said and some things he didn't. She wondered how Dakota took the news about One Bear and if she decided to do something about it.

Chapter 16

Sam spent a restless night at the Westin, punctuated by dreams about men with guns committing mayhem. Finally, in the last go-round, she imagined a beautiful woman with platinum hair who froze them all in place simply by pointing a finger. Better results than most of her nightmares, she had to admit.

She lingered in bed, savoring the extra five minutes she'd granted herself. Then she popped a pod into the room's coffee maker and ran through a series of sun salutations. That would have to do, at least until she got back home. Maybe she'd burn up calories by fighting the bad guys, whoever they were.

The Glock she'd purchased yesterday afternoon lay on the nightstand. Even used and even with the "law officer discount," it ran well over $300. She hoped not to need it. At the same time, she wanted to be prepared.

The coffee was decent, but its effect on Sam's mostly empty stomach was less than ideal. She threw her belongings into her duffle bag and headed downstairs for the free breakfast. Half an hour later, she was on the road to Forsyth. It was not yet eight in the morning.

On the ninety-minute ride up, she considered reaching out to Cat Two Moons. She wanted to get the woman's take on the arrest of Townson One Bear for the murder of Undersheriff Scott. But then she'd have to address the issue of the aunt's missing niece. Sam wasn't ready to spin more stories, not yet.

She'd never been to Montana before. She knew to expect a flatter terrain, but the vastness amazed her. At the edge of the Great Plains, the mountains were replaced by prairie land. The Yellowstone River ran alongside the highway. Even from the car, she could see miles out. In the distance, she spotted a herd of antelope. This part of Montana was indeed Big Sky Country.

Not a great place to hide out, she thought.

Forsyth was a pretty little town, low to the ground and with the requisite Main Street. The place billed itself as the "city of trees," although Sam figured anyone who lived on the coasts or closer to the mountains would scoff at the idea. Still, the foliage provided some topographical variation and the hint of a vibrant autumnal palette.

Sam had read that area housing prices had skyrocketed, fueled by a variety of people fleeing crowds and high taxes or seeking a simpler way of life. She wondered how the local population felt about the newcomers.

She drove along Main Street at a leisurely pace and parked. Not many people were out and about. Nothing was open except a hardware shop and a place called Caffeine High. She ducked in and had an excellent cup. The good people of Montana seemed to appreciate a quality cup of java. So did she, especially since last night's bad dreams still lingered.

No one paid her any mind. A woman dressed in beat-up jeans and boots didn't raise any eyebrows. She located the sheriff's department in a low-slung brick building off Main Street. The desks were empty save one, occupied by an impossibly young deputy who scrolled through his phone. He jumped to attention when Sam walked in.

"Can I help you, ma'am?"

She peered at his badge. Deputy Hutton.

"Good morning. I'm Sheriff Sam Tate. Sheriff Greene and I met a while ago and spoke on the phone just last week. I'm passing through on my way to see friends and thought I'd drop in. Although I'd guess he wouldn't be in on a Sunday. Probably out fly-fishing."

"Sheriff Tate, nice to meet you. Yeah, the sheriff ain't in on the weekends unless there's an emergency."

Sam gave the young deputy an easygoing smile. "I can understand that. He out with his kids somewhere?" She was riffing off what she'd gleaned from her online research. His home address was public as well, described as a four-bedroom split-level on two acres at the edge of town.

"Doubt it," Hutton was saying. "His kids do their own thing on Sundays. You know, they're teenagers, got their interests, their friends." This from a young man who couldn't have been more than nineteen or twenty. "He might be up at his house or maybe his cabin. Too bad you didn't come in yesterday."

"He worked on a Saturday?"

"Yes ma'am. Seeing as we're kind of short-staffed."

"Yes, I heard about Undersheriff Scott. Must be hard for everyone."

"Mac was one of the good ones." He swallowed. "Also, we're down another deputy, Melvin Cork. He's the acting undersheriff, but he's been out since Thursday. Says he's got the COVID, although some of us reckon he got bit by the love bug after he caught sight of the seriously good-looking woman who was in here the day before."

Sam covered her gut-wrenching certainty with a chuckle.

"What, you don't get good-looking women in the office, Deputy?" she teased.

The young man flushed. "Well, yeah, I mean, you're here."

"It's fine, Deputy Hutton. Tell me, what was so awesome about this particular woman?"

"Let me think how to say it. She looked like she'd been made from the most beautiful parts of women from all over the world, you know? Like if you took the finalists from the Miss Universe contest and combined them to make someone, what's the word?"

"Exotic," Sam finished for him. "What did this goddess want?"

"No idea. She asked for Sheriff Greene. She didn't have an appointment, so Marla at the front desk told her to wait while she called through. The woman didn't, though. Wait, I mean. She just walked right into the sheriff's office without a word."

"Wow, no one tried to stop her?"

"Melvin Cork jumped up, along with a couple of others. Mel followed the woman into Sheriff Greene's office and shut the door. He was there a good five minutes. Then he came out smiling and shaking his head, so we figured the sheriff had the situation under control."

"No yelling or fist-fighting?"

"Nothing I could hear. She was in there for an hour that I know of. That right there is peculiar. I went out on patrol during that time and when I got back, she was gone. No one seemed to remember when she left." Hutton shrugged. "I was gonna ask Mel, but he'd gone home sick."

"Huh." Sam had a lot of questions, but she knew if she started asking them, the deputy would grow suspicious.

"Sounds like an exciting day," she said. "Anyway, I'd better get going. Sorry I missed the sheriff. Maybe next time I'm in the area. Thanks for your help."

She stepped outside and walked around to the back of the building where she found a second door.

Easy in, easy out, she thought. But out to where?

Time to make a home visit.

Chapter 17

The Greene house was set on an incline and fronted by mossy grass and an ancient-looking pine tree. A deep gray Volvo was parked in the open garage with its hatchback up. A woman in a fleece vest with her hair pulled into a hasty ponytail carried grocery bags into the house. She appeared to favor one arm. Sam saw her wince each time she hoisted a bag.

Sam hopped out of her rental. "Hello," she called out, hoping not to cause the woman to startle. "Can I help you with those groceries?"

"Who are you?"

She was cautious, Sam realized. Understandable.

"Hi. My name is Lieutenant Sam Tate. I met your husband at a conference a while back." The first statement at least was true. The lying was becoming too challenging.

"Was he expecting you?" Still not giving an inch, although her arms must be killing her. Small town caution or something more? Sam scolded herself for not preparing for resistance.

"He wasn't. Look, I can show you my credentials or you can go inside and get him. It's just, you look uncomfortable, and I'm trying to help."

The woman appeared to relax ever so slightly. "Maybe you can grab whatever's left."

Sam picked up the last bag and a sixpack of beer. She went inside and took a discrete glance around.

The house was homey without falling into kitsch, well-appointed but not ostentatious. Cozy yet classic, with comfortable-looking furniture. Fabrics and textures suggested a lodge without resorting to any of the familiar motifs, such as an oversized fireplace or a ceiling with wooden beams. A large picture window at one end of the space provided a view of a small grouping of trees that still retained some of their fall foliage.

She headed into the updated kitchen and put the bags on the counter. The woman was struggling to put groceries away. She seemed fatigued. Sam cleared her throat.

"I dropped by to say hi—Jarrod said to do that anytime. Still, I guess he didn't intend for me to take it so literally."

The woman turned around, a thin smile on her face. "Sounds like Jarrod. I'm Cindy Greene, his wife. He's not here. And I'm sorry to be so rude, it's just ..."

"You're hurting and I'm intruding. I get it."

Cindy Greene suddenly looked vulnerable. She was Sam's age or maybe a little older. Average height, a bit thin. Dishwater blond hair with a hint of silver and blue-gray eyes. No doubt pretty in high school and on her wedding day. Now, she seemed faded and worn, as if she'd lost her step or maybe her dreams.

Then there were the fresh bruises on her face, neck, and wrist. She felt Sam's gaze and put a hand to her face. "Stupid misstep off the front porch," she explained. "I'm lucky I didn't chip a tooth."

"I hope you get that arm looked at."

"I will if it doesn't stop hurting. Most likely it's just bruised. This kind of thing heals." Her expression cleared. "Let me make you a cup of coffee to make up for my inhospitable greeting."

"Easy as pie. The kids got me a fancy java machine for Christmas Brews one cup at a time."

"Black, if it's not too much trouble."

While her hostess busied herself with the coffee, Sam settled on a stool at the kitchen's center island, which looked new, and glanced around. She caught sight of a family photo and found her next opening.

"How are the boys? JJ was bragging on them, as I remember."

"Here's your coffee. Yes, we're both very proud of the boys. Honestly, they're my everything. Toby is seventeen, almost eighteen. Star of the football team. Got himself a scholarship to Montana State next year. Bart turned sixteen. He runs track and does the most amazing drawings on the computer. They're good boys—popular, smart, athletic—but not jerks if you catch my drift."

"I do. They take after their father, I'll bet."

Cindy Greene's face clouded. She touched her injured shoulder absently. "I suppose they might, Lieutenant," she faltered.

Sam recognized the signs. She wanted to reach across the table and grab the woman's hand. She wanted to give assurances, promise safety and assistance and a life free from fear and pain. She couldn't do that. Not until she had answers.

"Call me Sam. Listen, Cindy—may I call you Cindy?"

"Go ahead." Her guard had gone back up.

"Okay. I'm a cop, just like your husband. It's a tough profession. Tough on a woman because we're in the minority. Tough on a man because there are certain expectations. And sometimes we cops bring our work stresses home. I just wondered if perhaps your injuries aren't from an accident."

"What are you implying?"

Sam took a deep breath. "Has someone hurt you?"

The woman responded with shock and anger. "What gives you the right to come in here and throw around such accusations?" she demanded.

"I'm not accusing, Cindy. I'm asking out of concern. If I'm off the mark, I'm truly sorry."

Greene's thin veneer of righteous indignation slid off at Sam's words, delivered in a careful, gentle tone. "He's a good man, Sam. Gruff at times, stricter with the boys growing up than I would have liked."

"You're talking about your husband."

"Jarrod never hit them," she went on. "Not once. Maybe it was because they got big fast. Before you knew it, they'd matched him for size and strength."

"But you never did."

She shrugged. "JJ gets worked up from time to time. He has no place to put all that anger, so he lashes out. That's no excuse for what I did."

The gut instinct that served Sam so well, that operated like an algorithm to sort, assess, and apply experience and information buried below her immediate consciousness, floated an idea to the surface.

"How well did you know Mac Scott, Cindy?"

She looked away. "He was a friend."

"I had a colleague once," Sam replied quietly. "We partnered on several cases. We got close. He was deeply involved with someone else. I was unavailable. We tried to stay just friends. It didn't work out that way."

Greene hung her head. "Mac had troubles at home. Nothing physical. He and his wife simply didn't talk. We did. It felt so natural. But we called it off, mainly because I was scared Mac might want to confront Jarrod."

Or the other way around, Sam thought. She decided not to burden Cindy Greene with the idea her husband was a murderer on top of everything else.

"Where is JJ today?"

"He went to his cabin. I mean, it's the family cabin but now that the boys are older, he mostly goes up there alone to fish."

"That's quite a bit west of here," Sam guessed.

"Near Greycliff. Almost 150 miles but JJ says the fishing's better in the mountains." She wore a concerned expression. "You're not going out to see him, are you? I don't think he'd want to be disturbed."

"No, no. Let's leave him be." Sam stood. "Thanks for the coffee. Go ahead and let JJ know I stopped by. And take care of yourself, okay?"

"I absolutely will. Thank you, Sam."

Sam climbed back into her rental and waved goodbye to the woman who never expected to be unsafe in her own home. Then she plugged in her phone and asked Siri for directions to Greycliff.

Chapter 18

To get to Greycliff, Sam had to drive back through Billings, then on to Columbus. At least it was mostly highway, although even with her foot hard on the pedal, she needed about two hours to traverse the 142-mile distance.

As she drove towards her destination, the land rose, the temperature dropped. Sam felt as if she'd crossed into a different world. In the near distance, she could see mountain ranges to the south and to the west. The number of trees increased. More than half of them had already changed over to gold, orange, and burgundy Here one could live with some degree of privacy, despite development in the region.

Signs for fly fishing and river excursions proliferated along the highway. She passed at least one campground. At Greycliff, she got off the highway to grab a sandwich and figure out how she'd find the man she suspected of all sorts of things.

As luck would have it, JJ Greene was a familiar presence in the area, according to the kid who worked in the convenience store next to the gas station.

"Sheriff Greene? Yeah, I know him some. Nice guy. He invited me up to his cabin once or twice when he'd bring his sons. I was a little older, but I liked playing big brother."

Sam looked at the young man with his shock of light brown hair that fell over his pale gray eyes. She figured him to be no more than eighteen. Amazing how significant a year or two was to a child.

"You see him recently?"

"As a matter of fact, he stopped in yesterday with a friend of his."

"A woman?" Sam asked too quickly.

"Didn't see a woman, just another fella."

"We're colleagues," Sam told the young man, flashing her widest smile. "I was hoping to surprise him. I don't suppose you have an address?"

"Not an address but I got an idea where it is.

The young man pulled out a piece of paper and started drawing. "Here's what I remember," he said when he'd finished."

He handed her a simple map. ""There you go. It's really close. Shouldn't take more than ten minutes."

She needed twice that. Some of the roads were unmarked. Homes were few and far between. The ones she passed did not display numbers or names. People liked their privacy, she decided.

After several false turns, she came upon a one-story log cabin with a stone chimney, set inside two acres and hidden by Ponderosa pine.

Sam pulled off the road and parked well back from the house. She scanned the old trees, looking for overhead cameras. Any security features were well hidden or, she hoped, absent. All she had to do was exit the car without slamming the door or tripping over any roots buried under the dry needles.

The deciduous trees sprinkled among the pines had begun to change color. Reds and golds were splashed gaudily against the muted and shadowed earth tones that predominated. The quiet was its own soundtrack. Bird song and the wind that stirred the pines. She heard nothing human—no cars, no planes, no buzzsaws or mowers. Even the air was different, clean, clear, and cool, almost arid. Quite a change from the late-summer swamp that was Washington.

She pulled on a cap and gloves, zipped her jacket, and retrieved her weapon from the glove compartment. She decided to leave her Ray-Bans in the car. Her phone and keys went into the bag around her waist, which already held her ID, a pen flashlight, and an all-purpose Swiss Army knife. She had a second weapon in her boot, a Schrade 19 knife she'd carried ever since her stint in Afghanistan. It was small but lethal.

The cabin looked to be well-built, with a tidy front porch and a sturdy foundation. A perfect weekend retreat. She'd noted a lake in the vicinity. A sliver of dappled blue suggested it was close by.

A newer model black Jeep Cherokee sat out front. As Sam made her way to the house, she spied another vehicle, a tan Kia with out-of-state plates and a sticker from a rental agency.

Sam's heart began to race. She slowed her breathing and crept to the side of the house and up to a smallish window. She wondered if the Greene family had a dog and if it might have made the trip out here. She should have asked.

Peeking inside, she caught sight of a decent-sized kitchen that opened into a sitting area with couch, chairs, lamps, several outlets, and what looked to be a wall vent. The sheriff's hideaway was equipped with the infrastructure needed to make it livable year-round.

No creatures, human or animal, moved. The breeze had stilled, the birds had stopped calling to each other.

Maybe everyone's out fishing, she thought, but she couldn't make herself believe it. She kept moving, gun at her side (she didn't want to shoot someone by accident) and searched for a low window or a set of stairs leading to a lower level.

When she rounded the corner of the house, she nearly bumped into Jarrod Greene standing in front of a worn set of sloping doors with a bowl in his hand.

He was even bigger than he appeared on the Facetime call, tall and wide like the linebacker he was back in his glory days. In early middle age, he managed to look both softer around the shoulders and chin, and harder around the eyes.

He covered his surprise with a smile. "Sheriff Sam Tate, as I live and breathe. My deputy mentioned you'd stopped by the office earlier today, although I didn't expect to see you in my neck of the woods. And this literally is my neck of the woods," he added and dropped the smile.

"I wanted to be sure to catch you before I left, Sheriff. Looks like I interrupted a meal delivery. Or are you having an outdoor picnic in front of your cellar?"

"A sense of humor. I like that in a woman. Shows character."

He moved his eyes to her firearm, to the dish he held in his hand, and back again in her general direction. "Seems you brought a gun to a food fight," he said with a chuckle. "Doesn't seem fair."

Sam heard the crack of a twig and whirled, her gun raised. A mustachioed man with jet-black hair and dressed in a navy parka trained a rifle on her. He was close enough to blow her away even if she got off a shot.

"Mind dropping your weapon, ma'am? Toss it behind you if you please."

Behind her, she heard Greene grunt as he bent to pick up the gun. Then, without warning, he came up behind her, reached under her jacket, and yanked off her waist pack. In that moment, she felt both violated and vulnerable.

She could hear Terry's voice in her head, reminding her that going it alone isn't always advisable. Her own internal nag was asking why she didn't invite Ethan Puhl along on this little episode with her. Was she afraid he'd decline or tell her she needed to go through "proper channels"?

That would have been preferable to finding herself out in the woods in the foothills of Montana in the company of two armed men with plenty to lose.

You're here for Dakota, she reminded herself. Remember that.

"Sorry to relieve you of your tools of the trade, Lieutenant," Greene was saying. "Can't be too careful out here in the woods."

Sam fixed her gaze on the man with the rifle. "Deputy Cork, I presume," she said. "Or is it Acting Undersheriff Cork now?"

"How 'bout you call me sir?" Cork sneered. "Better yet, keep your mouth shut."

"Now Mel," Greene said. "Let's try to be polite to our unexpected guest, never mind she wasn't invited to the party. She's been outfoxed. Probably doesn't sit well with her."

"You know what might not sit well with your new undersheriff, Greene?" Sam said. "Prison time for kidnapping a federal agent. Or killing one, if it came to that."

She caught Cork's frown. Maybe he hadn't thought that far ahead. She might be able to use that.

Jarrod Greene chuckled. "Federal agent? That's not you, Lieutenant Tate from Talbot County, Maryland. And if you're referring to the woman who barged into my office last week, I don't recall her showing any ID. I figured her for an irate member of the Cheyenne Nation come to complain about the lawful arrest we made. We get a lot of those visits."

Sam turned her back on the rifle-toting man and looked Greene full in the face. "I came here after meeting with Cindy, your wife. I'd say she's being abused and you're the abuser. You might think that makes you a real man but no. It makes you a coward and a bully. Can you blame her for seeking comfort and satisfaction from someone who is? Someone like Mac Scott?"

Greene slugged her hard enough to send her down on one knee. Sam kept herself from falling further through sheer determination not to humble herself before this man.

"Hold on." Cork kept his gun on Sam but looked at his boss. "Jarrod, you said Mac was the one beating on his wife. You were going to talk to him, set him straight. Then things got outta hand. I figured self-defense, not straight-up murder. That ain't right."

"Melvin, come on," Green said. "After all I've done for you, you're gonna quibble about details?"

"This ain't no small thing, J.J."

"No, it ain't," Greene agreed. He lifted his rifle and shot the other man right between the eyes. "Damned idiot," he complained. "Come to think of it, he would have made a terrible undersheriff."

Sam had seen a lot in her years, but the ease with which her adversary took out the man who'd risked his career for his boss chilled her. If, as she strongly suspected, he'd broken the neck of his undersheriff, he was likely capable of anything.

She stood, moving slowly, fighting off nausea and trying to ignore her aching jaw. "Why did you brand Mac Scott?" she asked. "Were you trying to imitate the MO from the serial case he solved?"

"Funny you should ask. I didn't think about the Cattleman Killer when I used the brand. I found the branding iron out by the fence. With its big A against a mountain range, kind of seemed appropriate, kind of like in The Scarlet Letter. Perfect for the son of a bitch. We only met near the ranch because it's halfway between his place and mine. Mel got it half right; there was a struggle, although I came in hot."

"Why didn't you let the FBI believe the death was connected to their larger investigation?"

His expression darkened. "I don't need the feds coming anywhere near Montana. We do our own thing out here. Call it prairie justice."

"And One Bear is part of that system of justice?"

"A useful substitute. A drunk with a history of disorderly conduct. No love lost between him and Mac." He looked around and sighed. "I'm gonna end up with a couple more bodies than I bargained for, but I got a plan for that."

"Is Agent Williams alive?"

He shrugged. "She was the last time I checked. Either way, you two are gonna end up in the same place." He grabbed her by her arm. "In you go."

Sam stumbled and yanked Greene off-balance. As she anticipated, he loosened his grip. She reached into her boot to retrieve her knife. She swung the weapon to Greene's gun hand and sliced his wrist almost to the bone. Greene dropped the Glock with a piercing scream. It hit the ground without firing, which Sam considered nothing less than a miracle. She snatched the weapon and pointed it at the man who crouched on the ground, writhing in pain.

"Montana DCI!" yelled a familiar voice.

"Over here, Push. 'Bout time you showed up."

Chapter 19

"Sam, are you okay?" Ethan Puhl came running up from the opposite side of the house, followed by four men in windbreakers with matching insignias. "Are you bleeding? Wow, that's some punch you took. What's the other guy look like?"

"See for yourself." She was on the ground but still held the gun on her quarry. "Sheriff Greene here has sustained a serious wound. Maybe we could apply a tourniquet. Or we could just let him bleed out."

"Help me!" Greene screamed. "I'm hurt!"

A slender bearded man ran up with a black bag and dropped to his knees beside the wounded Sheriff. Two other men stood over him, arms crossed.

"Stop yelling and let Doc Linter work his magic," Puhl ordered Greene.

"You brought a doctor?" Sam asked.

"Sweet Grass County Sheriff's reserves. They've got a doctor, a teacher, a mechanic, and a trucker."

"How did you find me?" Sam asked.

"Cindy Greene called the office. Seems she was a little concerned about you. Not that she needed to be."

"I still wish you'd shown up ten minutes ago," Sam replied, touching her jaw and wincing.

"You should have asked me to come with you."

"That thought did occur to me."

" You need some ice for that?"

Sam holstered her gun, picked up her pack and strapped it back on. "Not yet. We need to get into the cellar. Give me a hand." She and Puhl, along with one of the volunteers, lifted the heavy sloped doors, which opened to a pitch-black space.

Puhl held a flashlight as she eased herself down the shaky ladder with one hand. When she hit dirt, she pulled out her flashlight, her heart pounding.

The space was small, maybe six by ten feet. No utilities or storage, basically a hole in the ground with one concrete wall meant to provide reinforcement. Her beam caught the figure slouched against it, attached by a chain that bound her arms to her sides above the elbows. Head lolling to one side, long hair falling across a bruised face. A plate of uneaten food on the ground, along with a collection of water bottles and a few candy wrappers.

"I've got her," Sam called out. She squatted beside the woman and found a pulse, weak but steady. "She's alive, but she's chained. I could use a bolt cutter."

"On it," Puhl replied and issued instructions to his team.

"Agent Williams. Dakota, can you hear me?" She brushed back the woman's hair and shook her shoulder. Gently at first, then a little more forcefully.

Williams gasped and sat up straight. She struggled against the chains, ready to fight despite her weakened condition.

"Easy does it, Agent Williams. You've had an ordeal, to put it mildly."

Williams murmured something. Sam leaned in to catch the barely audible words.

"No shit," Williams croaked. "To put it mildly."

Sam laughed with relief. "How about we get you out of here?"

As if on cue, a young man with dusky hair clamored down the ladder with a pair of sturdy bolt cutters. He strode over as if he freed kidnap victims every day. Two well-placed clips and some gentle tugging and the chain fell away. He helped Sam get Williams to her feet.

"Much obliged, Deputy."

"Norton, ma'am. Glad to help."

The two of them guided the federal agent up the ladder, where she sunk to her knees on the ground. Then she caught sight of Greene. With a feral cry, she pushed to her feet and rushed him.

Sam grabbed her arm, and Puhl caught Williams as she staggered against him.

"You have every right to feel like murdering this man, Agent Williams. But we gotta do this another way."

Williams sunk to the ground, spent. Sam fished in her belt bag and retrieved an energy bar.

"I want you strong enough to walk to the car, okay?"

"All I want," Williams insisted, "is food I can trust, coffee I can drink, a shower I can stand in for as long as I want, and a warm bed I can sleep in."

"We can make that happen."

Williams leaned against Sam. "Might need a shoulder when the shock wears off," she whispered.

Sam held her friend tightly. "We can make that happen, too," she said.

Greene had finally stopped wailing, helped by a shot of painkiller administered by Linton. Another deputy handed Sam an ice pack wrapped in a towel, which she applied to her jaw with a minimal amount of cursing.

Puhl officially arrested Greene and read him his rights. Doc Linton recommended they run the sheriff up to the 24-hour clinic before transporting him back to Billings.

"The cut is nasty and it's deep," Linton reported. "His artery was nicked. He may have severed a tendon. I can't be sure. What I did was triage, but he needs that hand x-rayed and sewn up."

"He's a dangerous man," Puhl said. "Killed two so far."

"I'm a reserve deputy as well as a doctor, Agent Puhl. This man can be my patient and my prisoner at the same time. I've got three more of my brethren on hand who are willing to come with me to the clinic, then transport him back to Billings. We're all armed."

Linton looked at Mel Cork's body. "We'll take him to the morgue. Your DCI people can take it from there." He stepped over to Williams, peered into her eyes, moved her head, pressed on her abdomen, and squeezed her ribs, his movements swift and sure. "This young woman seems to be in good shape, all things considered. Mostly scrapes and bruises. Still, she needs to be checked out."

"I want to go to Billings," Williams declared. She surveyed the skeptical faces. "I survived four nights in that hole, I can make it another hour."

"St. Vincent's," Puhl recommended. "I'll call ahead."

"I'll get her there," Sam replied.

"Fine. I'll meet you there. Agent Williams, we'll get your car back to the rental agency. Lieutenant Tate, keep ice on that jaw."

"You want me to drive one-handed?"

"It's Montana. You can drive any way you please."

Chapter 20

Sam tucked the agent into the car with a coverlet she'd "borrowed" from the hotel. Williams pulled the blanket up over her head and promptly fell asleep. Fine by Sam. She needed some quiet time to get her adrenaline under control. She popped some Advil supplied by the resourceful doctor.

She hadn't used her knife like that since combat training. Combined with the shock of seeing Greene execute his loyal second and the relief of finding Williams alive, it was a lot to take in.

Half an hour into the drive, she put in her earbuds and called Terry.

"Hey, I thought we weren't going to talk until tonight. Any luck with the search for my agent?"

"We found her, Terry. I found her. We're on our way to the hospital in Billings. She's going to be alright. There's a lot more to tell you, and I will tonight. Sheriff Greene is as dirty as they come. He killed Mac Scott and one other, but he isn't our serial killer, and this isn't our case."

"Can you come home soon?"

The simple request soothed her. She exhaled, and the tension began to slip away.

"Depends on who needs to talk with me."

"Let me make some calls. Get back to me as soon as you've got Agent Williams settled. And tell her to take all the time her doctors tell her she needs. We want her back whole and healthy."

"Yes, boss," Sam said with a grin that hurt. She disconnected and noticed Williams had her hazel eyes open.

"Do me a favor, Tate. Call my aunt. She's my next of kin. She'll be all over the doctors like nobody's business. You go home. I'll follow as soon as I can. And keep ice on your jaw." She yawned and nodded off again.

Sam placed a call to Cat Two Moons and filled her in as concisely as possible. The aunt asked only where her niece would be taken and how soon they'd arrive.

"St. Vincent's," she said with obvious disdain. "Fine, I will allow my niece to be examined by their doctors. Then I'm taking her home to the reservation."

Sam didn't argue. She suspected Cat Two Moons was a force to be reckoned with, but a force for good as far as Williams was concerned.

A team waited at the emergency entrance to St. Vincent's. As they transferred Williams to a gurney, Sam offered a summary of the woman's ordeal. She left the keys in the car, grabbed her bag, and followed, with Puhl right behind her.

"Sam, you need to be checked out."

"Me? I'm fine."

"Your jaw says otherwise. This is my jurisdiction, Lieutenant Tate, and I'm making the call."

Sam bit her lip to keep from laughing. She let herself be led away by a nurse. As expected, she was fine, except for a fist-sized bump that hurt like hell. Her blood pressure was slightly elevated, but nothing like what it must have been a couple of hours earlier. A local injection eased some of the pain. The nurse offered

Vicodin. She reassured the woman that the Advil she'd taken was working fine. It wasn't, not really, but she needed a clear head.

Ten minutes later, she escaped the exam room to find Cat Two Moons in the lobby. A small, lean woman, her dark hair threaded with gray, she might have been anywhere from fifty to seventy. Her handshake was firm, her manner matter-of-fact.

"I want to see my niece, but there seems to be a problem."

"She's an FBI agent who was kidnapped," Sam said. "Just means there are hoops to jump through. Also, it's a Sunday. Let me see what I can find out."

"There are always hoops for us to jump through," Two Moons sniffed. "You rescued her?"

"I located her," Sam replied.

"Leave it to a woman," Two Moons said before adding, "Thank you."

Puhl appeared with a young doctor as Sam and the aunt stepped up to the admitting desk. "Ms. Two Moons, I'm Agent Ethan Puhl with the Montana Division of Criminal Investigations. This is Dr. Abdallah Ahsan, who is overseeing your niece's case."

The woman eyed the trim, neatly bearded Ahsan. She inclined her head, a sign of approval. The good doctor was apparently good enough.

While the two of them discussed patient health, Puhl took Sam aside. "Agent Williams is fine. Bruises and cuts and she's pretty dehydrated, as you might expect. Nothing broken. No internal bleeding. She doesn't even need stitches."

"She's lucky to be alive," Sam noted. "Greene doesn't seem to have a problem disposing of inconvenient people. I should go see her."

"The doctor gave her something to sleep. The aunt's going to stay. I imagine she'll have something to say about how long her niece stays." He looked at Sam with concern. "Maybe you should take a seat."

"Good idea." She sank into the nearest chair. Puhl went to get her a glass of water.

"I'm supposed to debrief you," Puhl continued. "Then, the brass up in Helena want to talk with you. There are a few ruffled feathers about jurisdiction and overreach. However, there's the matter of finding justice for the wrongly accused Cheyenne man, which looks good on DOJ's ledger. Assistant Director Sloan will take responsibility for sending both Williams and you. I understand he's spoken with Ned Blackwolf. The point is, none of this has to happen in person, and none of it has to happen today."

She told him, "Maybe you'll get a promotion or at least a gold star for giving up your weekend."

"Are you kidding? I assisted in the capture of a rogue cop, found evidence that will free a wrongly convicted man, located a missing FBI agent, and got to work with the infamous Sam Tate. It was a great weekend. Beats sitting in front of the TV."

Sam was suddenly bone tired. She looked at her watch, shocked to discover it was nearly 5 pm Mountain Time.

"I need to make a call," she said. "Then I need to find a hotel. Maybe I can check back into the Westin."

"Make the call. You might not need the hotel." He stuck out a hand. "Nice to have worked with you, Lieutenant Sam Tate. See you online, and if you're ever back in Montana, please look me up." He walked away just as her phone rang.

"You ready?" Terry asked.

"For what?"

"Got you transport back to D.C. Your ride to the private airfield is sitting outside. If you hustle, we should have you back here just after midnight. Dinner is included."

"How the hell did you manage that?"

"I called in a favor from one of the senators from the great state of Montana. The wealthy one. He was delighted to fly a hero home, although I left the identity of said hero a little vague."

"I can't believe you arranged this all for me," Sam said as she raced out the door to a waiting Escalade with federal plates.

"Believe it, Tate," he said. "Fly safe."

Chapter 21

The billionaire senator from Montana had made his fortune in construction and real estate. Those businesses were now run by his adult sons, though he retained a seat on the board. He still availed himself of the company jet or loaned it out for special occasions. As he told Terry, this was one such occasion.

"Our people aren't generally fond of anything to do with the federal government. But this case is a win for a lot of folks. The fact that your agent on the ground is a Native American originally from Montana doesn't hurt. I assume that's who's returning."

"I think it best we focus the credit on the state's DCI people, especially Agent Ethan Puhl," Terry recommended. He and Sam had agreed they should maximize Puhl's involvement and make no mention of hers.

"Sure, we can play it that way," the senator chuckled. "You just tell whoever you're bringing home to get herself some well-deserved rest."

So much for discretion, Terry thought.

Sam called when the flight was en route. She sounded tired but happy.

"This is the most amazing ride I've ever had, Terry," she enthused. "And that's not the wine talking, although I am enjoying a very fine red."

"I hope they're serving dinner with that."

"Chateaubriand with asparagus and Yukon gold potatoes. I'm starving. Luckily, I have a very nice cheese platter to tide me over. Tell me, how can I ever thank the senator?"

"Don't mention it. I mean that literally. The senator is being rewarded by positive publicity, which he's going to exploit for all it's worth."

"My lips are sealed. Well, except to eat and drink."

"You deserve it. How's Dakota?"

"She's going to be fine. They're keeping her overnight, then the aunt is driving her to the reservation for a couple of days of R&R. She'll be back before Friday."

"You're not expected until Tuesday, right?"

"Right. I can pick up Jax and head back."

"You're coming to my apartment and crashing. Tomorrow you'll sleep in. I'll get Jax to doggy daycare."

"Let him stay. I'll have someone to cuddle with when you go to work."

"It's best you lay low anyway," Terry said. "My goal is to keep you out of the news. Not sure Agent Williams will be so lucky."

"She's pretty safe from the media right now. I'll shoot a message to my boss and my team to play it close to the vest until I get back. I didn't exactly fill them in."

"Do that. Enjoy your meal. Drink your wine. Maybe grab some shuteye. I'll see you in three-and-a-half hours. And don't worry about serial killers. Nothing's going to happen tonight."

* * *

When Terry left for work the next morning, both Sam and Jax were zonked out. Terry generally enforced the "no pets on the bed" rule when he and Sam were together, but the dog had been almost frantic with joy at the arrival of his mistress. When the humans tumbled into bed at 1:30 am, he lay on the floor, softly whimpering until Terry relented. Jax jumped up and made himself comfortable at the foot of the bed. His paw rested on Sam's ankle, perhaps to reassure himself she was there.

Terry met with his boss as soon as he got in. He was requested to explain why he sent an FBI agent to investigate a local murder. The Director had questions and the media outlets would soon be pressing the Bureau for details. Terry's goal was to deflect attention away from any improprieties Agent Williams might have committed.

Sam's name never came up, although everyone knew who was on the plane. The FBI had nothing to say about a non-employee who flew on a private jet. Her adventure might or might not go over with her boss. Presumably, she knew how to handle him.

Fuentes popped his head into Terry's office at about 9:30.

"Morning," he said. "Good news, I hear."

"Agent Williams is safe, thank God."

"And Sam Tate executes another GOAT move." He rolled his eyes. "Maybe she should be working for us."

"I'm not sure she's primed to go back to training, even for a year. Besides, you've got a pretty gutsy partner yourself, as I understand it."

"Yeah, Williams did a good job. The Montana case is off the table, right?"

"It is," Terry agreed. "We still have a serial killer to track down."

"True enough. I'm headed to Atlanta this afternoon. I guess you know the bodies were found in with the vultures." Fuentes grimaced. "Headless bodies. Agents are still processing the scene."

"Which suggests the killings took place in the zoo, right?"

"That's the working theory. The problem is, when exactly? And where? And where are the heads?"

"I trust GBI to come up with those answers, Mike. If they require forensic assistance, we can give it to them. Our focus is on uncovering patterns and then finding the son of a bitch who's doing this."

"One more thing, sir. GBI thinks they might have a witness, someone who may have seen our killer."

"You're kidding! That's hopeful news. Maybe we can get a general physical description."

"It's a child, sir, an eight-year-old boy. He was at the zoo with his mother when the agents were attacked. He went silent for a week before speaking last night. Whatever he said had his mother calling a hotline and then a counselor, not necessarily in that order."

"Christ almighty. Just when you think this can't get any worse."

"It can always get worse, sir," Fuentes said. "In our line of work, it usually does."

Chapter 22

Sam returned to work a day early and not even close to rested. Gordy, ever the detective, sized her up as soon as he saw her at her desk.

"Back a day early and you look beat up. I thought you'd be horseback-riding or fly-fishing, not used for bait."

Sam flinched at her sergeant's keen assessment. "You know me, Gordy. Work hard, play hard."

"Uh-huh. Well, let's hope things stay quiet around here so you can recover from your so-called vacation. By the way, something came for you. I kept it safe."

"What is it?"

"Beats me. It isn't ticking. That's all I know."

Sam unwrapped the brown box he handed her. Inside was a mug with an image of a medal. The mug said, "Well done."

"Someone is yanking my chain," she complained.

"Don't look at me," Gordy protested.

Sam put the mug in a desk drawer and promptly forgot about it.

Two days later, Talbot County caught its first homicide in more than a year. A teenager back from school found his mother stabbed to death in the living room. Sam canceled her trip to D.C. and accompanied Gordy and Pat to the scene. While her detectives questioned the distraught young man, Sam made sure she gave space to the forensic investigator. Martin Lloyd was well-known to her not just from work but also because he was dating her department's CSI.

"Thoughts?" she asked the tall and taciturn Lloyd when he leaned back.

"Homicide. Stab wounds are varied and erratic, almost frantic. And sloppy. No weapon, but I'm betting on a missing kitchen knife. And probably a print or two."

"Crime of passion?"

Lloyd shrugged. "That's your department, Lieutenant. Though if it walks like a duck ..."

"It's a homicide on the Eastern Shore," Sam quipped. "Thanks, Martin."

By the time two detectives from Maryland State Police arrived, Gordy and Pat had already learned from the son that his mother Anna had an ex-boyfriend with a violent streak. A quick canvas of the neighborhood produced a single witness who remembered seeing an unfamiliar car parked in front of the house. A recovered print tied the ex-boyfriend to the car, and a statewide APB went out.

Within a week, the suspect was found at his uncle's home in Oxford, a good-sized town in a neighboring county. Pat and Gordy were part of the takedown, which went off without a hitch.

"Criminally easy," Gordy told Sam later. "McCready was thrilled to be part of the entry team."

"Take the win, Sergeant. Both of you. Most cases don't work that way. Now if you'll excuse me, I'm headed to D.C."

"More work?"

She smiled. "I hope more play."

She arrived at Terry's at six with Jax in tow. The balmy temperatures meant they could dine outside at their favorite burger place with the thankfully well-behaved dog. After a long stroll, they all returned to the apartment where Jax worked on his new bone while Terry and Sam made their own kind of fun.

* * *

DNA confirmed that the victims in the Springfield and Uvalde homicides were likely killed by the same person. The Sacramento and Atlanta murders, on the other hand, yielded nothing usable for comparison.

That soon changed.

The day before the latest task force meeting, an unexpected downpour swept through central Georgia and flooded parts of the city. An inquisitive Australian Shepherd out for a walk came upon an unmarked grave of sorts and began digging the soft earth. What she uncovered delighted the dog but traumatized her owner.

"Both of them?" Terry pressed when Fuentes came to report that morning.

"Yes, sir. Wrapped in a bag. Significant decomp had occurred, and whoever buried them likely used gloves Somehow the forensic team was able to extract a sample of unidentified DNA from one of the, um, heads."

"One small piece of good news," Terry noted. "I suppose we should be relieved he didn't put them on display."

"He put a ribbon on the bag, sir."

Terry slapped his desk. "I hate this fucking guy," he said.

"At least this gives us something to report," Fuentes said.

"And a decision to make."

"Time to go wide, sir?"

"I think so."

* * *

Sam got to FBI headquarters with plans to surprise Terry, only to learn that he was tied up in a meeting with his boss. No lunch date. She decided to grab something to eat in the cafeteria. Maybe she'd pick up a sandwich for Terry as well.

On the way out the door, she caught sight of the mysterious blond woman Terry couldn't or wouldn't say much about. Suzanne something. Today she wore stretch trousers and an unstructured jacket, both in heathered charcoal. She paired these with a rose-colored silk shirt, gemstone earrings, and several small silver necklaces. Short black boots completed the outfit. She looked chic, confident, and dressed for success.

Sam looked down at her black denim pants, white shirt, and serviceable blazer and shrugged. She'd reached the point where she could admire and even covet the way other women dressed without holding herself to the same standards.

"Hi. We, er, bumped into each other last week. I'm Sam Tate."

"My name is Suzanne Foster," the woman said with a friendly smile. "Good to see you back." She stopped there, leaving Sam to wonder what the woman knew about Sam's recent trip.

As if reading Sam's mind, Foster added, "I understand you split your time between Washington and eastern Maryland. That must be quite the commute."

No reference to Montana, which relieved Sam. "That's right," she replied. "Do you work here?"

"I'm in business with my son. I work here as more of a consultant, primarily with the cybersecurity and counter-terrorism divisions." The smile grew wider, but Sam knew she wouldn't get any more information.

Then Foster surprised her by saying, "Perhaps we can have lunch at some point."

"I would very much like that."

"Good. I'll be in touch." Foster typed something into her phone. Sam's own device pinged a second later, a text with a digital contact card that read, "Foster and Foster, cyber investigations." No address, but two telephone numbers and an email.

"How did you know my cell number?" She looked up, but Foster had vanished.

Sam headed to the cafeteria, content to be distracted by the mystery that was Suzanne Foster. Terry's unit, Criminal Investigations, was under the Criminal, Cyber, Response, and Services Branch, which also contained BAU and NCAVC. The National Security Branch stood adjacent and oversaw counterintelligence and counterterrorism units. The two branches frequently collaborated, as violent crime and domestic terrorism often overlapped.

Sam wondered how well Terry knew Suzanne Foster.

Chapter 23

Sam caught Dakota Williams on the way into the Friday meeting. The two women hugged, although Sam was careful not to put too much strength into the embrace.

"It is so good to see you back," Sam told her.

"It's good to be back."

"You look well." She did. Her bruises had nearly faded, and her face was beginning to fill out.

Williams smiled. "Auntie Cat and her coterie of medicine women took excellent care of me."

"I can believe it."

Williams put her hands over her heart. "Sam, I owe you."

"You owe me nothing. This is what friends do for one another."

Williams hitched an eyebrow. "Mm, I'd say more like friends with special training."

The women burst out laughing.

"Inside, you two," Fuentes chided, though he couldn't hide his pleasure at seeing his old partner.

Sam took her seat and looked around the table and onscreen. Full house. She imagined everyone had heard about the discovery of the two severed heads. They'd want guidance on how to proceed, or maybe they'd just want to express their opinions.

"Let's begin," Terry said without preamble. "You heard that a civilian walking her dog discovered the heads of the two murdered officers in a park in Marietta. As hideous as this is, the discovery has inadvertently provided us with definitive proof that four of the slayings were committed by the same person, or at least that the same person was present at all of the murders. Agent Grisby, is there anything you'd like to add?"

"Yes, sir. There's every reason to believe we're dealing with a serial killer who works across state lines. Isn't it time to bring more people into the loop? We're already national news down here. Our citizens are frantic. Maybe we can ease their concerns if we can put these murders in the context of a larger event so that folks know the killer isn't targeting Atlanta."

"I can't see how knowing that will ease anyone's mind except maybe the citizens of Atlanta," Lindsay Block protested. "People will wonder if their city is next. They'll be more fearful. Since it seems this spree, if that's what we want to call it, began in Sacramento, attention on us will increase. Everyone will assume we birthed this monster."

The room erupted in angry and anxious back-and-forth as the officials tried to contend with what a publicly advertised nationwide investigation would mean to their jurisdictions. Sam kept her eyes on Terry. He allowed it to play out for a few minutes before he intervened.

"All of you are making valid points," he said. "On one hand, we have to let law enforcement nationwide know that this case is officially under the purview of the FBI. A notice has already been drafted by our communications department and approved by DOJ. That will go out later today. At the same time—"

"The general public is gonna find out sooner or later," Steel interrupted. "Cops talk to each other, their wives, their friends, hell, their bartenders."

"Public outreach needs a little more coordination," Terry admitted. "We have to strike a balance between releasing information and causing a panic. The hard fact is that all evidence indicates the targets are specific to law enforcement, to a specific kind of investigator who handled a specific kind of case. It's a big pool, don't get me wrong, but it's not the kind of need-to-know that might be necessitated by a nuclear strike or a once-in-a-century weather event."

"I assume your alert to law enforcement includes the FBI," Williams said. "Aside from those of us in this room."

"Yes. Federal investigative agencies will also receive notice. That includes retired and active BAU members."

Terry glanced at Kinney, whose wan smile didn't mask her unease. He noted that many of the attendees on and off-screen were fairly twitching.

"All right, just a few questions. Keep them general. Remember, we haven't begun to fill you in on certain significant details. Ranger Steel."

"I assume we're all taking a supporting role at this point. Especially," he moved his finger across the screen, "seeing as you've added agents from another six or seven regional Bureau offices to the mix."

"No, not supporting at all. Think of it like this. We're all working on the same puzzle. Each of you has a section to complete. Your investigations are ongoing and far from cold. Work with our field agents in your region because anything that turns up could help us put it all together. At which point we'll see what all the evidence reveals."

"The face of our killer," Kinney said, and no one disagreed.

Chapter 24

On a nearly perfect early October day, the lunchtime crowd at Fiola Mari included more tourists than politicians. That suited the two diners seated at the secluded end table with a view of the Potomac.

"I'm glad you found the time to meet, given your schedule," Suzanne Foster remarked as she tucked a tiny piece of branzino into her mouth. How's your ricotta?"

"Delicious," Terry replied. "And I'm thrilled to be whisked away from work. This lunch is long overdue. Although I should have been the one treating you instead of the other way around."

Foster made a dismissive gesture. "Don't be silly, Terry. It's a company expense for me, never mind I co-own the company."

"It's not about the money, Suzanne." Terry put down his fork. "I should have been more present for you last year. I guess I was taken by surprise."

"So was I." She blinked and looked out the window. "People die in their early seventies. Healthy men can have heart attacks. He was older than me. Still, I wasn't expecting it, not for a while." She sighed. "He was so happy teaching at American University and at the Farm."

"The Company was smart to snap him up."

Foster smiled. "Brian's background made him a desirable commodity. He left MI6 on good terms, more than ready to follow Michael and his wife across the

Atlantic." She smiled. "And no one was running from anything."

Terry knew the story. Suzanne Foster had been a college student with a bright future when she ran afoul of a ruthless criminal. For decades, she worked as his full-time marketing director and his part-time assassin. Then she met Brian Foster, an MI6 agent working undercover to bring down Suzanne's boss. His love offered her a way out, but one that risked his personal safety and that of their only child, Michael.

She blames herself, Terry thought. She'll always blame herself.

"You and Michael have made quite the splash in this town," he said.

"Our little start-up has done well for itself," she said, her eyes twinkling. "He's the real cybersecurity genius. I'm the client relations side of things."

"I heard something to that effect. How long do you intend to keep your enterprise going?"

She arched an eyebrow. "Terry Sloan, you know perfectly well the Bureau's cybercrimes division has dangled a tantalizing proposition in front of my son."

"Do you think he'd be interested?" Terry asked. "Government pay can't hope to approach his current income."

"He won't need the money if we sell. The potential for meaningful projects is exciting. And he'll work fewer hours." She smiled at Terry's expression. "Okay, then he'll be home more, which will make his wife Kate very happy."

"And what will you do?"

Foster considered her answer. "I don't know. I'm not quite eligible for Social Security and have no interest in retiring in any event. We shall see. Meanwhile, what are your plans vis-à-vis that remarkable woman you're seeing? You don't want to keep someone like Sam Tate waiting. She is one in a million."

Terry blushed. "She is. She's also skittish when it comes to commitment. I'm planning a strategy."

"Good. I'm here for any advice you may need."

"But that's not why you invited me to lunch, as delightful as that has been."

"How well do you know Senator Sean Parker?"

Terry couldn't keep the surprise off his face. "He's a rising star who sits on the committee that makes recommendations to the committee that funds my unit. Anything else I know is from his bio. Raised in Providence, attended Brown and Harvard, made money in New York, moved to Maryland."

"Ever notice a resemblance to Sam? Who is gorgeous, by the way. I'd seen pictures, but they don't do her justice."

"She is. As for any resemblance to the senator, they both have green eyes."

"A singular shade of green," Foster observed. "Parker seems to have a particular interest in all things Mafia related. Almost anachronistic to imagine the organization has that kind of power."

"He's not wrong," Terry countered. "While La Cosa Nostra may have morphed over time, the group remains operational and exceedingly dangerous."

"I noticed you said, 'raised in Providence. 'Not born there?"

"He doesn't hide the fact that he was adopted, Suzanne. What are you getting at?"

She took a sip of water. "I support the idea of mulligans, do-overs, whatever you want to call them. I'd be a hypocrite if I didn't believe in rehabilitation, even for those who have done the most awful things. Case in point."

"I'm not following."

"My former criminal employer, Victor Kemp, had various psychological tactics for keeping me in line. For example, he'd threaten to 'remove and replace 'me. Those were his words: remove and replace. He even had someone in mind, he told me. Someone able to blend in perfectly in any environment. Someone cold and also a little crazy. A green-eyed monster named Quinn."

Terry nearly choked on his food. He tried to laugh it off, but Foster was too smart.

"You recognize the name," she said.

"I ran across the name during my investigation of organized crime activity on the East Coast," he answered, somewhat truthfully. "Mostly in a historical context. Haven't heard that name connected to anything over the last twenty-five or thirty years."

"That would track," Foster replied. "I think he retired from the life. The point is, this Quinn was at a party I went to with my boss. It was a work thing."

"No judgement," Terry assured her.

"I know. Anyway, Victor made a point of walking up to the man, who treated him with a deference I found frightening. It was Quinn, of course. Good-looking, as I recall, and young, about my age. That was my first surprise."

"And your second?"

"The man's eyes were a shade of green I'd never encountered. Sam's are the same color, as I'm sure you've noticed. The look he gave me was absolutely chilling. And I knew this was the man who could remove and replace me."

"You think the man at the party was an assassin and that man is now a senator."

She sighed. "It sounds flimsy when you put it that way."

"No, it doesn't."

"I suppose that whatever his past, he is entitled to a second chance. I'd be a hypocrite if I said anything else."

"Your situations weren't morally equivalent, Suzanne."

"We don't know that, Terry. Perhaps he never was the monster my employer described. He could have been forced into the life. He might have changed. Perhaps he's attempting to make amends, a do-good senator bent on bringing down an evil organization."

"Perhaps," Terry managed to say. "In any event, your information is invaluable, Suzanne. In more ways than you know."

Chapter 25

Sam groaned at the sound of Terry's phone. She'd been having a peaceful night for a change, lulled by the gentle breezes off the Chesapeake, the warmth of a familiar body beside her, and the soft snores of a contented dog who slept nearby.

"Tell them it's a holiday," she mumbled into her pillow. "Senior FBI officials get time off, don't they?"

"We're a full-service, twenty-four-seven kind of operation, kiddo," he teased. He pushed himself up, swung his legs over the side of the bed and picked up the phone. "Assistant Director Sloan speaking."

"It's Rob Stein, sir. I'm sorry to bother you on a holiday. I didn't think this could wait."

"What's happened?"

The simple question jolted Sam upright. Jax stirred in his bed in the corner as Terry switched to speakerphone.

Stein spoke, his words tumbling over one another. "I created an algorithm to track and flag any news items relevant to our current case. It's a little bit irregular and outside my job description. But it seems warranted."

"Don't worry about it. You're not the only one who collects news online." He glanced at Sam. "Go ahead."

"An item popped up this morning from the Exponent Telegram out of Clarksburg, West Virginia. It's long. Do you want a text or an email?"

"Text is fine."

Jax scratched at the door. Sam let him out. Terry followed, eyes on his phone. He scanned the attachment and passed the phone to Sam.

Clarksville Detective Slain at Medical Center

by Sue McCarthy

Clarksville, WV, October 9th. Detective Connie Pratt, 52, died unexpectedly Friday night after routine hip replacement surgery performed at the Louis Johnson VA Medical Center.

The cause is believed to be a fatal blood clot. Pratt's family asked the court for an expedited autopsy. That request was granted over the weekend. The autopsy will be performed Tuesday after the holiday.

Pratt, an Army veteran and mother of two, was described as fit and healthy. "Something went wrong," her husband, Vernon Pratt, told this reporter. "We need to find out what that was. MY kids did not deserve to lose their mother."

Pending the outcome of the autopsy, both local and federal officials will hold a press conference. The hospital released a statement that said, in part, "The administration is working closely with the local police and The Department of Veterans Affairs to provide answers about this unforeseen tragedy."

Pratt, a detective with the Clarksburg Police Department for the past thirteen years, may be remembered as the investigator who helped catch notorious serial killer Ronnie May Lawson, aka Nurse Death. Lawson, who is serving life in a federal penitentiary, murdered nine patients by lethal injection over a three-year period. The victims were all patients at the Johnson VA Center, where Lawson worked at the time as a nursing assistant.

We will update this story as information becomes available.

"Holy hell," Sam mouthed, handing the phone back.

Terry nodded. "Rob, thanks for this information," he said into the phone. "Stay on top of it. I'll see you tomorrow."

"Who do you know at the Clarksburg field office?" Sam asked when he'd disconnected.

"Dennis Vann is the special agent in charge. I'll see if I can reach him today. Other than that, we can't do much until we see the autopsy report. People do die in the hospital. Doesn't mean it's homicide or even negligence."

"Come on, Terry! The woman was another serial-killer hunter and a cop."

"The hospital is a federal facility, which should give us more investigative leeway. I'll reach out to DVA and the locals so I can have the report in hand as soon as they do. I'll lay the groundwork, but we have to establish that a crime was committed."

Sam turned away and ushered Jax into the house. She started the coffee and fed the dog without speaking.

"I expected you to have more to say, Tate."

"I'm thinking." She poured two mugs and handed one to Terry. "I do have a question for you."

"Which is?"

"Do you believe this woman's death was a medical accident?"

He blew on his coffee, sipped, and swallowed, every movement a deliberate stalling tactic. "I don't," he finally answered.

"Do you believe this is the work of our judgmental psychopath?"

"That's two questions." She glared at him over the rim of her cup. "Fine. My gut tells me it is. I still want proof."

"My gut agrees with yours," Sam said. "Which means our guy is on the move. Worse, he's moved into our backyard."

"I'll set up a conference call for tomorrow." Terry locked eyes with her. "For the first time since I don't know when, I want to be wrong about this."

"You're not wrong, Terry. We're not wrong."

They weren't.

Chapter 26

The mood in the room was grim. The air was both stifling and artificially cold. The fluorescent lights gave off a blue cast. The interior windows kept out sound but not light, so that passersby could steal furtive glances. Sam wondered if they pitied the people within, a dedicated group of law officers who couldn't stop a serial killer.

"Thanks for making yourselves available so late in the day," Terry began. "I wanted the core group to meet before we convened the larger one on Friday. With us today are Special Agents Rob Stein of ViCAP, Molly Kinney of BAU-4, and Agents Dakota Williams and Mike Fuentes of CID. Lieutenant Tate, thanks for making the trip from Easton, Maryland. Hope the traffic was bearable."

Sam figured that almost everyone in the room knew she and Terry were an item. Still, she appreciated the formality. And she had gone into work and left an hour-and-a-half earlier to make the trip in.

"It helped that I was heading in as everyone else was heading out," she said.

"On speakerphone, we have Clarksburg Chief of Police Trevor Lockhart along with Special Agent Dave Padilla, a homicide investigator with the Bureau's Clarksburg office. Gentlemen, the people in this room are aware of the incident in question. And thank you, Chief Lockhart. for getting me the requested information so quickly.

"Not a problem," Lockhart replied in a flat tone that owed more to official Washington than rural West Virginia. "This was eventually going to land on your desk, Assistant Director, but I assumed 'eventually 'was too slow. I also took the liberty of sending a copy to your office here in Clarksburg after we spoke, even though I could have walked it over since they're located around the corner."

"Will you summarize, Chief?"

"The short version is we've classified the Pratt murder as a suspicious death, one that was made to look like a natural occurrence, or at worst, negligence."

"How could they tell?" Kinney asked.

"Pratt died from a blood clot that was, how do I say this, created. She was given anti-coagulants, which is routine in major orthopedic surgery, but the dose was tripled, though not recorded as such. Although the victim was hooked to a self-administering analgesic pump with morphine, which is standard, the cut-off was broken."

"She OD'd?" Sam asked.

"No," Agent Padilla chimed in, his West Virginia accent strong. "But she was pretty out of it."

"Wasn't there a night nurse on duty who checked in on her?" Terry asked.

"Lockhart here. In answer to your question, yes, her floor was covered by a nurse by the name of Jerry Anders. At least that's what his ID says. His picture shows a sandy-haired bearded man with either brown or hazel eyes and chunky glasses, and that matches the description of the man who worked that night. His paperwork is aboveboard. He doesn't usually work the night shift, so the other staff members didn't know him well. They described him as standoffish. The day shift claims he's anything but."

"The night nurse deliberately administered the wrong dose," Sam said. "Have you found this Jerry Anders person?"

"That's just it. He hasn't shown up for his last three shifts. Someone purporting to be Anders called to say he'd be out for a couple of days due to a family emergency."

"Never to be seen again," Stein whispered to Kinney.

"We're trying to track him down," Lockhart said. "We can go ahead and issue an APB, although the phony Anders may have been wearing a disguise."

"Go ahead anyway," Terry said. "Your department should be the public face of this investigation. I have no doubt the hospital will want to issue a separate press release about the fake nurse with access to real patients. Don't reference the other cases, though."

"You don't want to let the general public know about this guy?" Lockhart demanded.

"Here's my concern, Chief. This guy could be a murderer, but not a serial killer. He could be a serial killer but not our serial killer. I don't believe that, by the way. I do think he's the person we're looking for, but I'm not ready to let the world know yet. Law enforcement across the country is staying vigilant. We'll take it one day at a time. For the moment, it's a local murder."

"We'll present it as a one-off."

"Right. Meanwhile, please share whatever information your team gathers with Agent Padilla and with NCAVC. Images will be helpful. We have another witness in another case who might recognize our suspect from a picture. If anything changes to solidify the fake nurse's connection to our cases, you will be included in our briefings going forward. At that point, we will alert the public. Thanks."

He disconnected. "Molly, any off-the-record thoughts about what it means that the unsub has decided to show himself, assuming that's what's going on here?"

Sam's phone went off. A text. She ignored it.

"He's making himself more visible," Kinney said. "Maybe he's getting bored. And reckless. The question is, why now?"

"Maybe he wants more attention," Stein said.

"Do you think he wants us to go public?" Terry addressed his question to Kinney.

"It's possible. He believes he's seeking some perverted form of justice, but he also needs to have his efforts acknowledged."

Sam's phone pinged again. She rolled her eyes and glanced at her phone. "Holy shit!"

"Sam?" Terry asked. "What is it?"

"I just got a text from our unsub."

Chapter 27

Hello and welcome back from Big Sky Country. Heads got your attention? Or the VA hospital visit? Good. B2W

"How did he know about Montana?" Fuentes wondered.

Sam had that question and so many others. Where was he? Why was he texting her? Why now? She felt him as a physical presence through the phone.

She looked up, trying to contain her nervous excitement. "What should I say?"

"You need to learn as much as you can in a short amount of time," Kinney advised. "Be direct. Ask him what he wants."

Sam wrote,

How can I help u?

She read her words aloud. Everyone in the room nodded.

The reply came back almost at once.

I want u 2 catch a killer.

"Ask more questions," Kinney whispered as if the killer could hear her.

Can you be more specific?

The long pause was followed by an emoji of a yellow face with a closed slanted mouth. The sender was skeptical, confused or frustrated. Or he didn't like her questions.

Finally, he replied,

do your job

what do you think that is?

protect and serve adults and children

Why did he bring up children? Sam looked at Kinney, who scribbled something down on her notepad, then nodded. Sam then typed,

which children?

Wrong question, she thought. She deleted the two words and asked,

from the killer?

that would be a start

Sam looked up from the screen, exasperated. "He's talking in riddles."

"You're doing fine," Kinney assured her. "Keep asking questions."

Sam looked down at the screen and started to type, but whoever was texting her had more to say. When the dots finally stopped bouncing, she read,

do what you do best, Lieutenant. Stop the killing. Be the hero. Save lives

He disconnected and she looked up to find five pairs of eyes fixed on her.

"He's offline."

"What the fuck was that?" Fuentes exploded. "Sorry, boss, unprofessional. But that's pretty unexpected."

"Trust me, I'm thinking the same thing. Sam, are you okay? Drink some water." He pointed at her bottle. Sam took a generous swallow.

"I'm not sure," she replied. "I just heard from a serial killer who knows far too much about me, beginning with my cell phone number. He knows I went to Montana. He might know I'm in a meeting just now."

"It's not illogical to assume the task force would meet concerning the latest murder," Terry said. "Or that there'd be a task force."

"Does this change how you feel about the latest murder?" Fuentes asked Terry.

"I'm persuaded that our person of interest and the Clarksville killer are one and the same."

"First of all, Sam, kudos to you," Williams chimed in. "Not sure I would have kept my cool. Second, is it possible the text wasn't from the serial killer but from someone with insider knowledge who doesn't like how the case is proceeding?"

"Maybe our killer has insider knowledge," Fuentes said.

"Let's not make assumptions about what our killer knows just yet," Terry said. "I'll authorize a secondary sweep of the conference room and burner phones for all of you that you will use exclusively for this case."

"What about the other team members?" Fuentes asked.

"From now on, the brainstorming will stay within this working group. We'll convene the full group only when we have information to share. New people will come on if and when a new case arises."

"Which we all hope won't happen," Stein said.

"I wonder what he meant by protecting children?" Williams mused. "Whose children did he mean?"

"Do you think he has children?" Fuentes asked. "Does he want someone to protect them from him?"

"Molly, you look like you have something on your mind," Terry said.

Kinney looked at her notes. "We need to look for adults who might have been witnesses to serial murders going back twenty-five or thirty years. Maybe he's talking about protecting the child he used to be."

"I was thinking the same thing," Sam said.

"Any idea why our unsub contacted Sam in particular?" Williams asked.

"She's got a reputation for solving serial cases," Kinney suggested.

"He might resent that," Fuentes offered.

"Or he admires her," Kinney said. "Maybe he sees her as good at stopping people like him. Maybe he's counting on her to end his killing spree."

"Not by herself," Terry declared. "Here's what we need to do before Friday. Molly, continue to develop your profile. Rob, see if Molly's work gives you any ideas about opening up the database to cast a wider net. Mike, you're the point person on West Virginia, Williams can take Atlanta. We've got more to learn from those two crimes."

"Are we at least sharing the news about the text with the bigger group?" Williams asked.

"I need a couple of days to run it by the higher-ups." Terry rubbed his forehead. "Ever since we alerted the law enforcement community, I've been getting pressure from people in the AG's office. Never mind. Let's dig in. Thanks."

"When do you think we can get those new phones?" Kinney asked.

"Tomorrow, if I can cut through the red tape," Terry replied. "For now, keep our business off your mobile phones and watch your back."

"Head on a swivel," Stein joshed. "Got it."

No one laughed.

Chapter 28

Sam and Terry hung back as the others exited the room.

"I've got to go back to Easton, Terry. Tonight. Sheriff Tanner deserves to know what's going on."

"I understand. First, though, we need to find someone in cybersecurity to do some magic on your phone."

Terry punched a number. "Kevin? Terry Sloan. You're working late, I see. Look, I have a red flag situation involving a compromised cell phone. It's evidence, yes, but it also needs to remain operational. We're going to need ... Yes, that's right." He listened. "Really? You would? Thank you. We'll be right down."

He turned to Sam with a tight smile. "Kevin Wolcott is the AD for Cybersecurity. He'll get a tech to take care of us."

The floor that housed cybersecurity featured fewer offices and more shared workspaces dominated by screens of all sizes and shapes. Sam was reminded of a school visit she'd made to NASA. The biggest difference was that the cybersecurity floor was much quieter.

A tiny woman with short blue-black hair and long bangs introduced herself as Agent Rhonda Invers. "If you have anything you don't want me to see on your device, please delete it now," she said with a grin.

"I'm good," Sam replied.

Invers took the phone and plugged it into a console. She typed, her fingers a blur across the keyboard. The message from the Judge appeared briefly, supplanted by lines of code. From what Sam could tell, the information was then condensed into a folder, which Invers opened and scanned.

"We've cloned your phone," she said, handing the device back to Sam. That means we can monitor anything that comes in or out. As for your most recent text, it came from a burner used in Akron, Ohio. We can't trace the location with any specificity, but we do know this one was powered down or more likely destroyed."

Terry and Sam exchanged glances. Akron meant the killer was either moving west or simply laying low.

"We've also assigned you a temporary phone for sensitive information exchanges," Invers went on. "You can and should continue to use your primary phone. Your inclination will be to avoid it, but you want to keep from arousing suspicion."

They thanked the agent and headed to Terry's office. Sam begged off dinner but promised she'd return Friday.

"Do you feel like you need protection?" Terry asked.

"I work at a police station," Sam replied. "Besides, I have a ferocious watchdog."

* * *

Sam rose at dawn to run with a delighted Jax. After a quick breakfast for both of them, they headed into the office, where Jax accepted head pats and ear rubs before he curled up on his bed with a contented sigh.

She made an appointment to see her boss, then spent an hour reviewing the county's latest crime statistics. Murders were down and serious drug-related crimes had been slowed thanks to a cooperative partnership with the Maryland State Police. Domestic violence was still a problem and so was theft at every level, from consumer fraud to home break-ins. She'd have to talk with Gordy about the outstanding caseload and the best way of deploying both deputies and her few detectives.

Her trusted second appeared just then, looking equal parts apprehensive and amused.

"Don't take this the wrong way, but you don't look rested."

"There was a lot to do in a short amount of time."

"Right. With your friend in need. Everything resolved?"

She'd already assumed that Gordy didn't believe she was on any kind of personal business.

"Actually, yes."

"And things are good with your D.C. colleagues?"

She reminded herself that nothing got by her second.

"I don't need to know everything you're doing, Lieutenant," he continued. "Except if it's work-related. Or life-threatening. Then I should be informed. And, with all due respect, I don't want to find out from McCready. Not that he confided in me, not right away, so don't give him a hard time."

"Did you beat it out of him?" Sam questioned.

Gordy flashed his vulpine grin. Sam stared at him until he dropped his eyes.

"Okay, Sergeant Gordy. You deserve some information. Give me ten minutes to meet with Sheriff Tanner. Then come back, close the door, and I will let you in on what's been going on. And then we'll get back to work. Deal?"

"Deal," he replied.

She only needed five minutes. Tanner, like all department heads, received the outlines of the case when the FBI alert went out.

"Are you in danger, Sam?"

"Before yesterday, I would have said no more than the hundreds of other cops, detectives, agents, and analysts who've handled a serial-killer case. But yesterday, I heard from someone, likely the killer some are calling 'the Judge.'"

She told him about the text.

He leaned back in his chair, his lips compressed. "This is concerning, Sam. The killer knows who you are and how you're connected to this case."

"I'm just consulting, along with a dozen others."

"Does he also know what you were really doing in Montana?" Tanner chuckled at her surprised expression.

"County sheriffs are connected in official and unofficial ways. Workplace gossip is inevitable, although no one seems inclined to include the media in any confidential discussions. Did you Lone Ranger things a little? My guess is you did. On the other hand, you came upon a problem, and you acted. You took a bent cop off the board. Good."

"Thanks."

"What do you plan to do about your current situation?"

"Not much to do except work my job. I'll alert my detectives about the text message but let's see if we can keep the rest of the department out of it for now. I don't want to worry anyone. Meanwhile, I'll go to the

Bureau's task force meetings in D.C. on my day off, or I'll jump on a Zoom call. Nothing changes."

"Until it does."

"Until it does," she agreed.

Chapter 29

Sam took care of herself over the next few days. She went out to dinner with Gordy, McCready, CIS Carol Davidson, and Carol's boyfriend, Forensic Investigator Martin Lloyd. She told them about the texts and swore them to secrecy. In turn, they all volunteered to watch her house. Even though she turned them down, they ignored her. Sam was good at spotting strange cars in her neighborhood, or familiar ones belonging to friends. She felt guilty but also lucky.

Meanwhile, she ate smart, avoided alcohol, ran, and practiced yoga. To her relief, the anonymous texter didn't make an appearance.

She went into Friday's meeting feeling refreshed. The same couldn't be said for Molly Kinney and Rob Stein. No doubt the burden of profiling a killer who might have them in his sights was wearing.

"We have a lot to share with you," Terry started. "First, the latest murder. You all know by now that Clarksburg, West Virginia police detective Connie Pratt's death was ruled a homicide. We believe her killer is our suspect who masqueraded as a night nurse in order to administer a fatal dose. We're waiting for a way to connect him definitively to the other cases. However, several people saw him and that's good news. Clarksburg Police Chief Trevor Lockhart and Special Agent Dave Padilla are here to fill in the details and will be part of the group going forward."

"Anybody wonder how large this group is gonna get?" Ranger Steel asked.

"I expect not much larger," Terry answered. "I say that advisedly since the person we're trying to catch is wily."

"And busy," Stein put in.

"I thought we had a witness in Atlanta?" The question came from Lindsay Block.

"A young boy saw a light-skinned man in a baseball cap who he remembered as big and tall, though not as big as a football player or as tall as a basketball player," GBI's Grisby replied. "Not much to go on."

"He made himself visible at the hospital," Lockhart said. "True, he was likely wearing a disguise. But his body type, his voice, even the way he walks, those things are hard to fake. We had one of our sketch artists mock something up." He passed around copies of the sketch. Terry put up the digitized version for the Zoom callers to see.

A youngish man glowered from behind a full beard and thick glasses.

"Three witnesses put him between five-ten and six feet," Padilla added. "He's described as on the stocky side, with glasses, sandy hair and a beard, possibly fake. Early to mid-thirties. As to eye color, two voted for brown, one for hazel."

"Great, a big man wearing a disguise," Block griped.

"Something else," the Clarksburg chief went on. "The floor nurse noticed our unsub was dragging, and his eye was twitching. Seems he went to the bathroom a lot and visited the candy machine more than once. She put it down to fatigue since the nurse he was impersonating usually works the day shift."

"Is he sick?" Steel asked.

"I couldn't say," Padilla commented. "We've recovered DNA from the crime scene we can test."

"A serious illness would explain a lot," Kinney said. "Like why he's getting careless about showing himself."

"You're saying he's not thinking clearly?" Lockhart asked.

"Maybe not."

"Any chance you found a blood sample?" Sam asked.

"Not in this case," Lockhart, replied. "Why?"

"You have more options for identifying certain illnesses with blood than with DNA. Like diabetes."

"Bathroom breaks and candy cravings," Stein said. "Makes sense."

"Now we have to determine if he's killed prior to this year," Kinney added.

"Has he?" Williams asked.

"It's worth considering that he killed before Sacramento. Perhaps not as often or as refined, for lack of a better word."

"How far back are you thinking?" Terry asked.

"Rob and I looked at cases over the past ten years. Remember, we originally checked on lead investigators for solved serial-killer cases, not open ones. We went back and opened up the parameters a little bit."

"And?" Terry pressed.

"The investigators were alive and well with three exceptions," Stein interjected. "A female detective who was investigating a set of serial murders by cyanide died the same way seven years ago in Bellingham, a town about two hours north of Seattle. Two years later, another detective died in a building collapse near

Tacoma. He'd been trying to solve a rash of homicides at a construction site. Two years after that, a detective drowned at a beach down along the Oregon coast near Tillamook. And yes, he'd solved the case of a killer who was pushing people off a rocky ledge into the ocean for fun. But his death was ruled an accident as well, although the family is pushing to reopen the investigation."

"And no one ever connected these murders to each other?" Block demanded.

"They were far enough apart, they took place in two different states, and there was no obvious evidence to tie them to the earlier cases. It's possible these murders were trial runs for the Judge while he refined his technique."

"Your theory is worth exploring," Terry said. "We may be able to establish the killer's point of origin. Great work, you two."

Sam looked up from her notebook to ask, "What month did these three deaths take place?"

Kinney smiled. "You caught that. The Bellingham murder happened on Memorial Day, the Tacoma incident on Thanksgiving, the Tillamook drowning on July 4th."

"Wait, what?" Fuentes asked.

"All our victims died on holidays," Sam said.

"Maybe that's the only time our killer can take off work," Steel wisecracked to scattered chuckles.

"Possibly," Kinney said. "His choice of the holidays may be part of his ritual. My point is, if he committed these earlier murders, this year marked a turning point. He's killing more frequently, more publicly."

"He's getting cocky," Padilla said. "Or needy."

"Which is why he reached out to—ow!" Fuentes added as Williams elbowed him.

"Excuse me?" Block interjected. "Reached out how? Has someone heard from the Judge?"

Sam and Terry exchanged glances. "I was getting to that," Terry said. "Lieutenant Tate received a text from someone we believe to be our suspect."

He'd expected the outburst. Even filtered through the conference room's sound system, the clamor from the online participants raised the decibel levels.

"All right, everyone, quiet down, please." Terry made a gesture that served to lower the volume if not the intensity. "This is a significant development, I'll grant you," he continued. "The text may be a one-time thing, or he may be reaching out to other people."

"Like us?" Powell asked.

"We can't know that. It's vital, however, that we keep this amongst ourselves. Any publicity would be unfair to Lieutenant Tate and unproductive. I hope we're all good with that."

"Can we hear what he wrote?" Steel asked.

Sam read the words back, keeping her voice even.

"How do we know this message came from the Judge?" the Marietta chief asked. "Nothing in there you couldn't pick up on the news."

"He sent it to me," Sam said. "My involvement, such as it is, has not been made public."

"What that tells me," Kinney said, "is that our killer has identified Sam as someone uniquely suited to understanding his message."

"What it tells me," Steel said in his rolling baritone, "is someone has the inside track on what we're doin ' here."

Chapter 30

While Williams followed up with Grisby and other contacts in Atlanta, Sam persuaded Millie to find her a small workspace. She pulled out her laptop and tried to catch up with work-related items, but her mind kept wandering. Just before five, she gave up and popped her head into Terry's office.

"I need to stay another two hours," he told her. "Believe it or not, I'm overseeing other cases, including an investigation involving our favorite mob, still kicking."

"You'll have to let my half-uncle know," Sam said, using air quotes around the designated relationship.

"I'll do that. Are you going back to the apartment?"

"Jax is in daycare until seven. I'll see if Dakota is free."

Williams was finishing up a call. "Perfect timing," she said. "I want a beer or maybe a burger. Or both."

They headed to Denson's, an establishment that was both less overtly chic and much quieter than most places on the Hill. As soon as they sat down, Williams put out her hand. "Hand it over," she said.

"What?"

"Your phone. I want to read the texts."

"I read them out loud not three hours ago. And while they were coming in a few days ago."

"I just need to see them for myself," Williams insisted.

Sam handed her phone to the agent, who located the exchange and took her time reading before she handed the device back. "Very cheery opening. It's like you're already friends."

"Perish the thought."

"It's not unheard of, though, right? Killers trying to bond with the people investigating them?"

The waitress appeared to take their orders and returned in a minute with two frothy brews. After she left, Williams sat back, tapping the table.

"What would make him reach out to you? Is there something about you besides your crime-fighting expertise that makes him think you're the one who can understand where he's coming from?"

Sam fought down the dread that came from feeling she might be over-exposed. Some aspects of her past life were a matter of public record, like her name change or her army service. She'd tried to bury her history as the survivor of a horrific act of violence, but how successful had she been?

A smart investigator like Dakota Williams could dig if she chose to. And so could someone else.

She covered her distress by taking a large swallow of beer. "I had a lot of the same experiences growing up as other American kids. I skinned my knee, went to church, went to weddings and funerals and school, watched Powerpuffs on TV, thought NSYNC was cool, and developed a crush on my math teacher."

Williams snorted. "I wouldn't brag about some of those choices, girlfriend."

"Haha. My point is, I'm not that unusual. I don't see the Judge reaching out to me based on a real or imagined childhood experience we had in common."

"You're not sick, are you?" Williams worried. "Someone at our last meeting suggested the Judge might be dealing with some sort of disease."

"I couldn't be healthier, I promise." Sam decided to sprinkle in a bit of truth. "Unless you count bouts of insomnia, brought on by a job that veers between tedium and unpredictable adrenaline rushes."

"You mean like challenging a couple of guys with guns while trying to rescue a hapless agent held hostage in a cellar?"

"Something like that," Sam laughed as they fist-bumped. "I don't know why the Judge chose me. Maybe I'm only the first, and he'll contact the rest of you. Which begs the question, how does he know who's on the team?"

"Do you think we've sprung a leak?" Williams asked.

"I don't believe anyone is deliberately trying to help a killer. Maybe someone let something slip."

"Not on our team, Sam. Maybe the unsub assumed you're working on the case because you have a connection to the FBI. Maybe some random clerk heard about the meeting and shared that information. Gossip at the agencies is a thing. I don't know how the CIA protects their people."

"Maybe," Sam said.

"I want to go back to motivation. Did the guy have a crummy childhood? Deadbeat or cruel dad, unloving mother. Was he bullied at school, or always in trouble? Maybe he was snatched out of his house and kept in a cellar by some perverted backwoodsman. Or he could have had a normal millennial-era childhood before some defining event switched it all up."

"That's why we follow the evidence and leave the profiling to people like Molly Kinney. Listen, Dakota." Sam leaned forward and took hold of the startled agent's hands. "If you and I are going to forge a friendship that will last a lifetime, we have to find something to bond over besides serial killings and your undying gratitude to me for saving your ass in Montana."

Sam stared at a stunned Williams for a second before she let go and grinned. "You should see your face."

Williams snorted. "You got me," she said. "Tell you what, no more talking or thinking about the sleaze who is occupying too much space in our lives. I'll pay for the beers, and we'll call the Montana rescue even. What's our next topic?"

"We could talk about books or movies or weapons."

"Or other people. Isn't that what besties do? God, we need practice, Tate. Maybe we could start with some lighthearted gossip."

"I'd rather talk about weapons," Sam said. "But I am curious about your impressions of some of our newer teammates."

"Let me hit the ladies 'room first." Williams took a long draught and pushed back from the table. As soon as she was out of sight, Sam pulled her notebook out of her bag and scribbled:

kid trauma = adult trauma

Well, sure. Everyone brings a piece of childhood forward for good or for bad. But there was a big difference between having bad dreams or commitment issues and killing a slew of people in the name of some twisted sense of justice. Sam could attest to that. So could Dakota.

"Protect your people," he'd written. If only she could.

Chapter 31

One week before Halloween, the Judge wrote Sam to say he'd be unavailable for some time but expected to see progress. She asked him where he was going, not that she expected a reply. She just wanted him to read the message. The dots appeared briefly, then disappeared. Good enough.

She called the tech who'd cloned her phone. "Did you get a location?"

"Barely. He's already disabled the phone, but we caught a ping off a tower in the general area of Des Moines."

The Judge was moving west, but why?

Molly Kinney was her next call. "Sam, to what do I owe the pleasure?"

Sam recapped the exchange.

"Sounds like he's off to take care of personal business. He could be back to work or seeing a doctor."

"How do we know that?" Sam asked. "The DNA tests we had the lab run didn't reveal a genetic link to any known diseases."

"Our suspect could still suffer from something that requires medical attention."

"Maybe he's visiting family. Maybe he has a wife or kids."

"It's possible, but I wonder. He does lecture you a bit. He could be mimicking a parental style but not necessarily his own."

"Maybe he's got father-figure issues," Sam stated. "Unfortunately, that puts him in the company of at least half the men in the world, maybe more."

"It's a place to start."

Sam hung up and stared into space. Would a man with father issues choose a female member of the task force chasing him as his point of contact? Or did he choose her for her name recognition? What did he know and how did he come to know it?

She made a note to tell Terry about the latest text and put the Judge out of her mind.

Two more weeks passed pleasantly enough. Sam met with five recruits, all of whom hoped to work in her division. She gave a lecture at the police academy, an experience that initially unnerved her as much as facing down a serial killer. The kids 'Halloween party held in the department's parking lot turned out to be a fun time, especially for Jax. Sam went as a green-eyed witch, which took very little effort. Jax wore a bandana and worked himself into a state of happy exhaustion.

Terry decided the task force would only meet every couple of weeks or if new developments came up, which left her with a free Friday early in November. She scheduled a session with Putnam and accepted a lunch invitation from, of all people, Suzanne Foster.

They met at an elegant French bistro on 9th Street near Bureau headquarters. Sam was glad she'd worn a nice blazer and slacks. At least she appeared well-heeled, although she didn't think her credit card would survive the restaurant prices.

Foster arrived just ahead of her, elegant as usual in a dove gray suit paired with a mustard yellow sweater and mixed metal necklace. Her earrings were subdued, and her bag was a pebbled leather that inspired in Sam an unfamiliar pang of envy. She tucked her convertible backpack underneath her chair and made a subtle effort to smooth her hair.

"Thanks for meeting me, Sam. Lunch is on the company, by the way. Believe it or not, this isn't the kind of place I frequent, but the combination of top-notch service and food is excellent."

Suzanne seemed sincere if guarded. It occurred to Sam that this lovely self-contained woman might not have that many friends.

"I appreciate the invite," Sam said. "My lunch tends to be takeout from Harris Teeter, Easton's nearest grocery store."

"Your job keeps you busy, then."

"Yes and no. More hours are given over to administrative chores, leaving less time for investigation. I delegate, as I'm supposed to. It's the nature of running a division, even within a county sheriff's office."

The waiter glided up to them with menus. Foster ordered a chicken club and white wine and Sam followed suit.

"From what Terry Sloan says, he faces the same issue," Foster continued. "I imagine he misses fieldwork. Do you?"

"Sometimes. How do you know Terry?"

"Through my late husband Brian."

"I'm sorry for your loss. He was in intelligence, right? Your website refers to your late husband's distinguished career. Not that I'm not looking for you to divulge anything."

Foster smiled. "It's fine. Brian was former MI6. We followed my son when he moved to the states, but neither of us stayed retired for long. Brian taught classes for the CIA and delivered the occasional lecture."

"And you work with your son."

"I do. Although he's the brains behind the operation. I suppose I represent the experienced elder. Anyway, what about you, Sam? Catching killers wherever you go. That must be exciting."

Foster had done her homework. Terry never shared Sam's information with colleagues, but her professional data was easy enough to discover, as much as she might wish otherwise.

"My first position was exciting and my second presented change and opportunity," Sam explained. "Then a death in the family necessitated my move to the East Coast."

"Sometimes we don't have a say as to where we end up," Foster said as the waiter brought the wine to the table. "With all your moving around, I can see why you'd want to stay put. You don't strike me as someone who wants to settle, though. Are you happy where you are? Content?"

"I like having a job," Sam replied. "To be fair, it's more than that. I genuinely like the people where I work. I'm good at what I do. The reality, though, is that the job market is unusually tight for someone whose command experience is limited to smaller departments. Not so many options."

"There may be more than you think, Sam. You're not that old."

"You sound like Terry. He was trying to get me to apply to the FBI. I can't imagine starting at the bottom any more than I can imagine climbing a ladder while simultaneously contending with paperwork and politics."

"Heaven forbid. You're an investigator by nature."

"Maybe. Command has some perks. I like to mentor, but yes, I miss being on the ground more often."

"People do start over, though," Foster insisted. "Not necessarily at the bottom. Sometimes they parlay their skills into a parallel line of work. You never know where and when the opportunity might arise. Oh look, our food is coming. Cheers." She lifted her glass in a toast and Sam reciprocated.

Over lunch, talk turned to restaurants, meals, and the best and worst meals they'd ever had. All in all, Sam was happy to spend a few hours with a smart and affable companion who had more than lunch on her mind.

Chapter 32

"Excuse me, Lieutenant, got a minute?" Pat McCready stood in the open door, studiously ignoring the dog who thumped his tail at the prospect of a potential playmate.

Sam was back in the office after a surprisingly relaxing Veterans Day weekend, one without reports of staged homicides or murder of any kind.

"How can I help?" Sam pulled her eyes away from her screen.

"I wanted to run something by you. It can wait, though."

Sam sat back, interlaced her fingers, and pushed her arms out in front of her. "Happy to listen, Detective. I could use a break. Believe it or not, I'm working on a lesson plan."

McCready grinned. "I heard your lecture was a hit. I guess they're trying to get you back."

"Just once more, or at least that's what I promised myself," she chuckled. "What's up?" She gestured to the chair. McCready sat and worried a piece of paper he held in his hand.

"It's about the FBI case you're working on, LT. I guess everyone's calling the unsub 'the Judge.' My friend in the Bureau's Atlanta office and I are still checking the discussion boards about this case on our own time. We thought maybe someone who would reach out to you might also get online to see what people are saying about him."

Sam looked at her detective with respect. "Smart thinking, Pat. Anything jump out at you?"

"Nothing yet. He could be lurking. Maybe he enjoys the speculation. No shortage online."

"That's to be expected, I'm afraid." Sam waited. McCready wasn't done. "Is there something more?" she prodded.

"Just another article about a cop's death. This one appeared to be an accident. Still, it got me to thinking. Has the FBI already checked to see if anyone working on an open serial case has died?"

"We did. Our search has included officers who closed their cases and those who didn't. Believe it or not, the list isn't that long." Sam gave her detective a long look. "Do these questions have to do with the paper you're clutching so tightly?"

McCready glanced down at his hand as if he'd forgotten what he was holding. "Yes. No. I'm not sure. It's probably nothing, just a news item about a cop who was run over and killed the day after he officially retired."

"Was he someone who had previously handled a serial case?"

"The article doesn't mention anything. But it's possible he had an open case, right?"

"Anything's possible," Sam said, thinking of the early cases presented to the task force. "Are they calling his death a homicide?"

"Hit-and-run," McCready replied, looking sheepish. "But it was on Veteran's Day."

"That's interesting but not conclusive." Sam took a breath, as a thought occurred to her. "Where did this happen?"

"Everett, north of Seattle."

"Let me have the information. I'll have the FBI people run a more detailed search. Okay?

When he didn't move, she added. "I promise to pass along this news, Detective."

She waited until he walked out and closed the door before reading the short piece from the Everett Herald.

Everett Detective Dies One Day Into Retirement

by Ryan Yu

A decorated detective and thirty-year veteran of the Everett Police Department was struck and killed by a car outside his home in the Port Gardner area early Saturday evening. Thomas Hansen had officially retired just the day before and had been feted by fellow officers in the department.

Hansen died of his injuries at the scene.

Traffic cameras in the quiet residential community caught images of a late-model dark-blue Honda careening through the neighborhood prior to the accident. The rain and the fading light created hazardous conditions that hampered visibility and prevented a definitive look at the driver, who continued after impact without slowing.

Police are tentatively classifying the incident as a hit-and-run pending further investigation. They ask that anyone who might have any pertinent information contact Everett Police Department's North Precinct at the number listed below.

A full obituary will appear Monday.

A hit-and-run, or h&r. A recently retired cop who was mowed over by a drunk or tired or inattentive driver going too fast in bad weather with low visibility. A driver who didn't stop. Maybe in a stolen car, maybe not. A death. Probably a Class B felony, although, as with all such cases, it could play out in one of several ways once they locate the car and the driver.

The holiday angle was a coincidence, wasn't it? So was the location: Washington State, where Kinney and Stein had uncovered two earlier cases they thought might be tied to the Judge. No reason for Sam to give it another thought. The poor detective hadn't worked a serial case. Or had he? Maybe she'd call into Everett PD, poke around a little.

Or maybe you'll act like a team player, she scolded herself. She reached for the phone and punched in a number closer to home.

Chapter 33

Dakota Williams called two days later. "Got something," she announced.

"What took so long?"

"You'd better be joking, Tate. You would not believe the amount of tracking I had to do. Then there's the time change and the fact that our guy is retired but he's not the sort to sit home."

"Yes, I'm kidding. What did you find?"

"Well, your instincts are good. So are the ones belonging to your newbie detective. Maybe we should get you both over to the Bureau, sort of a package deal."

"Dakota, please."

"Okay, I'll stop torturing you." Williams went into official mode. "Your detective was correct. According to the Everett police chief, Hansen never handled a serial case, open or closed. He couldn't recall any serial cases passing through his precincts, though he tagged a couple in Seattle. No one had threatened Hansen as far as he knew. The department is leaning toward vehicular manslaughter, or it was."

"What do you mean?"

Williams made a snorting sound. "You know how hard it is to call into a precinct, identify yourself as FBI, and not explain what you're after? It helps that the cops all know about the Judge and his victim preferences. That doesn't mean I convinced the chief to reclassify Hansen's death as murder or even as suspicious."

"Did you mention accident clusters?"

"I did. Everett hasn't experienced a spike in the number of poisonings, roof collapses, drownings, falls, mishaps involving heavy machinery, or any of the sad and stupid ways people die. Nothing out of the ordinary."

"Damn. I feel as if I've sent you on a fool's errand."

"Ah, but I'm not done."

Williams reported that she'd gotten a call from the chief later that day with the number of Hansen's old partner, Lonnie Friedman, now retired. After a couple of missed calls, they connected. Friedman confirmed neither he nor Hansen had ever handled anything over the years but routine cases. "Crimes of passion, robbery, murders over drugs or money, an occasional random crazy," he'd told her.

"Then he comes up with a recollection from maybe sixteen or seventeen years ago. A teenager came in claiming he had information on several murders. Hansen, who was still a rookie detective, took the report."

"Did the boy provide specifics?"

"Friedman says the kid came in with spread sheets, photos, a couple of receipts, even some articles he claims the killer kept in a drawer. Hansen was apparently very impressed. He promised the boy he'd look into it."

"What happened?"

"Friedman told his partner he was wasting his time, but Hansen took the information to his sergeant. He was instructed to walk it over to traffic."

"Traffic?"

"Every one of the deaths—Friedman thinks there were ten going back five years from that date—had already been classified as a hit-and-run."

Sam had somehow expected as much, which didn't stop her small gasp.

"You like that?" Williams asked. "It gets better."

The young man came in twice more, Williams reported. Each time, he insisted the police launch an investigation. He promised to reveal a name once he knew that was happening. Friedman believed the boy wanted attention. He told Hansen to call the parents.

"The father came in," Williams continued, "Nice man, quiet professorial type, according to Friedman. Taught at UDub. That's what the locals call the University of Washington. Said the boy had some issues following his mother's death a few years earlier. Acting out, I guess. He'd been diagnosed with some chronic condition that needed regular monitoring. The father promised to get his son some help. That was it. Hansen wanted to follow up, but the sergeant warned him against taking it further."

" But you got the names of the father and son, right?" Sam couldn't help but ask.

"Let me finish. Friedman couldn't recall any more details. I thought I might have to go back to the chief or someone above him on our side for some sort of a warrant since, as you know, everyone's very touchy about jurisdiction. But Friedman stepped up. Said he had a special friend in records, and he could go to her with a story about writing his memoirs and get the information I needed. He seemed excited, bless his heart."

Despite herself, Sam burst out laughing. "You have a soft spot for the veterans, Dakota."

"I respect the wisdom of the elders, Tate. And if I can make an old man's day, it's a victory."

"So?"

"The boy's name was Derek Baker. The father was Dr. Henry Baker, a professor of mathematics. And before you ask me to track him down, he died when Derek was a junior at UDub. Killed by, of all things, a hit-and-run driver."

Chapter 34

Sam drove in from Easton Wednesday after work to meet with Terry and Agent Williams. The mid-week commute was a pain, but she didn't want to use Zoom for something this important.

Not that the development would be shared with a wider audience. Terry had called off Friday's meeting, suggesting in an email that group meetings would take place only when significant advancements were made in the case.

Every now and then she glanced at the manila envelope on the adjacent seat. Inside were the coroner's reports on Henry Baker and Tom Hansen, along with a copy of Derek Baker's high school yearbook photo, the only image Williams could find. He looked average, perhaps a little soft around the face. Not a jock and not a murderer, at least not back then.

To pass the time, Sam reviewed the list of questions whose answers would guide future inquiries. Was Henry Baker's death an accident or a coincidence? Was he murdered by the same person the teen tried to report? Where was his son now? Did the boy grow up to be a killer or a future victim? She itched to dig further, preferably in Everett. Something about the place had drawn their unsub back. She was certain of it.

"Is this everything?" Terry asked, tapping a collection of papers on his desk. He seemed subdued, maybe because he got the documents and Dakota's summary earlier in the day.

"That's all we have so far," Williams answered. "I've compared the sketch of the night nurse 'Jerry Adler 'to the photo. Hard to tell if they're the same person. The tech wizards should be able to age the boy in the photo up fifteen years."

"Rob can run the name Baker through CODIS," Sam added. "Father and son. Maybe Baker senior was a victim of a crime or committed one himself."

"When was the last time you heard from the unsub?"

"Three weeks ago, remember?" She gave him a puzzled look. "I would have reported anything new."

"No indication he'd committed another murder or planned to do so," Terry said. He pushed up from his desk and went to his window. It was fully dark outside. The traffic indicated the nightly exodus from the capital, though Sam knew many others would work well into the evening on behalf of the government or private contractors.

Terry continued to look out the window. Sam cleared her throat. "Given these significant developments," she said, "we think a trip to the Seattle area is warranted."

Terry turned around. "You're talking about a troubled teenager who comes into a local precinct some fifteen years ago with a story about a serial hit-and-run driver whose name he won't or can't provide. Then what? Did he report his father's death as a murder? Did he hire someone to look into it?"

"We don't have that information, sir, but we might be able to follow up by talking to people that knew him. His high school, the university he attended. Maybe he changed his name. Maybe he's still living in the area. Is he in hiding because he is a target or a killer?"

"Remember the Judge seemed to be heading west when he last texted," Sam added. "What if he's ill, as the night nurse witness suspected, and is heading home for medical treatment? What if he timed it to catch and kill Detective Hansen the day after his retirement? We can learn a lot by being out there. I can clear things at work to take a few days."

Again, silence. Terry folded his arms across his chest and looked at the floor. Working things out, Sam supposed.

"Here's how I'd like to proceed. I've got a bit of agency business in the Seattle office. Might as well get that off my plate. While I'm out there, I'll speak with the Everett police chief and see how he feels about using our resources to re-investigate a series of h&rs from two decades ago. If he's willing to do that, I'll hook him up with our office out there, providing the bureau chief can spare someone."

"You're kidding!" Sam blurted before she could stop herself.

"I'm serious. I appreciate the effort you two put into this lead. However, I also need to consider cost and deployment when it comes to an out-of-state lead."

"At least take Dakota," Sam pleaded. "She already knows some of the players."

"Agent Williams is covering Atlanta right now. If necessary, she can also work with whoever we get from the Seattle field office. That's assuming there's anything to work with, which I will determine while I'm out there. Thank you both for this background. Sam, a minute?"

As soon as Williams left, she whirled on him.

"What the fuck was that about?"

"It's about me doing my job. I'm sorry you drove all this way just to be disappointed by my decision."

"You treated us like amateur teen detectives in an after-school special," she sputtered.

"No, I treated Agent Williams like someone who works for me, and you like someone whose role is to contribute valuable insight."

"Thanks for the shout-out." Sam hated to sound like a petulant brat, but she pushed on. "I'd like to think I'm more than carrying my own damn weight with the help of Detective McCready. Granted, Montana turned out to be an anomaly, but we got Williams back and put away a bad cop."

"What is this 'we 'business?" Terry snapped. "McCready isn't FBI. You're not FBI. Both of you have full-time employment elsewhere. As for Agent Williams, she's lucky to have a job after Montana. Her instructions were to observe, not engage."

"She was just trying to—"

"Pull a Sam Tate?" He'd gotten louder. "For Christ's sake, what makes you think I could send you, even if I thought it was a good idea? People above my pay grade know what happened in Montana. While they're happy we didn't lose an agent, they're not pleased with what precipitated the need for a rescue mission."

"I'm sorry if my so-called mission got you in hot water."

"Are you, Sam? I think a part of you loved the action, so much so that I can't help but think you might pull a similar stunt in Everett."

"You're saying I have a problem controlling myself or following orders?" Sam retorted. "May I remind you which of us served in the armed forces?"

Her remark hit; she could see it in his face. Fine. They'd both delivered low blows. Now they stood, legs apart, doing battle with words that wounded.

"You can't expect to jump feet first into a case like this," Terry said after a pause. "We're in Washington D.C., not Tennessee. Everyone is watching. Besides, you have a job. You're responsible for your people and the cases they investigate. I'm sorry if you don't find it exciting enough." He immediately regretted his last statement. "Sam ..."

She was past the boiling point. "Are you suggesting I go back and do my job, Terry? Funny, that's what our killer expects me to do. Only he thinks my job is to catch a killer, to catch him. And since he contacted me and only me, I'd like to oblige. Because I have a goddamn bullseye on my back, so excuse me if I don't have the luxury of observing while bureaucrats like you make sure we adhere to the fucking process."

She grabbed her coat and flung it over one shoulder.

"I'm going home."

"Wait, Sam, please. At least have some dinner." Terry reached out to touch her arm.

She pulled away. "We have food in Easton."

"I hate that we fought about this. How about I come out this weekend and we can hang out? Talk about work or don't talk about it."

"No thanks. I've got to tend to my professional responsibilities. Maybe you can get a head start on your investigation. I'm sure you'll have fun being back in the field."

She left in a state of righteous indignation that drove her all the way to the parking lot where she'd left her car. Only when she'd climbed inside did she allow herself to shed hot, angry tears.

Chapter 35

The heated argument left Terry sick to his stomach. He and Sam had never had a knock-down drag-out fight like that before. With all the cursing and yelling, he was surprised neither of them had thrown a punch.

She's scared, he told himself. So are you.

Sam's abrupt departure was a further gut-punch. He allowed himself a flash of anger. Fine, she was pissed off. She couldn't expect him to send a part-time consultant to do the work of a field officer, could she? She had no personal ties to Everett. Sure, it was her lead, but so what?

Regret soon took over. Sam had been personally impacted. The Judge specifically sought her out. The mere fact that he contacted her constituted a threat. She wanted to hunt him down.

If only she'd come to work for the Bureau. When she turned down Parker's offer to jumpstart a career with the Secret Service, Terry suggested the FBI. She wasn't too old to be a rookie, and her experience counted for something. Sam demurred, claiming her current position gave her more responsibilities and opportunities. He never quite believed her. There was just one opening above her, filled by a career officer who had a dozen good years left and no apparent interest in retiring.

Maybe Sam Tate, fearless in the face of danger, was afraid of commitment. To a job that offered professional advancement. To a career that paralleled his, notwithstanding his head start. To being with him every day. To living with him.

He had other concerns. He was keeping something from her. At some point, he had to sit her down and let her know what he knew. They were a team, or at least he hoped they still were.

* * *

The jet landed in the fog and drizzle that was vintage Seattle on a mid-November afternoon. During the flight, he called Sam and reached her voicemail. He kept his message professional, letting her know he'd taken her advice and was heading out west. As if he hadn't been part of the blowup that scotched his weekend plans and maybe his relationship. Miss you, love you, all unsaid.

He also called the Everett chief of police. Much to his surprise, Marko Bortnick was anxious to meet him.

"Call me Mark," Bortnick told him. "I thought about the case after speaking with your agent Williams. We may have some information about the old h&r and how they compare to what happened to poor Hansen. Can you meet tomorrow morning?"

"Absolutely."

An agent was waiting to bring him to the Bureau's Seattle office. Terry filled the SAC in on two earlier cases and asked him to assign an investigator to work with the local authorities. Rob Stein had already contacted the Tacoma precinct about the detective who died in the construction accident. The chief agreed to reopen the case, persuaded by the notion his detective might have been a target.

The Bellingham police chief needed some convincing that her detective's poisoning death could have been practice for a serial killer in the making, but she soon warmed to the idea. She also agreed to work with the Bureau.

He had dinner with the SSA and his husband, then checked into a hotel where he agonized over a text to Sam before settling on letting her know he'd arrived.

She didn't respond.

The next morning, he checked out, rented a car, and drove twenty-five miles north to Everett to meet the chief of police. Marko Bortnick was a solid, square man whose abundant brown hair showed just a touch of gray. He thanked Terry for making the trip and cut right to the point. "Is Derek Baker a possible match for the killer everyone is calling the Judge?"

"I don't know," Terry admitted, "but it's a lead we need to follow."

"We haven't had much time to look at the old h&r cases," Bortnick said. "Fortunately, we had an organized data entry process dating back before they occurred. Hansen kept his notes on Baker's complaints. Let me get the detective who spent most of the night putting together a report."

He placed a quick call. A willowy auburn-haired woman dressed in slacks, T-shirt, and blazer walked in a minute later. She looked none the worse for wear for having worked late.

"Joan Roberts," she said by way of introduction. No handshake. Not everyone was back to old forms of greeting. "Nice to meet you, Assistant Director." She took a seat next to Terry and crossed her long legs. Hard to ignore, and he was only human. Bortnick smiled.

"The Baker boy mentioned as many as ten h&r incidents he'd identified as homicides," Roberts began. "I located information on eight and they do bear some similarities. All occurred on quiet residential streets at dusk, specifically around 6 pm. All in either April or October, always in the rain, which, given where we are isn't that odd." She produced a dazzling smile.

"The victims were married men, varied age range, out for a stroll or a run. One was out to his mailbox; another was walking his dog. No witnesses, although just before the dog- walker was hit, neighbors heard a horn, which spooked the animal into pulling away, we think."

"The dog got away," Terry commented.

"Yes. I should mention a few people think they saw a late-model car in two instances, boxy, like a Subaru or a Volvo, of which there were thousands sold in the late nineties."

"Good work," Bortnick said. "Anything else?"

"Derek Baker was an only child. He was of age when his father died, so custody wasn't an issue. Derek had one more year of school, which he finished. I have nothing after that. I looked at Henry Baker's death and found something interesting. He was struck by a car in April at dusk while he was walking near the university in the rain." She rose without being asked and left the room.

"You think there's a connection to the earlier h&rs?" Bortnick asked.

"I don't know what I think," Terry answered. "It would help if we could find the son."

"If Derek is still in the area, he's using a different name. We can't even locate an image of him more recent than a dozen years ago. He had light hair and brown-green eyes, as I recall."

"Appearance can be changed," Terry said. "What about friends, romantic interests?"

"We can look into that. I'll ask Detective Roberts to run point on this."

"Great. The Seattle office will assign an agent to help if you're agreeable. Do you know if Derek Baker had additional family?"

"Let me pull up Henry's obit. There we go." Bortnick peered at his screen. "No survivors on his side but it mentions his late wife's brother. Sending you the link."

Terry opened the message, clicked the link, and skimmed the article until he got to the name of the late Vivian Baker's brother. He should have been shocked. He wasn't.

Chapter 36

Sam woke up with plans for the Friday she normally spent in Washington, D.C. First, a run with Jax, followed by a cup of coffee and a hard-boiled egg for her, and water and kibble for him. She could spend a couple of hours cleaning the house before she headed over to St. Michaels to do some window shopping. She and Jax could stop at the dog park. All that would use up at least half the time.

Or she could go into work, even though she had the day off. Not that she needed to adhere to a schedule. She was a senior officer with Talbot County's Sheriff's Department. She must have some pressing assignments to hand out, officer reviews to complete, calls to return, or any number of tasks for which she was responsible.

The word "responsible" operated like a trigger, taking her back to the fight with Terry. In the five years that they'd been involved—five years!—they'd never come at each other like that, verbal knives out and ready to wound. Words were said, exposing fault lines. Did he think she was reckless or irresponsible? Did she believe he was unfeeling and disrespectful?

The comment about the armed forces was a low blow. Terry had wanted to serve as his father did. Joint instability from an old football injury had sidelined him. Not fair, no matter how angry she'd been.

She had little experience in the minutia of a long-term commitment. She and Jay were engaged just a year before he died. Terry and she continued to be part-time lovers, except for one five-day vacation last year to attend a wedding so lavish it could have made a TV series. Not exactly daily life with a partner or a spouse.

What did she know about how partners moved on from a fight? What did she know about anything outside of work?

She knew she missed him. She loved him. She wanted to turn back time and she couldn't.

But she could have answered his text last night and she didn't. Was she prideful or embarrassed? She didn't even know. A call to her therapist might be in order.

As she predicted, housecleaning and the visit to St. Michaels occupied her attention until about 1 pm, which put her three hours ahead of the west coast. She drove back with Jax to her office. Gordy and McCready were both out and the sheriff's door was closed. Good. Fewer people to talk with, not that the Criminal Commander had to explain her schedule to anyone.

As messy as her inner life was, she tended to be tidy, especially at work. She filed or shredded papers, returned calls, answered emails and texts in a timely fashion, and made herself available to her detectives. She kept a physical day planner on her desk and a digital calendar on her phone and updated both regularly.

Which left her with nothing to do.

She pretended to rearrange a few items on her desk, drummed her fingers, then placed a call to Quantico.

"Hard at work, Agent Stein?"

"The work never stops, Lieutenant. At least they have me semi-sequestered, which allows me to run my searches in relative peace. Is there something I can help you with?"

"As a matter of fact, there is. Are you able to do a background check on a law officer?"

"Depends on who you're talking about and what you're looking for. If you're asking whether there's a national database of law officers, yes and no. The FBI administers the Uniform Crime Reporting Program, which collects data on law enforcement employees from reporting agencies. Note that UCR has the same problem ViCAP does. It's dependent on input from cooperating agencies. Even then, we're talking about hard data, like how many employees a department has and what they do. If you're looking for personal information on a named individual, you'd be better off starting with the socials. Almost everyone is on at least two. Then there are the professional organizations which can lead to bios and such."

"I should have started with those searches."

"I'm flattered you contacted me. Can you give me more specifics?"

"I was curious about some of the people outside the Bureau who make up our ad hoc task force."

"You're not the only one. I pulled together a packet for the Assistant Director just a few days ago."

"Was he looking for anything in particular?" The silence that followed her question spoke to his reluctance.

"I'm sorry, Rob. I didn't mean to put you on the spot."

"All I can tell you is the data I pulled together is all public knowledge, basic stuff. I didn't look on the dark web or uncover any devious or criminal behavior. That would have taken more work on my part, and that's not my lane. I was happy to do the director a solid, and I think it saved him time."

"Okay. Well, thanks."

She disconnected and scribbled out a list with the names of everyone at the Friday meetings, then crossed off Williams, Fuentes, Kinney, Stein, and Terry. She suppressed the pang his name generated. You wanted some distraction, she chided herself.

Half an hour and four names later she saw it. She finished checking the rest of the list, then went back to verify her earlier discovery. There it was, the connection that probably sent Terry to the West Coast. And very possibly into a dangerous situation.

Chapter 37

Terry turned down Bortnick's offer of lunch and headed back to the Seattle office. There he met with the Bureau agent assigned to the case, Zeke Gerrity, who he added to a conference call with Everett Detective Roberts to outline his requirements.

"I'd like you to work together to track down and interview any professor or friend from Derek's university days. Look for people who might have known his father, Henry. We'll also need Derek Baker's juvenile health records. Since he's a person of interest in a series of violent crimes, you shouldn't have a problem."

Next, he placed a call to Kinney to fill her in on everything he'd uncovered.

"I hate asking you to sketch this out off the top of your head, Molly."

"Quick thinking is my specialty, Director. What do you need?"

He shared his findings.

"The story about his going to the police brings to mind several questions. Did he invent the story about the homicidal h&r driver to get attention? Was he telling the truth? And if he was, what kept him from naming the person he thought was responsible?"

"I still can't say. The evidence we have to support his point of view is all circumstantial. The accidents have several things in common, including time of year and time of day."

"Vehicular homicide indicates rage. It's an outlet, like punching a wall. On the other hand, the presumed killer chose the time, the place, and the circumstances, which indicates planning." Kinney paused before asking, "When did the mother die?"

"Maybe five or six years before Derek made his report. She died of breast cancer, not an accident."

"Doesn't have to be an exact match for trauma to occur."

"The boy was maybe ten, Molly. Not exactly driving age."

"I'm thinking about the father. Terry, let me get back to you. I need to work this through. It won't be long, I promise."

"I trust you," he said and disconnected. Despite his exhaustion, he felt the familiar electricity akin to seeing a puzzle piece fall into place or recognizing a move in chess. They were close.

He had one more call to make, a request for a meeting that was more like a command. At 3:15 pm PST he was wheels up, on his way to Springfield, Illinois, a single file open on his laptop and three-and-a-half hours to make more calls.

The background checks of the non-Bureau personnel felt like an unnecessary intrusion. These law enforcement professionals had all gone through their organization's vetting process, many more than once.

Terry wasn't looking for evidence of a crime, only a connection. He found it in Timothy Powell's file.

Major Timothy Logan Powell, 53, had a sterling record at the Illinois State Police, where he'd served for nearly thirty years. An Illinois native, he'd stayed close to home to earn a bachelor's and master's degree, taking two years to serve in Desert Storm before joining ISP and climbing to the rank of major within the Division of Criminal Investigation in charge of the southern third of the state.

Powell's personal life was less successful. Two marriages and two divorces. His second union lasted twenty-five years and produced two daughters. The split was relatively quick and drama-free. The girls were by then grown and lived out of state.

Powell didn't seem to have any other family close by. His only sister had stayed in the Pacific Northwest after college. There she met and married a promising graduate student named Henry Baker.

Derek Baker was the major's nephew.

That didn't mean that Powell was close to the boy or in touch with the adult. It certainly didn't suggest that Powell did anything wrong, at least not until they had more information about Derek Baker. As Kinney had pointed out, they couldn't even say if Baker was hunter or quarry or a victim of his own unfortunate circumstances.

Terry was normally a cautious man. His new position made him keenly aware of the obligations and limits of his position as a senior FBI official. So why was he headed to Springfield? A gut feeling, a judgment call, his need to get ahead of the evidence he suspected was coming. Maybe a desire to prove that he took Sam's insights seriously. All of the above.

Fortunately, two calls he received within the next two hours gave him a lot more confidence.

Gerrity called first. "I honestly didn't expect to get back to you on a Friday afternoon, Director, but we lucked out. Actually, it was Detective Roberts 'idea. We knew it would take time to find which pediatrician had treated Derek and then get an administrative warrant to see the health records. But Roberts located the boy's school. Turns out the same nurse has worked there for twenty years. She remembered Derek because he had type 1 diabetes, and that's rare. Thinks he was diagnosed around his twelfth birthday. Unfortunately, she doesn't have a blood sample stored or anything like that. But she promised to look for the name of his pediatrician."

"That's great work, Agent Gerrity, and thanks for giving Detective Roberts credit. Let me know what else you find out."

No definitive proof, but the missing man had something in common with the relentless cop killer.

He shared Gerrity's news with Kinney when she called just fifteen minutes later. He told her about Derek's diagnosis.

"Type 1 diabetes is very rare and, believe it or not, less often the result of genetics than type 2," Kinney told him. "I will tell you that any chronic illness is very stressful for teens and young adults, especially when added to the physical and physiological changes they're going through. What do you know about the father?"

"Not much, why?"

"I'd like to know how he handled his wife's death. Here he was, a widower with a son who suffered from a form of diabetes with fewer treatment options eighteen or so years ago. Did he get any counseling? Did his son?"

"I have investigators looking to interview old friends or colleagues of his. I can also find out what Powell knows. Do you have a theory?"

"I do," Kinney replied. She delivered a brief outline. She finished to silence on the other end of the line. "Terry, you still there?"

"Damn, Kinney, it works. You're a genius."

"I know," she replied, but he'd already disconnected.

Chapter 38

Terry pulled up to Timothy Powell's neat two-story brick house just before nine that evening. Exhaustion had replaced elation. He'd barely eaten since breakfast. All he wanted to do was return to his hotel, grab a Scotch from the minibar, and fall into bed.

He'd briefed the Bureau's Springfield office on his plans. They insisted on accompanying him.

"Fine," he said. "But you don't enter unless and until I tell you." He hoped his decision proved to be the smart one.

Powell answered the door in a sweatshirt and jeans, holding a tumbler of amber liquid. Out of uniform, he appeared leaner and less formidable, more like a middle-aged dad relaxing after work.

"Come in, Director. Can I get you something to drink? Water, coffee, beer, or something harder?"

"Beer is fine," Terry said. He entered a small hallway and passed through a living room to a cozy study behind, complete with a small built-in bar, a writing desk, a built-in bookshelf, and two comfortable chairs. Powell pulled a beer out of a mini-fridge and refreshed his drink. He brought both back and pointed to two leather chairs.

"I'm sorry to visit so late," Terry began, turning his chair to face the other man. "We've developed a significant lead in our case that sent me to the Pacific coast yesterday."

"Really," Powell replied. No "Why make a special trip to see me?" or "Why not tell all of the team at the same time?" Almost as if he expected to see Terry sooner or later.

"You have relatives in Seattle, don't you?"

"I do. A nephew, Derek, although he seems to travel a lot. Some kind of tech job."

"Do you keep in touch with him?"

"On and off. He had a rough time of it after his mother died. This was more than twenty-five years ago. His father was an exacting man at times, although I think he loved his family. He was unprepared to care for a young son on his own, especially one with a rare form of diabetes. I tried to be available to the boy even though I was halfway across the country."

"And while you were acting as a 'sounding board ' back then, did Derek mention he'd filed a police report about someone he suspected as a serial killer?"

"He did. Frankly, I viewed it as the act of a troubled young man. I encouraged him to see a counselor. I spoke with his father, who assured me he had everything under control. I assume he got Derek help. The boy never mentioned the story to me again. Why are you bringing this up?"

Terry ignored him. "Derek went to the police two more times, Major Powell. Yet you never gave his concerns any credence."

"I was worried about him. My wife and I had him out the summer between his junior and senior years. I thought that would be good for him and I think it was. Until it wasn't."

"What do you mean?"

"Derek announced at the end of the stay that he planned to remain with us through his senior year. I think he got it into his head that we might adopt him. It wasn't remotely possible. His health needs, his obvious emotional issues, the problems with his father at home—it was all too much. We had our girls to consider. Henry would never have allowed it in any event."

"I see. What happened next?"

"He stopped speaking to us. We sent him a gift when he graduated high school and another when he finished university. Nothing. We offered to attend his father's funeral. He sent word our presence wasn't necessary. No contact for about eight years. Then, a few years back, we reconnected. By that time, my marriage was on its last legs. Now he calls several times a year, usually from the road. He travels for work but is based in Seattle. He sounds healthy and happy."

"Does he talk about his father?"

"Not since ..." Powell faltered.

"Not since he shared the one piece of information with you that he couldn't tell the police: the name of the man he believed was the hit-and-run killer, is that right?"

"I told you—"

"You told me you dismissed Derek's version of events. Was that because he thought his father was the man behind the wheel in ten separate vehicular deaths over five years?"

"He was an angry kid," Powell protested. "Henry wasn't a killer. The reports were Derek's effort to gain attention."

"More like a cry for help. Or a plea that someone make the killings stop. When no one did, when the so-called accidents started up again after a two-year break,

Derek felt he had to do something. He ran down his father."

"What? No!"

"You didn't suspect?"

" No!"

"Then this next part will be hard for you to hear. We have reason to believe that Derek has turned his unresolved anger on the very people who he counted on to stop a killer."

Powell jumped to his feet. "Holy hell, you believe my nephew is the Judge."

"Everything is beginning to line up. We've gone back to see whether DNA can give us information on what disease our unsub might have. While Derek has been picking his victims seemingly at random, based perhaps on their visibility, he knew his last victim. The detective he spoke with all those years ago, Thomas Hansen, was run over just after his retirement, which happened to be around Veterans Day."

Powell walked to the bar and poured himself another drink. His hands were trembling as he downed the beverage. He returned to the couch and collapsed.

"This is insane, Sloan. You're saying Derek killed his father, then went on a seven-year killing spree that took him across the country? How does he finance his— Jesus, what would you call them? Activities?"

"We think he has a job. I'm not sure how he gets time off; he may work remotely or travel for work. As for his meds, it's possible to buy certain kinds of insulin without a prescription. He may have a doctor that knows him by a new identity he built for himself. It's possible, although medically inadvisable, that he hasn't seen a doctor in the last year or so."

"Why kill on holidays?"

"If Henry became detached from the idea of family, he might have ignored milestone occasions like holidays, birthdays, graduations. These rituals are important to a child."

Terry locked eyes with Powell. "Derek is circling back to deal with the people who rejected his claims. Hansen. Maybe even you if you've outlived your usefulness to him."

"My usefulness?" Powell sputtered. "If you're accusing me of helping my nephew by feeding him information on task force activities, you're mistaken."

Terry stood and pulled out his phone. He typed in two words, then returned the device to his pocket.

"I'm not accusing you of anything right now, Major. We'll leave that discussion for tomorrow. I've asked a small team of forensic investigators to go through the house. I know it's late, but they should be out before midnight. You'll get enough sleep before I return at 8 am to take you to our regional office so we can continue our conversation."

"Will I need counsel?" Powell asked, his eyes averted.

"That's up to you. Might not be a bad idea."

As the forensic investigators entered the house, Terry said, "I don't know if you were culpable, careless, or simply duped. We'll leave a car outside the house all night in case it's the latter."

Chapter 39

At 9:30 am, Sam had already slowed down. She'd started her day with good intentions and vigorous exercise. Ten sun salutations and a five-mile run with Jax. She made sure all her bills were paid and her subscriptions up to date. Now she noticed a creeping despondency trying to make its way into her subconscious mind.

She'd argued with herself about whether to check in on Terry since Thursday evening. She'd seen his texts and obsessed more when they stopped. Her anger had faded, replaced by concern that spilled over into dreams of lost chances and missed connections. She sipped cold coffee and willed the phone to ring. Then it did.

Power of positive thinking, she told herself and answered.

"Sam, are you okay?" Terry sounded frantic.

"I'm fine. Where are you now, Seattle or Springfield? What's all the noise in the background?"

"How did you know? Never mind. Have you received any text messages?"

"Not for weeks. Terry, you're panting. Take a breath. Tell me what's going on."

"I'm in Springfield at Major Timothy Powell's home. He's dead, Sam. I found him this morning. He was in his garage under the wheels of his car. The local and state police are here processing the scene. Goddamnit, I just saw him last night. I even left an agent parked outside his house."

"Tell me what you can," Sam insisted.

Terry recapped the evening's conversation.

"Wow, that's a lot to process even for me, and I knew some of it. How did you center on Derek's father as the hit-and-run killer?"

"It was Molly Kinney's theory. There's no way to prove it, but it almost doesn't matter."

"Right, as long as Derek believed it was true. The boy suspected his father of being a serial murderer. He tried to report it to the police without identifying Henry. Whatever he brought with him in the way of evidence wasn't enough for anyone to pursue, especially without a name. He must have been afraid of his father. And frustrated with the local police."

"It's possible. Powell mentioned that Henry was difficult even before his wife's death and inconsolable afterward. Beyond that, he didn't suspect anything was off where Henry and Derek were concerned."

"He may have engaged in denial." Sam took a beat. "Let me go back to the scene. You said Powell was under the wheels of his car. But no one saw or heard an engine, is that right?"

"Apparently so. And the garage door was closed. Someone got him under the front right wheel and pushed the car over him. He might not have been dead when he went under but he had to be unconscious. And after seven hours of the weight on his chest ..."

"You think Derek did it." She stated it as fact.

"It's a reasonable assumption."

It's also reasonable to assume Derek and the Judge are one and the same, she thought to herself. Terry might be headed toward that conclusion. She was already there, but she wasn't going to push him.

"What now?" she asked instead.

"Every officer in the county seems to be here, including one of our agents and Powell's commander from the state police. She's pretty much looped into our larger case. I've got to spend a couple more hours here, then I'm heading home."

"You must be tired."

"I'm ..." Terry couldn't finish the sentence.

"Where and when are you landing?"

Terry gave her information on a commercial flight he'd managed to book.

"Jax and I will come and get you," Sam stated.

"You don't have to."

"I do, Terry. We'll get you back to your apartment. We'll get you decently fed. And then we'll get you safely tucked in."

"I might need you two to stick around."

"Jax and I are at your service, Assistant Director."

She could almost hear him smile.

* * *

Later that night, after Korean takeout, a shower (for Terry), a stroll (for Sam and Jax), and much needed though brief lovemaking, Sam lay on her elbow with her head propped and watched Terry as he slept, his breathing slow and regular.

She envied his ability to put the stresses of his work and life to bed when he turned in. As far as she knew, he'd never had a nightmare or a bad dream. His job was wearing, it had to be. Yet he seemed to take it in stride, at least when he was with her.

They had talked a little about the events of the last few days. Mostly about her guilt at thinking she could ignore the constraints of her position and charge out to Seattle, his remorse for shutting her out of his plans and treating her not like an equal but like a rookie.

"I'm not sure I had any more business going out on my own than you did, Sam," he told her. "Sure, I head the Bureau's CID, but my job comes with responsibilities and limitations. Fieldwork is supposed to be something I delegate, not undertake."

He looked so sheepish, his broad shoulders slumped, that she'd thrown her arms around him. "We both have some adjusting to do, Terry. At some point, we might have to let the kids kick ass while we issue instructions." They both laughed.

Adjusting to each other also meant sharing information. Sam had promised herself she wouldn't keep anything from Terry, but timing was always an issue.

"I need to tell you something," he murmured just before he fell into a deep sleep.

His news would have to keep, as would hers, but only for tonight. In the morning, she would let him know about the ominous text she received as she was on her way to the airport:

so close and yet so far

Chapter 40

The day before Timothy Powell's murder, Suzanne Foster entered through the glass doors that fronted the K Street offices of Foster & Foster, where she was greeted by Stuart, the firm's reliable front desk receptionist. Though slight of stature, he possessed a low, resonant voice suitable for promoting a political thriller, an American-made car or, her son claimed, a "we mean business" security firm.

"Good morning, Ms. Foster," he greeted her. He started to say something more, but just then the phone rang. Nine on a Tuesday morning and the calls were coming in. Always a good sign.

She pushed through a second set of doors and turned down a corridor to the office next to the one occupied by her son. As always, she took a moment to study the lettering etched on her door. Suzanne Foster, Chief Operating Officer. She took responsibility for obtaining and retaining clients, reviewing income and expenses, and representing the firm to the public so her brilliant son Michael could design and implement state-of-the-art systems to thwart even the most talented cybercriminals.

The firm employed ten other full-time people, most of them talented coders who worked directly under Michael. A director of communications had been recently added. Legal and financial matters were handled by reputable firms on retainer. The small size worked well, especially as the senior Foster was a credentialed consultant on a wider variety of topics involving counterterrorism.

Much of their work came from the federal government. Once the largest employer of cybersecurity personnel in the world, the government had been losing specialists to the private sector even as the need for protection had increased. Foster and Foster promised and delivered expertise via lucrative temporary contracts that sometimes lasted up to twelve months. They had worked, at one time or another, for DOJ, the FBI, the CIA, the Department of Defense, and Homeland Security.

Another piece of their work involved cyber threats against individuals. These contracts, initiated by monied clients, were both less straightforward and more fraught. Whenever possible, the firm tried to partner with local law enforcement or, in one or two rare cases, with the FBI.

Foster and Foster did not function as private investigators. Once they identified the source of an internet story, they would turn that information over to the client. Oftentimes they would recommend one of three private investigators or a highly capable public relations firm plugged into what went on in D.C. political, social, and media circles.

They'd recently been presented with a potential client, a politician who felt his situation rose to the level of cyberterrorism. Both Michael and his mother had reason to doubt those assertions. However, this particular politician interested Suzanne Foster.

Sean Parker came to them with demands but also ill-disguised fears concerning certain stories about him circulating online. Most of these stories offered no evidence, although future reveals were promised.

Washington was rife with nasty rumors, some based in truth and far many more rising to the level of slander. Parker's attackers were not hinting at sexual proclivities, padded resumes, or inappropriate interactions with foreign governments (although there were rumors about his involvement with Eastern European mobsters). No, these accusations centered on his supposed earlier career as a murderer-for-hire.

Parker approached the firm without a clue about Suzanne Foster's early history. She looked nothing like the young woman from the party who barely earned a glance from him. They never ran into each other again, although she heard he had retired. At that point, she was dealing with more pressing concerns.

Then the hit man known as Quinn—or his doppelganger—appeared in Washington as a junior senator from Maryland.

She initiated a search into the senator's past not long after her lunch with Terry. She considered Assistant Director Sloan a good friend, but he had shut down when she remarked on the resemblance between Parker and Sam Tate. Something was going on that she wanted to understand, something that concerned the younger woman.

Parker's official website contained constituent-friendly and carefully curated content. Visitors could learn about his upbringing as the adopted child of a middle-class couple from Providence. His biography skimmed through his education, his time in finance, his entrepreneurial successes, and his entry into politics. There was a folksy section designed to humanize him with images of him eating a crab cake, cheering at a

Baltimore Orioles game, playing tennis, and smiling with a group of children at a spelling bee.

Both on the campaign trail and in interviews, Parker fielded questions about his marital status. He made mention of someone he was "seeing" and occasionally referenced a long-ago love interest whose death left him bereft. Sometimes he used the word fiancée, although Foster never found an engagement announcement. That didn't mean anything, especially if neither had been from families who would send a notice to even the local papers. Without the name of this dead lover, she couldn't find an obituary either.

She also ran a search of the name Quinn with the hashtags "eighties," "New York City," and "assassin." Nothing came up. He was anonymous, invisible. Yet her boss knew of him, and so, she assumed, did other people who might use his services.

The present-day stories about Parker's secret past were still confined to fringe media, still seen as outrageous tabloid fodder. But not for long. Rumors sparked into wildfires before anyone could hope to put them out, especially online. Foster and Foster could only trace the origins. Someone else would have to take on the task of stomping out the flames. Sean Parker suggested he would then assume the task of shutting them down.

Who knew the truth about the senator and what was their goal? Without proof, it was innuendo. With it, Parker faced the end of his career and likely the beginning of criminal charges. His supporters would back away. His constituency would demand his resignation.

A man such as Sean Parker could be compromised, she guessed, but not cornered. He would fight back with everything he had. Inevitably, innocent bystanders would get caught in the crossfire.

Chapter 41

Sam and Terry spent part of the Sunday following his return in what he called a "reset" mode. Before long, they were enjoying their usual mix of chitchat and work talk. The fight was not forgotten, Sam realized, but neither did it mark an endpoint. The relief she felt caused her to break into giddy laughter from time to time.

"I love your laugh," Terry said as they strolled around Georgetown with Jax in tow. "So full, so deep, kind of like a happy longshoreman."

"At least I don't bray," Sam teased with a gentle elbow to his ribs. "Count yourself lucky."

"Believe me, I do."

The unusually warm weather, which they agreed might not be so unusual anymore, allowed them to pick a brunch spot in Georgetown outside at a café along the river. Jax was content to lie by their feet.

"I have something to tell you," Sam said as they sat down. "I heard from the Judge last night just before I picked you up." She relayed the brief message.

"He's taunting us," Terry said. "I can't tell if he's referring to his movements or how he rates our ability to catch him."

"Could be both, although his judgment tends to extend to the way I'm handling or not handling the case to his satisfaction. Ah, coffee," Sam said to the server who appeared with two mugs and a pot.

"Do you think Derek is the Judge? Did he kill Powell?"

"Yeah, I do. I just can't prove it yet. Powell's death was a homicide. But h&rs don't generally yield DNA samples."

"Fingers crossed he slipped up," Sam said. "If Powell was disabled before he was run over, then the driver exited the car."

"There was a bruise on his jaw that might have been made by a fist, not a bumper."

"I can see that Derek might hate the two people he confided in—Hansen and his uncle—enough to kill them. They let him down. Death by car, even in a garage, might be an acceptable alternative to running over Powell. But I don't see the holiday angle here."

"November 17th was Henry Baker's birthday."

"You're kidding."

"Nope. The date stuck with me for some reason. Holidays can be interpreted as special occasions. As if that weren't enough, November 17th is also something called National Adoption Day."

Sam's eyes went wide. "Jesus, Terry."

"We still have a ways to go, Sam. We need Derek's DNA to positively identify him as the Judge."

"If he was in Springfield, where is he headed next?"

"He's coming East."

"I suppose," Sam mused. "The question is why?"

She didn't miss the change in Terry at her question. He folded into himself like a crane and averted his gaze.

"Come on, Terry. I know you and Molly have discussed this. What does Molly think he wants?"

"Let's order," he said as the menus arrived. They quickly settled on the brunch special.

"To answer your question," Terry said when the server left, "Molly and I agree that Baker wants to find you."

"I know that." She forced herself to smile, although the words chilled her. "I'd argue that he already has found me. I can't figure out why. Isn't that Molly's department? I mean, does he think my involvement with three serial cases makes me an expert? Am I an obvious choice for a guy who wants to be caught because he's ill or looking for someone to pass judgment on him? Does he think I'll be more sympathetic because I'm a woman?"

"Maybe he relates to you because you both lost your mothers when you were about the same age."

Sam's face clouded. "That's not something I want to hear. Are you saying the killer is bonding with me over our past traumas? What else does he know about me? What does the rest of the world know, starting with Molly Kinney?"

"Sam, listen. You've been in the spotlight on and off for five years. Your childhood records are supposed to be sealed, but we know at least one person gained access. And journalists can be very good at ferreting out information. I'm amazed we haven't seen a story or better yet, a graphic novel about a girl who lost her family and rose from the ashes of her tragedy to become a Super Sleuth."

She cracked a smile. "Perish the thought, Sloan."

"Enough people are aware of your backstory, though. Your Aunt Rosa. Your cousin, Karen. Dr. Putnam. At least one person from the Army, likely more. A couple of important people within each of the departments you've joined. At least two people with the Bureau, including Paula Norris, our crack cyber investigator. You even met with a NYPD cop to learn more about the day Arthur Randolph shot up your brother's wedding. The list goes on."

"It's a lot of people," Sam admitted.

"Let's not forget Sean Parker. Speaking of whom, I need to tell you something."

"Saved by the bell," Sam said as Terry's phone rang.

He held up a finger. "This is Assistant Director Sloan. Yes, go ahead." He listened, all his concentration centered on the person who spoke. At one point, he gave a silent thumbs up.

" That's an incredible break. Who's the lead? That's good for us. Ask him to please ask the lab to compare it with the sample they collected last summer while investigating Trooper Lasky's death. Yes, that's the one. I also want them to collect DNA from Powell so they can ..." He listened. "That's exactly what I'm looking for. Lay it all out for them. No need to hold back. Nice work, Special Agent. Thank you."

"Good news?" Sam asked when he ended the call.

"More evidence linking everything together. Our investigator with the Bureau's Springfield office is representing us on the scene. Somehow, Powell got a piece of his assailant under his fingernails. Minute sample, but probably enough to run against the other."

"A match to the DNA found in the trooper's death will tie Powell's murder to the rest of ours. But we still ... oh my God," she exclaimed as the pieces fell into place.

"Yup. A sample from Powell's DNA could tell us if there's a familial match to the person who murdered him."

"To Derek Baker," Sam exclaimed. "Damn, Terry, we might have him!"

"We might have a name. We still have to find the man or at least find someone who's seen him recently. But you know what? I'll take it."

"Good," Sam replied. "Our brunch comes with champagne, and I want to celebrate for a minute. So, what will we talk about?"

Terry put his chin on his fist, his amber eyes glinting with amusement. "Why don't you regale me again with how you brought down a corrupt Montana sheriff? Don't leave out any details."

"Glad to oblige, G-man," she guffawed. "Once upon a time out west ..."

The story proceeded, punctuated by laughter and accompanied by food and drink and enough entertainment to push back the dread, even for an afternoon.

Chapter 42

Thanksgiving came and went. Sam held the holiday dinner at her house. She surprised herself by pulling things together in under a week with help from friends. The guest list included three work colleagues and their significant others, along with Agents Williams and Fuentes. Ten people and a dog showed up between one and three, moving back and forth between the living room, where they watched football, or the kitchen, where they jostled for the privilege of saying they helped.

Sam allowed herself to believe in a future where holidays were celebrated not with death but with friendship and love. That didn't stop her from listening for a text message, a phone call, or some other harbinger of unpleasant news about the killer they called the Judge.

Two days earlier, Terry had received confirmation that Timothy Powell's DNA was a familial match to the sample found under his fingernails and the sample collected from the slain state trooper. Even better, forensic investigators found an old baseball in the garage with trace DNA that matched the sample found at the scene.

"Powell and his nephew played ball one summer sixteen or seventeen years ago," Sam marveled at the time. "That seals the deal, right?"

"It brings us closer. Maybe Powell's ex-wife can confirm that no one touched the ball except her late husband and his nephew. She's been hard to reach."

He took her in his arms. "We've got an APB out naming Derek as a suspect in two or three murders, Sam. That'll be enough to hold him. Then we'll nail him."

"Do you think he knows what we know?" she asked, leaning her head on his chest.

"It's likely. He's self-righteous and arrogant, so he may believe he'll always triumph. Or he may have another endgame. Especially if he's ill. Detective Roberts and Agent Gerrity are looking for his juvenile health records and any doctors who might have or are still treating him. Let's hope they turn up something next week."

"Let's hope he doesn't decide to kill before then," Sam replied.

While Sam played the part of hostess, she wondered if her guests felt as anxious as she did. "We do not talk about he who shall not be named," Terry intoned as he greeted the arrivals. Everyone embraced the idea. Pat McCready checked his phone every half hour, it seemed, probably to see if a news item had popped on any of the feeds he monitored. He'd catch Sam's eye and shake his head.

As the afternoon progressed, most people relaxed, helped by wine, food, and camaraderie. Sam remained caught between relief and apprehension, even after she said goodbye to the last guest.

Tomorrow, she thought as she and Terry cleaned up. The bad news will come tomorrow.

She was wrong. The rest of the weekend passed uneventfully.

Well, almost uneventfully.

"We made it through the holidays without an emergency," she said Sunday morning over eggs and bacon.

"True. But there is something I need to talk with you about." Terry put down his fork.

"Uh-oh, this seems serious." Sam tried to grin, although her stomach lurched.

"It's interesting, at any rate. I ran into Sean Parker at a Homeland Security and Government Affairs committee meeting two weeks ago."

"Did you talk with him?"

"More like he spoke to me. He congratulated me on prosecuting Mickey Civella."

"You're catching his bad guys," Sam replied. "I'm sure he's thrilled."

"That's not the headline. As the room was clearing out, I swiped his glass. As far as I can tell, no one saw me, either in real life or on camera."

Sam's eyes widened. "DNA capture. You might have a future with the CIA. I assume you got it tested."

He pushed a sheet across the table. "Private lab, expedited results."

She scanned it and looked up. "This is definitive?"

"Yes."

She remained trapped for a minute by her shock. Then she jumped up and began marching back and forth until she could find words.

"You're saying Sean Parker isn't my uncle? Or half-uncle?"

"According to the private lab I asked to run the test—which I had no authorization to do, by the way, so this never happened—there is zero percent likelihood of a familial match."

"Shit!" She jumped up and went to pour herself coffee, more to have something to do while she tried to sort through her complex feelings. Jax thumped his tail in anticipation of a treat, settled for a head scratch, and lay down again.

"Honestly, I don't know if I'm more upset about the idea that we're not related or that he pretends we are." She glared at Terry. "And don't tell me he was humoring me. Something doesn't feel right."

"I agree. This doesn't discount the story your cousin Karen told you. Your great uncle George may have fathered a child out of wedlock. He may even have cheated with his brother's wife, your grandmother. But the product of that union, assuming there was one, was not the man who became Sean Parker."

She studied his face. "There's more, isn't there?"

"I'm afraid so."

Chapter 43

When Terry left, Sam continued tromping around the house, picking up and putting down objects and trying to settle herself. Finally she quieted, concerned not so much for her mental health as for Jax's. The poor dog had worked himself into a state of anxiety.

"Let's go for a walk, buddy," she told him. "Clear both our heads."

She and Jax strolled through the quiet residential neighborhood. No one was out. At 8 pm, most families had either returned from holiday events or had seen off their guests and were preparing for the beginning of a work/school week. The air was moist, though the wind was picking up. She was glad she'd brought gloves and a scarf.

Her brief flash of anger at Terry's disclosures had subsided. The knowledge that she wasn't related to Sean Parker left her with a sense of relief and also loss. She'd been operating on the assumption that he had a blood connection with her mother and therefore with her ever since she met him three years earlier. He didn't. Case closed. Except it wasn't.

The central mystery about what happened at her brother's wedding always concerned what nine-year old Sam claimed she saw: a man in a brown suit with a gun. Someone who may or may not have fired it. The same someone who she remembered lifting her out from under the body of her father. Parker's origin story wasn't the big reveal.

Sean Parker might have been an assassin.

Sam had plenty of questions after Terry shared with her Suzanne Foster's conclusions. How did she find out? Did she know Parker or work with him? Did he work for the mob?

"I can't tell you precisely how she came by this information, Sam," he said. "All I can share with you is she's confident he was the same man who, back in the eighties, was described to her as a paid killer by someone she had no reason to doubt. She didn't have details about his name or his employer."

"So, the person I saw at the wedding, the same one my brother's best man saw hanging around our house, was a hired killer who went by the name of Quinn. And is now a U.S. Senator. Good thing he's not a relative." She tried to laugh.

"It would appear so. Sam, I don't know what to say."

"Terry, do you trust this woman?"

"Suzanne? With my life."

That was all she needed. "I appreciate the risk you took to grab that sample and get it to a lab. Are you sure it won't come back on you?"

"As sure as I can be about anything. Are you sure you're okay?"

"Yes. I have you."

As expected, her words worked like a tonic. He gave her a lingering kiss. "Got your back, Tate," he said.

Now she stopped to let Jax do his business, her mind racing. The last thing she needed was something that would split her focus even more than it already was. But she needed answers. She wondered if she could get help from someone like Paula Norris to do a little off-the-record digging. Or better yet, she should ask Suzanne

Foster and her son. She'd contact the firm first thing tomorrow.

Sam walked into work Monday morning and involved herself with a major case. It seemed the minute they shut down one group of thugs, another popped up in its place. Armed robbery had increased in the county's wealthier neighborhoods. The new crop of thieves was tech-savvy enough to navigate the best security systems. Neither did they have a problem using violence. No deaths so far but it was only a matter of time.

For once, Sam was glad to partner with the larger and more well-equipped Maryland State Police. She worked late three days in a row and stopped Wednesday evening only because Gordy made her. Terry had scheduled the task force meeting a day earlier than usual and she didn't want to miss it. Her second promised he'd keep her up to date and would also make sure the state police didn't throw their weight around.

She had no doubt he would.

Despite her fatigue, Sam felt jazzed about the meeting, the first in a month. Now they had a suspect, a motive, and less happily, four more victims they could add to their tally. On the other hand, no one had reported a death on Thanksgiving, including the ever-vigilant Pat McCready. Sam hoped Kinney had a theory about that development.

She wondered, not for the first time, if the task force was redundant. Its dissolution would render her unnecessary to this case. Fine by her. She needed to put in more time at work and a little extra to learn more about Senator Sean Parker, whom she didn't trust. She wanted to spend more downtime with Terry and give more of herself to their relationship. It was time and she was finally ready.

As for the Judge, she didn't care if she was the one to catch him, as long as he was stopped. She wouldn't miss the creepy texts, the little presents, or the insinuations that they were somehow connected and that only she could figure out exactly what he wanted and expected of her.

No, she wouldn't miss that at all.

Chapter 44

Sam wasn't the only one who suspected the task force had outlasted its usefulness. Terry had to contend with twenty people who attended Friday's meeting. Even though fourteen of them were video conferencing, the space seemed too small to contain the mix of anger, frustration, and concern.

To begin with, Terry noted the addition of four new people including Detective Sergeant Corey Ames, sitting in for the late Timothy Powell, Agent Zeke Gerrity and Detective Joan Roberts of Seattle FBI and Everett Washington PD, and Lena Small, the special agent in charge of Atlanta's FBI field office, who asked to join the call.

The room was heavy with tension. Ranger Brodie Steel didn't help matters by noting that with two FBI regional agents, a GBI agent, and a police chief, the Atlanta area was flexing some impressive muscle.

To which Lena Small retorted, "This isn't a competition, Ranger. We've lost two agents. Do the math."

The bickering continued, primarily among the online participants. Finally, Terry roared, "Stop!" The sound of his raised voice startled everyone momentarily into silence.

"We have a lot to cover today and sniping at each other isn't going to help. Most of you, no, all of you are aware that Major Timothy Powell died a week ago at his home and that his death has been ruled a homicide. You've also heard his death is connected to this case.

Detective Sergeant Ames of the Illinois State Police's Division of Criminal Investigation will bring us up to speed on this piece of our investigation."

"Are we all sitting ducks now?" Lindsay Block asked.

"I don't think so, Chief Block," Terry replied. "Powell had a relationship with a man we now believe is a major suspect. In addition, a week before Powell's death, a detective in Everett was run over on Veteran's Day."

Another verbal barrage erupted, mixing questions and opinions. Terry attempted to speak over the ensuing din. "Take a breath, people. We'll connect the dots if you'll just listen. There'll be time for all your questions at the end."

Fuentes said, in the voice of a drill sergeant, "Excuse me, will everyone please shut up?"

Everyone did.

Ames provided a succinct report about Powell's death and the evidence that linked his killer to the Judge. Then Detective Roberts added details about Detective Hansen's murder and his encounter years earlier with the teenaged Derek Baker as well as what they knew about Derek's early life.

"The trail runs cold after Derek graduated. He was admired for his computer chops in school, according to an acquaintance. Knew all the tricks, could hack, spoof, back-door, clone almost anything. One professor swears the CIA came around to recruit him, but Derek opted for the private sector. We suspect he created a new identity for himself and has remained anchored to Seattle, primarily to receive checkups and such. He likely works in the tech sector, perhaps freelance, which would allow him to travel for work."

"And murder," Fuentes murmured.

Gerrity picked up the thread. "We've contacted all hospitals and clinics as well as doctors who treat patients with type 1 diabetes. Everyone has been slow to respond but we have a preliminary list of two thousand patients, most of whom are juveniles. When we narrow the search to men in their early to mid-thirties, our list shrinks to eighty in a metropolitan area of roughly three-and-a-half million. That's still a lot but we have more winnowing to do. We've also reached out to tech companies in the area. That's a much bigger pool to cull."

"Time for questions," Terry announced. "Steel."

"Do we think Powell was in on it? Or knew about it? Or leaked information? No offense, Detective Sergeant Ames and anyone else here, but it's a fair question."

"Let me address that," Terry said. "I was at Powell's house Friday night. I grilled him about his relationship with his nephew. He knew the boy suspected his father of being a serial killer. The rest of it was a shock to him."

"Clueless," Lena Small murmured.

"Clueless, hapless, unsuspecting, willful ignorance. Call it what you will," Terry said. "Keep in mind, Baker has the skills to obtain information on any of us without depending on his uncle. All the regional offices, my office, and this conference room are swept regularly. The computers are layered with safeguards. Cell phones, however, remain vulnerable. I swapped my work phone out when I got back from Illinois. You might consider doing the same. Rob, what's your question?"

"What do you need to move Baker from two-murder suspect to identification as our killer?"

"A DNA or blood match," Terry said bluntly. "Gerrity and Roberts have located his pediatrician, now retired to San Diego. His old records might help, although the office won't have any stored samples. We're going to rely a lot on visual confirmations or records of recent visits to a physician or an ER. Type 1 diabetes takes a lot of work to manage. If Baker is focused on planning and traveling to his executions, and especially if he still has some sort of regular job traveling, he may not be taking care of his health. He may have a trusted doctor or a pharmacy he uses. Easier than buying his form of insulin on the black market."

"We can check ER doctors in our jurisdictions," Clarksburg Agent Padilla volunteered. "He might have had a problem on the road."

"Maybe he's slowing down or getting worse," Williams said. "He missed a holiday."

Molly Kinney glanced at her phone and gasped. A small sound but so out of character that the others around the table looked at their devices.

"Molly?" Terry inquired.

"Sorry. I need to take this. I'll be right back." Kinney sprang from her seat and was out the door before the on-screen attendees processed her exit.

"A profiler's work is never done," Stein said.

"Let's hope it's a break in the case," someone rejoined.

Terry's phone pinged. Kinney had sent a message which read: End meeting now. Keep our people.

"We're going to cut short the questioning," he said. "We'll keep you up to date, you have my word. Thank you."

He ended the online call and looked around the table. "Please stay on a minute."

"This is never good," Williams whispered to Fuentes.

Chapter 45

As soon as Terry abruptly ended the meeting to a chorus of protests, Kinney reentered the room. Sam scanned her teammate for signs of distress. Something was bothering the woman, though she kept a lid on her emotions.

"I received a text," Kinney began. "No, not from the Judge," she added when she realized how her words had landed. "A colleague sent a link to an obit for my first boss and former mentor at the BAU, Harold Corte."

"I remember Harold Corte," Terry recollected. "The man was a legend in the field. Joined the faculty at Quantico when he retired from the BAU. I almost became a profiler because of him."

"I did become a profiler because of him," Kinney replied, "and I never looked back. We stayed in touch, though not a lot. Holiday cards, one or two calls a year."

"I'm so sorry," Stein said.

"He was eighty-four. He'd just been diagnosed with Parkinson's. Normally I wouldn't think anything of it, except the circumstances seem off."

"Explain," Terry said.

"The article says Corte died while visiting his daughter, Celia Corte Tamblin, and her family over the Thanksgiving holiday. Something about going into the kitchen for a turkey sandwich, remains of which were found along with a glass of milk. Apparently, he fell off a stepladder, hitting his head on the granite countertop." Kinney looked up. "That's impossible."

"It does seem far-fetched that no one heard a crash," Williams said.

"I'd like to know why he needed a stepladder to fix a sandwich," Fuentes added.

"No, I mean, Harold wouldn't have been downstairs eating a turkey sandwich," Kinney contended. "He became a vegetarian in college. I doubt even Parkinson's would cause a sudden craving for turkey after seventy years."

"Maybe the reporter got that detail wrong," Fuentes replied.

"Or maybe whoever the reporter talked with got it wrong," Stein added.

Sam had been listening intently. Now she said, "I'd like to know if the autopsy report mentioned finding turkey in Corte's system."

"Why?" Williams asked. "You think someone force-fed him? Oh, shit."

"Yeah, that's exactly what I mean. Another holiday death with just the right touch of perversion."

"Molly, can you guess why Harold Corte might have been a target?" Terry asked.

"He was a prolific and successful profiler. He must have worked on hundreds of serial murders over his career. He solved most of them."

"Do you remember any cases that particularly frustrated him?" Sam pressed, ignoring Terry's sharp glance.

Kinney looked off into space, then swore as a recollection came to her.

"There was one that frustrated the hell out of him, he told me. This was before I joined the BAU. The targets were all elderly. All the murders were made to look like accidents. All involved falls. The police missed it. Harold and his team finally saw a pattern, thanks to a persistent niece who insisted her uncle would never climb a ladder, let alone fall off. Still, it took another year before they made an arrest, during which time the suspect killed several more people. The perp was described to us as a perfectly normal young man with no trauma in his past who killed because he could."

Kinney paused before continuing. "Harold always presented the case as a cautionary tale about making assumptions. I think he took it more personally than he let on. He judged himself harshly."

"He's not the only one," Sam noted. "And he's a perfect candidate for our killer. One, he handled a case where he admitted he regretted not catching the killer sooner. Two, he served as a mentor, maybe something of a father figure to the younger profilers."

"Including Molly," Williams added.

The comment settled on them like a lead blanket.

Terry rallied. "Is a funeral scheduled?"

"Yes, for Saturday afternoon," Kinney replied.

"Crap. The body may already be at the funeral home. Molly, please find the daughter and explain the situation. It will be an uncomfortable, even shocking conversation, but it has to happen right away."

"What do I tell her?"

"That her father's death may be a homicide, same thing we'll have to propose to the Alexandria PD. The crime scene will have to be reprocessed. A second autopsy may have to be performed. I'll call over to Alexandria PD and clear the path with the chief.

Williams and Fuentes will then head over to the station and sit down with the responding officers and the detectives to bring them up to speed and share our concerns."

"What can I do?" Sam asked.

"I want you to deal with the local ME's office. We need that initial report. Don't mention a repeat autopsy; I'm hoping the suggestion comes from them. In other words, everyone, tread carefully but not lightly."

Sam swiveled to face Williams and Fuentes. "Ask the detectives if they bagged and tagged the half-eaten turkey sandwich. If Corte didn't take a bite out of that sandwich, maybe we can figure out who did."

Chapter 46

Sam hated funerals. Hated them. It didn't matter if they involved a fellow officer, a fiancé, a family member, or a complete stranger like Harold Corte. Nothing about the finality of the service sat well with her, nothing about the supposed peace and comfort, the better life, the end of suffering, resonated with her. What about those left behind to absorb the pain and carry its weight for the rest of their lives?

Yet here she was, sitting in a pew near the back in an Episcopal church in Alexandria's Old Town with Molly Kinney and a few of her BAU associates, dressed in a seldom-used black dress with suede Chelsea boots, along with 600 or so other people, only a handful of whom realized the polished wood coffin sitting in front of the altar was empty.

Her team had worked fast once Terry cleared the way with the police chief. While Williams, Fuentes, and two Alexandria detectives fast-walked each other through their findings, Sam contacted the local medical examiner whose office served northern Virginia. She had to explain the FBI's interest without accusing anyone of missing anything in his initial investigation.

"The fatal injury was to the left side of his head and is consistent with a hard fall, the doctor reported. "Detectives found an open cabinet door and a stepstool that appears to have tipped over. The victim probably turned to look over his shoulder as he lost his balance. He was a large man and would have hit the granite countertop with some force."

"Can you tell me about the contents of his stomach?" Sam asked. "Did you find he'd eaten turkey?"

"As a matter of fact, I didn't," the man admitted. "Or rather, none had reached his stomach. I did find a bit of the sandwich lodged in his throat. It never went down. Perhaps he took a bite, mounted the stepladder, and began coughing, which caused him to slip and fall. In any event, the food didn't kill him; the head wound did."

"You're saying he started to eat the sandwich, remembered something he needed from the cabinet, pulled out the stepladder and climbed, all without swallowing?"

"I'm no detective, but it's not as farfetched as you might think," the doctor retorted. "People move with their mouths full, or they eat too fast, or they literally bit off more than they can chew. For a Parkinson's patient, the simple act of swallowing can be perilous."

"Are there any marks on Dr. Corte's jaw? Bruising from someone forcing his mouth open?"

"Wait. You think someone might have pushed part of the sandwich down the victim's throat after he hit his head?"

"You tell me," Sam said.

"I will need to get that body back on the table."

"We can arrange that."

Kinney meanwhile pulled Celia Corte Tamblin out of a deposition. The lawyer was stunned but otherwise surprisingly level-headed given the situation. She gave the investigators permission to reexamine both her home and her father's body.

Terry came up with the idea to use an empty casket. "I want the killer to think we're a step or two behind," he explained to the team. Fortunately, Corte's daughter agreed to the ruse.

The detectives shared that one of the Tamblin sons ordered a pizza delivery a few hours before Corte's fatal trip to the kitchen. A quick check revealed the company used a substitute driver that evening. The son hadn't really looked at the delivery man, he admitted, but remembered that "he was sweating bullets, which seemed weird in November."

CSI was able to collect a minuscule amount of DNA just outside the door, barely degraded thanks to a cold weather snap that preserved the sample. A different medical examiner was looking for a match on Harold Corte's body, which was not in the casket but on a table in Richmond at the Office of the Chief Medical Examiner.

Now Sam, who had driven back to Easton late Thursday to spend the next day going over leads on the robbery ring with her team, found herself at a funeral for a man she didn't know who was likely killed by a man she wished she didn't know.

She looked around, forcing herself to appear as a curious onlooker and not a crime fighter. Was the Judge, aka Derek Baker here? Would this be his idea of a good time, watching the watchers, savoring his supposed victory before he announced to the world that he'd murdered another serial- killer-catching failure? Or did he plan to text Sam and rely on her to spread the word?

As much as she'd wanted to wear a drab pantsuit and a pair of sunglasses, and top it off with a hat, as much as she wanted to hide in plain sight, Sam had chosen to be visible. She wore her hair down and left her reading glasses at home. She remained standing until the last possible moment, searching the crowd, looking to see and be seen. Her distinctive features lent her some visibility. If the Judge was looking for her, he would find her.

The service lasted just under an hour. The speakers were eloquent and, for the most part, brief. A reception was scheduled for later in the day to make time for a private graveside service that wouldn't actually take place. Family members slipped out a side door, accompanied by Dakota Williams and another agent. The rest of the assemblage drifted to the church's main entrance.

Sam rose and pulled on her coat, half listening to Kinney chat with the couple who sat next to her. Idly, she scanned the crowd one more time.

And locked eyes with a killer.

Chapter 47

The man stood in the back just behind the section where Sam sat. Early thirties, sandy beard that matched the hair barely visible under a flat tweed cap. Pale face, weak chin, thin lips. Thick tortoise-shell eyeglass frames. A wool olive blazer hung loosely on his thin frame. He was tallish, slope-shouldered, and otherwise unremarkable except for the fixed way he stared at her.

Then he lifted his hand and wiggled his fingers in a small wave. Sam had no doubt, no doubt at all, that she was engaged in a staring match with Derek Baker, the man known as the Judge, a serial murderer with at least ten victims.

"He's here," she growled to Kinney, grabbing her small bag. "Let me by." She pushed her way to the far aisle, keeping her voice low and her movements small. She didn't want to create a panic or start a stampede. Not that it mattered. He was out the door before she exited the row.

"FBI. Move!" she called out, louder now, so her voice cut through the chatter. No time for niceties.

She bulldozed her way through the scrum, ignoring the outraged protests. Outside, she caught a glimpse of the olive jacket and gave chase. He had a head start, but she was faster, even in a dress and low-heeled boots.

He appeared winded as he sprinted across the street. She thought she might have a chance to catch him.

"Stop!" she yelled, but she was the one who had to halt for traffic. She watched him fling himself into the driver's side of a dark-gray Toyota. He took off, tires squealing, leaving Sam in the middle of the street as traffic screeched to a halt.

The horrified mourners who'd witnessed the last part of the pursuit had either moved away or whipped out their phones to record the wild-haired woman with a hand in her bag. She was glad she'd decided not to withdraw her weapon and try to get a shot off.

Kinney caught up with Sam, who briefly envied the other woman's loose suit and leather track shoes.

"Sam, are you alright?"

"I'm fine, but he's gone."

"The Judge? Derek Baker?"

"I'm sure of it."

Terry jogged up with Fuentes and another agent on his heels. "You saw him." he stated.

"I did," Sam agreed. "He got in a car with Texas plates," she told them. "LHT and then numbers I didn't catch. Probably a rental, although not one of the major companies."

"And you're sure it was our unsub?" Terry asked.

"As sure as I can be."

"Good enough for me. We'll update the APB, set up a hotline, and go to the media outlets."

"You'll be dealing with a flood of incorrect sightings and a rise in public fear," Kinney warned.

"We'll deal with the false calls," Terry said. "As far as scaring people, I think it's time the public knew what we're dealing with."

* * *

Sam and Terry headed to his apartment to change, then went over to headquarters to meet with the four others who formed the core team. Stein appeared with two pizzas, Fuentes with soft drinks, and Kinney with water. Williams showed up last.

"Still five agents at the reception," she reported. "Most of the profilers past and present have stayed away, per Kinney's suggestion. We don't need to provide him with a room full of easy targets."

While they feasted on the food (Fuentes, Stein) or ignored it (everyone else), they discussed Baker's appearance at the funeral.

"What do we make of that, Molly?" Terry asked.

"I think it's clear he wanted to lay eyes on Sam. We talked about that being a possibility, especially if he's hell-bent on reframing his quest for vengeance as a battle between two worthy adversaries."

"You make it sound like we're playing Mortal Kombat," Sam protested. "Am I supposed to be the bad guy?"

Before Kinney had a chance to answer, the conference room phone rang.

"Good, that's the call I was waiting for." Terry punched the speaker. "Agent Gerrity, Detective Roberts, thanks for phoning in on a Saturday."

"We have a lot to report," Gerrity began. "We circulated a description and sketch to a list of hospitals, pharmacies, and clinics that might be supplying insulin to Derek Baker. Detective Roberts had the idea to also approach tech groups. Believe it or not, we have something like thirteen thousand in the immediate area.

We started with the fifteen largest companies and hit pay dirt."

Roberts picked up the thread. "Second Gen is a software company that designs security programs. They have seventy full-time employees, down from 280 before the pandemic, and ninety-two remote workers who work flexible hours. Ineligible for most benefits except access to a private clinic and reduced-price medicine. One guy, who worked full-time before being downgraded, matches Baker's description. Sandy hair, brown eyes, no beard back then."

"Discount insulin would be useful," Sam observed.

"Did you get a name?" Terry asked.

"You won't believe it. James Moriarty."

"As in the archnemesis of Sherlock Holmes?" Stein asked. "Boy, this guy has a high opinion of himself."

"No doubt," Gerrity said. "But the big news is he was laid off last week. No golden parachute for contract employees."

"No more income for the insulin he needs," Fuentes said.

"I don't suppose the clinic gave you the name of the doctor who wrote the prescription?" Terry asked.

"Took a bit of persuasion, but they did," Gerrity answered.

"Two names," Roberts added with a touch of glee.

"Come again?"

"We have the name of the doctor and the name of her father, who happened to be Derek Baker's pediatrician."

Chapter 48

That evening, Sam and Terry were eating takeout from their favorite Taiwanese restaurant when she asked if he could imagine how Derek wanted the case to play out.

"I'm not sure how to answer that, Sam," he admitted, transferring a dumpling from the container to his plate. "Or maybe I should say, I think he may have several goals, some of which could conflict with one another."

They were in Terry's apartment, dressed in sweats, sharing a delicious meal while Jax snoozed, and Thelonious Monk played quietly in the background. Terry had been the one to suggest eating in, hoping to create an insularity that might hold the stress of the day at a distance, at least for a few hours.

But despite the relaxed setting, the comfortable clothes, the comforting food, the happy dog napping nearby, despite the trappings of safety, he knew Sam didn't feel safe.

The avalanche of news from Seattle gave the team everything they needed to haul Baker before a jury and lock him away for life. If he lived. The killer's relentlessness and lately his audacity had angered law enforcement nationwide. Death by cop was as likely as capture for the Judge.

Since the conversation was going to involve the case one way or another, Terry sought to steer it toward what they'd learned earlier in the day from Gerrity and Roberts. The interview with Baker's doctor, Monica Humphries, filled in a lot of the gaps.

"What a coup to locate Baker's doctor and learn he was once her father's patient," he began.

"It's interesting that Derek trusted her enough to confide in her about his visits to the police," Sam said, helping herself to more rice. She certainly seemed to be unwinding.

"Unlike almost everyone else, Humphries didn't discount his version of events, either. Seems she had a less than positive view of Henry's parenting style. Probably shared that with her father."

"Do we think she actively aided Derek in some way?"

"I trust Gerrity and Roberts," Terry stated. "If they say she was shocked to learn of the accusations, I believe them."

"Assuming she's telling the truth, can't she get into trouble for providing him insulin under an assumed identity?"

"I don't know about the legal ramifications, but the medical board might be unhappy. Unless Baker created a foolproof digital trail to give the appearance of a legal proceeding, then explained away the name change to his desire to make a fresh start."

"Gerrity said Dr. Humphries gave Baker a ninety-day prescription when she saw him in October. He should have enough to get him into January."

"Maybe. Meanwhile, we have everything we need to convict Derek Baker of eight or more counts of murder. And don't forget, the man may be clever, but he has several weaknesses."

"Several?"

"He's got a disease he may not be managing well. He's got a need to be noticed. And he wants something from you." Terry regretted the words as soon as they came out of his mouth. "Nothing we can't handle," he added with false cheerfulness.

Instead of responding, Sam took a large swig of beer.

Somehow, Terry got the evening back on track. They Facetimed with his mother, watched an old movie, walked Jax together, and prepared to turn in around 10 pm.

Which is when the text from @jmoriarty came in.

Thnx for not shooting me. U looked terrific, btw

U looked winded, Moriarty. I mean, Derek

so now I'm Derek

your birth name, amirite?

Ha, ha. Call me whatever u like, except the Judge

That's what u are. Judge, jury, and executioner

He didn't respond right away. Then he wrote,

back to today. A funeral without a body. How many people know where it really is? I do. What r they looking for?

He was even smarter than they credited him, Sam realized. She would have to stay on her toes, even as she pushed him.

We have evidence Corte didn't die by accident, Derek. The turkey sandwich in the throat was a clever misdirect. Too bad he was a vegetarian.

worth a shot. Parkinson's is so unpredictable

so is type 1 diabetes

Sam had decided to show her hand with that last comment. She wondered if she'd gone too far, especially when Baker paused for so long she thought he'd signed off, until he texted,

that's all under control.

Really? Must be challenging to score insulin

I'm good. Enjoy your evening, Lieutenant. g2g. So many plans to make for the holiday season.

r u heading back to Seattle or sticking around?

might ask you the same thing. I hope you're staying in town. We could have such fun and end the year with a bang. 'Tis the season to be noisy. Ho ho ho. cu soon.

She handed Terry the phone without a word. He read the texts. Then he put his arms around her. "Damn him to hell. I'm so sorry, Sam."

"I need this to be over, Terry." She leaned against him.

"I know, my love. I know."

Chapter 49

Sam always struggled with the holiday trifecta of Thanksgiving, Christmas, and New Year's Eve. Her Aunt Gillian and Uncle Kevin had tried hard to make the season as uplifting as possible for the orphan who came to live with them.

Eventually, she accepted the idea that the people around her were going to celebrate with food, festivities, and gifts. She wanted her guardians to be happy, so she feigned happiness. She decorated trees, exchanged gifts, sang carols, and baked cookies.

Sam left for college and managed, for six or seven years afterwards, to cocoon herself. She declined invitations to share the holidays. In Nashville she sang at holiday parties, which kept her from feeling lonely.

The army forced her out of her shell. As a second lieutenant, she led a platoon of women in close quarters, many barely out of high school and away from family for the first time. Morale was key to unit cohesion. She supported the plans and parties some of the more outgoing soldiers suggested to mark birthdays, special occasions, and holidays.

The previous year, Sam entered the holiday season on a high. She'd caught a killer and jump-started her relationship with Terry. The two of them spent Thanksgiving with his mother in Colorado and traveled up to New York for a joyful and noisy Christmas reunion with her Aunt Rosa and other members of her father's family.

This year, after an event-free Thanksgiving that turned out to be anything but, Sam wished she could hop a plane and fly out of reach. Instead, she snuggled with Jax and with Terry when they were together, seeking out whatever comfort and joy she could find.

The FBI issued a nationwide press release with the latest images of Derek Baker, aka the Judge. No task force members were named. A regional agent was assigned to each of the victims 'families, although their duties consisted largely of chasing away inquisitive reporters. Local authorities were directed to forward all media inquiries to the FBI National Press Office. The Bureau also set up a tip line, which was flooded with calls the first week.

Social media had a field day with the idea of a cop-killing vigilante. Comments painted Baker as either a "tool of the woke mob" or a "justice warrior." Memes recirculated a popular routine from the 1960s, "Here Comes Da Judge," with graphic depictions of a vicious slasher in judicial robes.

The Bureau brass considered that Baker might go after key members of the BAU and CID units. Molly Kinney moved into a hotel. Rob Stein moved back home. Terry refused a private security detail and so did Sam, reminding him that the killer probably knew where to find her. Besides which, she had several friends in the Talbot County Sheriff's Office surreptitiously guarding her house at night whether she wanted them to or not.

She might even welcome a confrontation with Baker. He was smart but not fearless, slinking from one murder to the next, hiding behind his computer skills, his beards, and his untraceable texts. On the other hand, he was fueled by his messianic desire to redress the wrong he felt had been committed against him, and the surge of power he probably felt after each murder.

He'd gotten under Sam's skin, and she hated that.

For that matter, so had the elusive Sean Parker. In his case, it was the absence of communication that made her anxious. He must have known they weren't related. Why did he pretend they were and then not follow up? And if he had been, in a past life, an assassin, was he at the wedding all those years ago to kill someone?

"On one hand, I have a serial killer who is communicating regularly. On the other hand, the man I remember from the wedding was probably an assassin. And is now a senator."

She sat in Dr. Putnam's comfortable office one rainy December afternoon, insulated from the damp cold if not from her fears.

"That's a lot to deal with," Putnam replied placidly. She'd dressed for comfort in bark-colored slacks and a pale-green sweater. Earth tones. The colors soothed Sam. She suspected they were meant to.

"Let me point out to you that while Senator Parker is an enigma, and his connection to your past is unclear, Derek Baker, aka the Judge, is a real person. He is a direct and present threat to you, to your team, and to members of the larger law enforcement community."

"I promise you, I know the difference," Sam said.

"Good. Now, let's talk about how you feel going about your daily life. Your work is removed from the frenzy surrounding this case. Does that help to lessen the tension?"

"Not really," she told Putnam. "Only one person in the department knows about my inconclusive history with Sean Parker but several others are aware that I've had direct contact with the killer. Even more suspect I might be a candidate for murder. They haven't said anything to me, but I can feel their trepidation. I told my boss I'd stay away from the office, but he won't hear of it."

"I suspect work's going to provide the best outlet for you." Putnam brushed an invisible speck of lint off her trousers. "You've taken all reasonable precautions, haven't you? The sheriff knows what's going on. Your closest friends have undertaken the task of providing some level of protection which you have accepted, if tacitly. What else can you do?"

"I can catch the son of a bitch," Sam said.

Chapter 50

While Sam worked to push Sean Parker from her mind, Suzanne Foster found it impossible. If Foster and Foster accepted him as a client, she might learn not only who was out to get him but also how they came by such damning and accurate intel.

No, she couldn't, not without damaging the firm's reputation or crossing her own ethical line, however faint. Foster and Foster maintained its reputation by scrupulously avoiding any action beyond online searches. They did not barter, trade, sell, or go public with the information they obtained. As much as she wanted to understand how Parker's past work for, and present antipathy towards La Cosa Nostra fit together, she couldn't jeopardize her good name, or Michael's for that matter.

"We promised to get back to Senator Parker before the holiday season, Mother," the younger Foster reminded her during their earlier breakfast meeting. "So, what do you think?"

"I think someone is out to get the senator," his mother replied.

"Surely not you?"

"Whyever would I?"

He regarded her with eyes so much like his father's it stung. "There's something about this potential client that doesn't sit well with you. Something you know that you're not sharing. Do you think Parker is a murderer?"

"What I think is immaterial," she replied.

"Not entirely. Not if you know or suspect he's dangerous. We're within our rights to refuse a client, after all. Do you want to work for him?"

"I'd like to know if these particular stories are true, but that's not within our professional purview."

He shook his head. "That doesn't answer my question."

"Give me a day or two to think about it, will you?"

The next day, Stuart buzzed her.

"There's a very handsome and very well-dressed gentleman in reception who's asked for ten minutes of your time to discuss 'an issue of mutual interest,'" he said in a low voice.

"He needs to make an appointment."

"I told him that," Stuart whispered. "I handed him the brochure and the new client form. He insists he isn't looking to receive help but offer it."

"Did he give you his name?"

"He handed me his card. It says, 'Terrance A. Kingsley, Esquire, 'and it has a phone number. I don't recognize the area code, 401. What should I tell him?"

"I'll be right out," Suzanne answered and sprang to her feet.

The man in the lobby cut a striking figure, with his tailored suit, expensive tie, his walnut face clean-shaven and strong-jawed. His well-tended hair showed a touch of silver, lending him an air of gravitas. If he wasn't a member of the bar, then he was perfectly cast as an actor playing one.

She ushered him into her back office and gestured to a chair while she took hers behind the desk, all business.

"I have five minutes, Mr. Kingsley. What can I do for you?"

"Thank you for taking the time to see me, Ms. Foster," he replied, handing her a card. His voice was as polished as his appearance. "I am representing certain interests who have information on a potential client of yours, information that might prove useful," he went on.

"Our client list isn't public."

"You know how it is in Washington. So much information, so difficult to contain."

"Who do you represent?"

He ignored her question. "Your clients seek to get to the bottom of online stories they consider damaging or malicious, don't they? These stories may contain information that is confidential in nature or even a threat to national security. Do you ever wonder if the stories are, in fact, true?"

"It's not our job to wonder, Mr. Kingsley," Foster snapped. "Perhaps if you tell me who you represent, I might better understand what you want. Or you could just tell me."

Kingsley leaned forward, placed his elbows carefully on the desk, and steepled his hands. "My clients are aware of certain stories circulating about a potential client of yours. They've asked me to let you know that the stories are true. This individual is a murderer and more."

If he expected her to show surprise or fear, he was disappointed. Instead, Foster made a show of looking at his card.

"Your clients have hired an attorney with a number in Rhode Island to come to Washington to warn me about an individual who hasn't even retained us yet. What do they expect from us?"

"Pardon?"

"What do your people want? An assurance that we won't work with whomever you think this is? Or that we will? Are there inducements if we comply or penalties if we don't? I'd like to know what's at stake here."

Kingsley listened and nodded as if he sat at a lecture of a professor whose work he admired.

"You're a very smart woman, Ms. Foster. Here's what I think. You know who I'm talking about, and you know the stories are true. By the way, my employers can prove it."

Foster didn't respond.

"Don't take Sean Parker on as a client, Ms. Foster," Kingsley continued, his voice low. "The man is an experienced killer. He's also driven by his conviction that my predecessor was involved in the death of his fiancée and the kidnapping of her infant girl."

"Is that what happened?"

"That was before my time."

"Do you know what happened to the child?"

"There was no child. The young woman was nine months pregnant when she died, along with her unborn child, in an unfortunate accident. This is fact, supported by medical records. That never mattered to Sean Parker."

"Why are you telling me this?"

"Parker's delusion poses a danger."

"To your clients."

"And to the woman he believes is his child."

Foster stood abruptly.

"Thank you for coming to see me, Mr. Kingsley. You've given me a lot to think about."

Kingsley followed her lead. "Happy to help." He gave a wide smile. "I'll see myself out."

Only when he'd left did she allow herself to sink back into her chair trying to decide what to do with the information he'd given her.

Chapter 51

Between the department's annual community kids' holiday event and the office party, Sam could almost keep her mind off Derek Baker and his whereabouts. The towns of Maryland's Eastern Shore went all out for the holiday season. Each town, decked out to the fullest, glittered in its own way. St. Michaels, with its cobbled pathways and historic architecture, looked like a 19th-century village, albeit with modern stores that attracted throngs of tourists.

Everyone at work participated in Secret Santa. Sam drew Betty Claiborne's name. The sheriff's administrative assistant was fond of scarves, which made shopping for her relatively easy, especially when Sam ignored the recommended dollar limit. Betty had been both helpful and welcoming to Sam over the years.

Sam received a set of No. 2 pencils and a Moleskine notebook. Whoever had drawn her name knew she had a habit of scribbling down her thoughts. The gesture gave her a sense of belonging, four years after she'd arrived from Tennessee.

Terry elected to spend the weekends with her in Maryland, arriving late Friday night and leaving Sunday. "Still more relaxing than staying in the city right now," he claimed. "I feel as if I'm on vacation."

Fortunately, the criminals also took the month off or at least cut back on their activities. Crime was down after a fourteen-month upturn. Even domestic violence ebbed, which was unusual during the stressful holiday season. Everyone in the department breathed a sigh of relief--everyone but Sam. It was all she could do to squelch her anxiety.

She heard nothing from the Judge.

Christmas Day finally arrived. Sam and Terry planned to spend a quiet and lazy morning, then visit her colleague Carol Davidson in the home she now shared with her forensic investigator boyfriend Martin Lloyd.

Sam padded down the stairs at 7 am, followed closely by an excited Jax. She turned on the coffee, pulled on a down jacket, and let Jax out back. Two minutes later, he was back, gobbling down breakfast while she peeked into the living room to admire the tree, the first in her new house. The pile of bags and boxes included those from Terry's colleagues and a couple for Jax. She'd have a hard time keeping the dog away once he sniffed out his gifts. Maybe the coffee would wake Terry and they'd sit around and rip open presents, something she hadn't done in thirty years.

For now, she sat in the kitchen and gave herself over to the warming sensation of being in a home she loved with a man and a dog she also loved.

Terry was soon downstairs, pulled by the scent of muffins and coffee or perhaps the dog's whining.

"Thank God you arrived," Sam laughed. "Jax is behaving like a kid at Christmas."

"He is a kid at Christmas," Terry replied. "Let me get coffee and we'll let our boy at his presents."

Another hour passed pleasantly as they watched Jax rip away the wrapping that covered his large chew bone and another that revealed a rope toy which he proceeded to throw around with great joy until Terry encouraged him to focus on the bone.

They'd agreed to limit their gift choices to one apiece. Terry received a pair of lined Italian leather gloves. Sam's was a delicate gold necklace with two entwined circles. She put it on, struggling to find something profound or poetic to say. She went over to sit on Terry's lap and whispered, "It's beautiful, and I love you" before delivering a tender kiss.

"Can we stay like this forever?" Terry asked.

"Nope. We need to get out and exercise ourselves and the dog."

Ten minutes later, they were warmly dressed and about to leave the house when Jax began to bark.

"What is it, boy?" Terry asked. "Ready to go out?"

"No," Sam said, drawing out the word. "That's his warning bark."

She and Terry exchanged looks. She reached into the drawer of the small table beside the front door and pulled out her Smith & Wesson Bodyguard 38, a small but effective gun. Terry held Jax by the collar as she opened the door.

On the front porch was a gaily-wrapped package with an envelope addressed to "Lieutenant Sam Tate."

Sam closed the door. "Thoughts?" she asked.

"Sorry we didn't get that security camera installed," Terry replied.

"Which means I don't know who this secret Santa is. Maybe I should call one of my Maryland State Police buddies."

"Just to be on the safe side, let's exit out the back door and move away from the house first," Terry suggested.

They walked down the quiet streets. Only Jax was able to enjoy the cobalt skies and the clean air.

Sam dialed Frank Weller, a homicide detective she'd worked with on a case three years earlier.

"Merry Christmas, Tate. Are you taking time off from chasing serial killers?"

"Thought I was. Listen, I hate to bother you, but I have an issue." She quickly filled him in, describing the size and shape of the package and reassuring him she hadn't touched it.

"I'll call into the Office of the State Fire Marshal. They have a bomb squad and someone's always around, even on Christmas. Stay away from the house."

Five minutes later, her phone rang.

"Lieutenant Tate? This is Ian Young. I'm a technician with the OSFD bomb squad. Detective Sergeant Frank Weller called. Can you give me your address? We can be there in ten. I assume you're out of the house."

"We are."

"Any pets?"

"We have a dog on a leash with us."

"Keep him close. We'll be coming with a robot and a bomb-sniffing canine. I can always guarantee at least one of them remains operational even during cold weather."

Sam couldn't help but smile. "We'll be close by," she replied. "Can you come in quiet? Don't want to spook the neighbors."

"You got it."

Sam and Terry walked up and down the block so they could look out for other people and keep the house in sight. They saw no one. Everyone was away or indoors celebrating.

Not us, Sam thought, and cursed the killer once again.

Chapter 52

Ten minutes later, an OSFD van came down the street, a single light flashing. Two men disembarked, along with a Labrador. Predictably, Jax reacted, assuming he might have a playmate. Sam held him back.

The older of the men, lean and grizzled, approached her. "Lieutenant Tate, Ian Young, bomb technician. We spoke earlier. My partner is Owen Lance."

The young man nodded.

"Thanks for coming," she said. "This is Assistant Director Terry Sloan. And this is Jax."

"How do you do, sir? Our dog is named Rocket. He's friendly, but he's working. Is that your house?" He pointed at her modest home, several yards away, and she suddenly feared for the structure as if it were alive.

She nodded.

Lance instructed Rocket to stay and went back to the truck to remove what appeared to be a drone with arms.

"A flying robot," Terry murmured.

"Roberta—that's what we call her—will take pictures and rudimentary x-rays which she will send back to us," Lance explained as the device took off. It darted around the package, capturing the "gift" from every angle.

"We can see some of what's inside," Lance said as they crowded around him to see what Roberta had found.

"Or in this case," Young added, "what's not inside. No evidence of wires or a timer, either analog or digital. Now, we're going to ask her to open the envelope and then the box."

"You're kidding," Sam said.

"No ma'am," Lance replied. Sure enough, the little robot cut open the envelope, removed a card, scanned it, and waited for further instructions.

"These seemed perfect for you," the sender had written. "I sent similar items to your friends. Enjoy."

"Does that make sense?" Young asked.

"I'm afraid it might." Sam clenched her fists. "Let's see what else Roberta finds."

The bot lifted the lid off the box. Inside were three items: a small knife, a book of matches, and an empty syringe.

"That son of a bitch," Sam said.

"Does this have to do with the serial killer you're chasing?" Young asked.

"It appears so," Terry answered.

"We have to make some calls." Sam started for the house.

"Hold on, Lieutenant," Young cautioned. "We're not done. Now we send Rocket over to sniff for substances on the surface of the box or the items that might cause harm. He looked at the dog and pointed to the house. "Rocket! Check for poison. Go!"

The dog took off running and stopped a foot shy of the open package. He sniffed, getting as close as possible without touching any part of the box or its contents. He didn't whine or bark. Instead, he gave a little wag.

"Good sign," Young remarked. "Now we go retrieve the package." He pulled on a pair of heavy rubberized gloves, strapped on a vest, trotted over to the porch, and returned with the box. "What do you want to do with these?" he asked.

"I'll take them into the FBI tomorrow," Terry said.

"Do you mind if I walk the dog around the house, just to be sure?" Lance asked.

"Go ahead," Sam told him.

Lance returned a few minutes later. "All clear, unless you want us to check inside," he reported.

"That's okay. I'm less worried about us than whoever received a similar package. I don't want to tie you up on Christmas, but we might have suspicious packages at two or three other homes in the area."

"Nature of the job, ma'am," Young said. "We can wait while you make those calls."

"Thanks. It'll just take a few minutes."

Sam and Terry retreated to the house. "I'm going to check in on Dakota, Mike, Molly, and Rob."

"I'll do the same with a few people around here."

While Terry texted his agents, Sam called Carol Davidson. She and her boyfriend had just risen. Sam realized it was only 9:30. A lot had happened in the last hour or so.

"Carol, hi. Please listen carefully. You might have a package outside your house. I don't know if it's marked from me or unmarked. Can you look without touching and let me know?"

"Sure. Do you want me to get my kit?"

"We've got a bomb technician on standby."

"Well, shit. Hold on." Sam heard her filling in Martin Lloyd. "Martin's headed downstairs now. He says yes, a wrapped package is sitting outside the door.

We'll throw on some clothes and get ourselves down the block. I assume it's from someone who doesn't like you or your friends."

"Something like that. I'll send over the team."

"Call my brother."

"Already on it."

Sam ran out the door. "Here's the first of three addresses," she told Young and Lance. "I don't know that for a fact, but I trust my gut on this. We'll text you the other addresses shortly."

She reached Gordy and learned he'd found a package on his front steps. He'd placed a blanket over it, shut the door, and moved to the back of the house. He was just about to text her when Sam reached him.

"Smart," she said. "As always. Maybe step out of the house. I have the team headed over to Carol's. Your place is next."

"Don't forget to call McCready. He tends to be ..."

Gullible? Trusting? Eager? Gordy didn't finish his thought, but Sam knew what he meant. Her heart pinched.

"Calling him now," she said.

Chapter 53

"Lieutenant Tate?" Instead of McCready, the call was answered by his mother, Constance.

"Mrs. McCready? It's Sam Tate. What happened? Where's Pat? Where are you?" she added as she registered the sound of voices, broadcast announcements, and footsteps on a hard floor.

"We're at Memorial Hospital," the older woman replied. A sob caught in her throat.

Sam made herself take a breath. "Did something happen to Pat?"

"No, he's fine. He's off talking to the doctor. It's Albert, my husband. Pat's father. He's having some sort of attack. Oh wait, here's Pat now. Do you want to talk with him?"

"Yes, please."

"Lieutenant? I don't know what my mother told you, but my dad's in a bad way. They've got him stabilized but it's pretty scary."

"Pat, did he handle a package that was left outside your door?"

"Yeah. It was addressed to me. He brought it into the kitchen where I was helping my mom. I told him to take a look inside. There was a syringe." His voice broke. "Then he started choking. I had my mom call 9-1-1."

"Did you or your mom touch anything?"

"No. I pulled on a pair of rubber gloves and put the package into a baggie. I've got it with me. It's the Judge, isn't it?"

"I'm afraid so. Gordy and Carol each got something similar. We have OSFD checking things out. This is not your fault, Pat."

"Thanks for saying that. It might help if the doctors knew what we're dealing with."

"I'm going to check in with the lead tech. He's over at Gordy's. I'll get back to you with the information. Or deliver it in person if you'd like company?"

"You don't have to do that," McCready said, although his tone indicated he'd welcome her presence.

"Not a problem, Detective. We'll be right there."

Terry had been watching Sam while he played fetch with Jax. She hung up and gave him a succinct summary. He in turn put the tired dog in the house with fresh water and locked up.

"I'll need directions," he said and opened the car door.

Sam plugged in the GPS coordinates for Terry, then called Young. He was at Gordy's house, he reported. The sergeant had received a box with a single item, a small knife that appeared to be coated with a toxic substance. Carol Davidson had received a similar package with a matchbook, also coated.

"Do you have any way of testing it?" Sam asked.

"We don't. But Owen here studied toxicology in college. He says some educated guesses can be made depending on the victim's symptoms."

"My detective said his father had difficulty moving and breathing, as well as a small rash. This box contained a syringe. He might have touched that."

She heard him relay the information to Lance, who said, "Farfetched, but the assailant may have used tetrodotoxin. It's usually ingested, not absorbed. Except, Owen is saying, if it's the new synthetic version it could work on several levels. Very nasty stuff. I'm sorry, Lieutenant. That's all we can do today."

"Go home, both of you. Deputy Young, you've done more than enough."

They found Pat's mother in the ER's waiting room. Bruce Gordy was also there. His calm presence filled Sam with relief.

"Pat is around here somewhere," the mother reported. "He can't seem to sit still. I sent him for snacks. He blames himself, as you can imagine."

"If anyone is to blame, it's ..." Sam was about to say, "me" when Terry cut in.

"It's the person who delivered the packages."

"Bastard," Mrs. McCready added for emphasis. She looked around at the startled faces. "Oh now, come on. You were all thinking it."

Her frank honesty worked to settle the group.

Pat returned with an armful of snacks and a tired-looking woman he introduced as Doctor Lane. She explained that Al McCready had been admitted to the ICU and placed on a respirator. They'd ruled out everything else and came back to poison even before the son told them about the suspicious package. The toxin appeared to cause muscle paralysis, which was affecting, among other things, the patient's ability to breathe.

"The next twenty-four hours will be critical," the doctor continued. "Machines should be able to support life-sustaining functions as long as he doesn't experience a mitigating event. Can you access his medical records online?"

"He was in good health before this," his wife said.

"That's good. Fortunately, paralytic toxins generally are less effective when absorbed."

"The techs that came to my house speculated it might be tetrodotoxin," Sam said.

"It might well be," Lane replied. "I've always associated it with pufferfish, which I would never knowingly order at a restaurant regardless of price or reputation. But I've learned there are synthetic variations, and I can't assess their effect except by observing how they work on this particular patient."

"When can we see him?"

"Half an hour, but just family and just for a few minutes. I hope you understand."

Sam, Terry, and Gordy trudged out the door. On the way out, she glanced up at the clock, shocked to see it wasn't even noon.

"Gordy, if you want to come over before Carol's, you're more than welcome," Sam said.

"Actually, I'm going to my sister's right now. She's already shaken up enough to try to cancel her party. I told her not to because we'll all need the free booze she plans to serve. Besides," he sharpened his gaze, "I'm guessing the Judge is done for the day. That's who this is, isn't it?"

"It is," Sam replied.

"Next time he texts you, ask him why he's targeting people who never chased or caught or even worked on a case involving a serial killer."

"Gordy, I'm sorry."

"Not on you, Lieutenant. But I'd like a word with this sick SOB. Or maybe a minute alone would do the trick. See you at Carol's." He turned on his heel and left.

Terry, standing behind Sam, put his arms around her. She wasn't sure it made a difference. She'd never felt more helpless.

Chapter 54

Carol Davidson had put a lot of effort into her party. Fresh-cut pine boughs intertwined with small white lights spread across the mantle and wound around the banister leading to the second floor. The ornaments on the trees were vintage, saved from childhood or perhaps purchased in an antique store. The table barely held all the food she'd prepared, even without the additional dishes brought by friends and relatives.

Even Jax, who got along well with their little dog Toby, had been invited, although the canines were mostly relegated to the backyard.

It could have been, should have been wonderful. Except that Sam had quite literally brought a serial killer to her friend's front door.

Terry had tried to assuage her guilt at home before they left for the party.

"Gordy was right, you know. It's not on you, Sam. You can't blame yourself."

"He's obsessed with me, Terry. With me."

"I know. That may be because you've been integral to this investigation, but it may not be. Look, you're skilled, experienced, and very good-looking. You cut an imposing figure. Quite a few people you don't know could be obsessed with you."

"Not helping, Terry."

"My point is, Baker's the one behind today's attacks, not you. There is nothing you said or did that caused him to alter his pattern and go after your friends."

"Fucking coward," she fumed. "If he wants something from me, why doesn't he come after me?"

"He is a coward, Sam. He also wants something. Maybe you can get it out of him when he gets in touch with you."

"You think he's going to reach out?"

"I guarantee it."

Two hours later, they walked into the party with a poinsettia, a case of Beaujolais, and an excited dog. The place was packed with people. Many she recognized from the department, including Sheriff Tanner and his wife. Some might have been Lloyd's friends or colleagues from the school where he taught part-time. Other guests might have been neighbors.

Fortunately, the mix of officers and civilians lightened the mood. At least half the guests didn't know that a murderer wanted in fifty states had dropped off a lethal gift hours earlier.

Jax made his way to his friend, accepting the inevitable head scratches as his due. Terry uncorked the wine. Sam found Davidson in the kitchen. With her long nose, chestnut hair, narrow gray eyes, and lean frame, Carol reminded Sam of a fox. The two friends hugged.

"I'm so sorry, Carol," Sam began, but Davidson stepped back and shook her head.

"No," she said. "Just no. Gordy said you'd try to apologize. This guy is trying to get to you through us, Sam. You are not at fault."

"I wish I knew why."

"You will. Now, can you carry this sweet potato dish to the table?"

Constance and Pat McCready arrived about an hour in. "I tried to get her to lie down," the younger man explained to the others. "She wouldn't hear of it. She had to bring the salad. I think she just wants to be around people."

"Did you see your father?" Sam asked.

"Yeah. Just about broke my heart to see him like that." McCready cleared his throat. "Well, he's being well taken care of."

"How about a beer?" Gordy asked. "I think your mom will be well taken care of. He gestured towards a slim couple in their sixties. Parents to Gordy and Carol, they'd swooped in and enveloped Constance McCready almost the moment she entered.

Everyone began to unwind. The members of the sheriff's department, from Tanner down to the young deputy, knew to steer the conversation away from the serial killer who was too close for comfort. Laughter punctuated the lively conversations. Holiday music played softly in the background.

And, as Terry predicted, Sam got a text.

Merry Christmas, Lieutenant. Hope you're relaxing after an eventful morning

Sam stepped outside into the chill air, her face hot with anger. She'd promised herself she would stay calm and neutral. She couldn't.

WTF, Baker? Now you're killing people at random?

Hello to you too. No one died, fingers x'd

She wanted to stomp on the phone or better yet, ram it down his throat. Instead, she took a deep breath, then typed,

Answer my question. Why these people?

Got your attention, didn't I?

You've had my attention for months, Derek. What do you want from me?

Isn't it obvious?

No

Sam watched the dots bounce and disappear, then start up again. Maybe he was composing a manifesto or making himself a sandwich. She wished she could tell him to send an email. Or fuck off.

Instead, she waited. Finally, he replied,

I don't want serial killers to be romanticized. Anyone can become one. Some are clever, others are not. Their capture isn't a victory. By definition, they've already killed at least three people. Most of the time they're caught because they slip up. Instead of preening or playing hero, the cops should get better at their jobs.

You think killing cops will change that?

I think it'll start a conversation

You self-righteous prick, she thought. She wrote,

You make some valid points. Maybe we can have a dialogue without more victims. I'll listen. I'll get other people to listen. You just have to meet with me.

Baker took another long pause. Then he responded,

nope. Playing the empathy card won't work

Sam calculated the risk of taking the conversation in a new direction. "Go hard or go home," her father used to say. She had no choice. She swallowed, then typed,

Fine. I'm sick of all this. Sick of you. You're a coward. You're not honest with me or with yourself. Find someone else to dump on. Stop contacting me.

She dropped her hand to her side, shaking. The anger was intentional. It was also real.

Within twenty seconds, a new text arrived.

whatcha doing New Year's Eve?

Chapter 55

His text message arrived on the morning of December 31st.

Sorry to be so late. Found the perfect spot: Salisbury, Maryland. The city planners are throwing a street party tonight. We're meeting a few blocks away at the site of the city's first hi-rise. Impossible to miss. 12th floor, 11:30. It's not fully built yet, so dress warmly.

How do I get up there? Sam typed.

You'll find a way. TTFN

Salisbury was about an hour south of Easton. It didn't have the charm of the smaller towns like Chestertown, St. Michaels, Easton, or Trappe. The city struggled with more urban problems like high crime, a lack of affordable housing, and a tight job market. Recent efforts to revitalize the downtown area included a mixed-use high-rise that promised to be the tallest on the Eastern Shore. Although the project had stalled during the pandemic, construction was once again underway. But not nearly complete.

"Damn him for waiting until the last minute," she stormed over breakfast with Terry, a meal he was eating while she ignored hers. "And he picks a half-finished building two blocks away from one of the city's busiest events. Why?"

She jumped up and began to pace, coffee in hand. Terry picked at a muffin and watched her.

"The celebration tonight is a big deal," she went on. "Live music, food vendors, restaurants open late, even a

259

ball drop. The streets will be filled with people. Police and fire units are on standby. He's insane!"

"And clever," Terry replied. "The event gives him cover. The police and fire departments will be occupied. And who's going to pay any attention to a construction site a few blocks from all the excitement?"

"Do you think he's going to stage a mass casualty event? Should the FBI recommend the city be put on lockdown?"

"As to your first question, I don't think so. Baker may have altered details, but his basic victimology hasn't changed. He's going after specific people who handled, or mishandled, in his view, serial-killer cases. Also, I'm not sure we could put the city in lockdown this late in the game. We'd require more officers to enforce it, we'd panic the residents, and we'd give Baker the chance to call it off. The meeting is a calculated risk but one we have to take."

"He could still pull something, Terry. I could be on my way to Salisbury and get a text with directions to a spot in Virginia or instructions to meet a block from my house."

"Sam, can you stop marching around for a minute?"

She did. He pulled her to him and put his arms around her waist. She looked into the face of the man she loved and trusted.

"Do you want to back out?" he asked.

"Not a chance."

"Good. Sit and eat while I make a few calls."

She had no intention of worrying Terry, even though the attacks on her and her friends left her feeling exposed. She didn't like being at the mercy of a killer.

She wanted to end Baker's game, maybe end him, she admitted.

McCready had accompanied his parents back home at Sam's insistence. Gordy and his sister, after a few days off, had returned to work. She showed up to the office to check on them.

"We've got it covered, Lieutenant," Gordy told her. "Go home. Try to enjoy your vacation."

As if.

She reminded herself that she had the advantage of access to FBI assets, beginning with Terry. Indeed, he returned after twenty minutes to report on a plan.

Three hours later, a van with the logo of a popular delivery service pulled up to the house. The driver hopped out and pulled three packages from the back of his vehicle. He ambled up the front walk, rang the bell, chatted with Sam, and greeted Jax as if he had all the time in the world.

The man was actually part of the FBI's Special Weapons and Tactics Team. The delivery was staged for the benefit of any prying eyes. One of the packages contained a device designed to detect newly installed hardware or software in and around the house. A technician slipped into the garage to check Sam's car. Another dispatched a remote drone to hunt for any of its kind hovering overhead.

Four sharpshooters were already in Salisbury, scouting for locations from which to surveil and, if necessary, remove any threats. Two of them planned to plant themselves directly inside the building, one huddled on the floor below, the other hidden inside the cabin of the nearest crane. They would spend several hours in the cold and wind without moving, something they'd been trained to do.

Sam left home at 9:15. She'd dressed in black pants and a dark wool shirt over which she wore a bulletproof vest. She pulled on a sweatshirt. No waist pack this time. No visible weapons either. A small revolver in one thick-soled boot, and her trusty knife in the other. Jacket, gloves, hat with a small LED light attached, all black.

She'd worn similar outfits on more than one New Year's Eve, she realized. Occupational hazard.

The team had given her two communication devices. The larger of the two went around one ear, the smaller, not much bigger than a dot, was placed behind her other ear. The idea is that the larger, more familiar-looking one would be discovered and surrendered without disrupting communication.

As she pulled out of the driveway, someone who looked like Terry but wasn't stood backlit in the doorway and waved. Perhaps the substitute might fool a camera or a second pair of eyes, although Sam was certain the Judge worked alone.

She hopped on Route 50, relatively devoid of traffic in the off-season. The road took her through a series of small towns, most of them deserted. Out here, revelers attended house parties or found their way over to Annapolis, which made for a long and potentially dangerous ride home across the Chesapeake Bay Bridge. The state police hated New Year's Eve and who could blame them.

Sam kept her phone mounted in front of her in case the unpredictable killer sent a text. Her burner—one in a series she'd been using since Baker first texted back in October—stayed in her pocket on vibrate.

Fifty minutes later, she pulled into a "No Parking" zone in front of the construction site and stuck an official Talbot County Sheriff's Office placard on her dashboard. A ticket would be the least of her problems this evening, but she didn't want to take any chances.

Two blocks over, the party continued in full swing. Sam felt no safer knowing that so many people enjoyed a vastly different experience close by. If anything, she felt exposed.

"I'm here," she murmured to whoever was listening.

"We've got you, Lieutenant," came the reply.

Chapter 56

In addition to the sharpshooters stationed inside and outside the building, Terry managed to get two of his agents onto the construction crew that worked on the building until 3 pm. No mean feat, considering they didn't show up until late morning. Sam was pleased to learn that one of them was Mike Fuentes.

The two men had scouted the place, trying to learn as much as possible. Terry filled Sam in on what they'd learned.

"The building is still in the skeletal phase. Further along at the lowest levels but otherwise steel pillars and concrete sub-flooring all the way up. You'll have something to stand on, but it's pretty much open air."

"How do I get up to twelve?"

"Fuentes spotted two platforms suspended by pulleys at the front of the building. One's outside level seven, the other's on the designated floor. In addition, the contractors installed two hoists. The one on the left side of the building is used to lift materials. The personnel hoist, which looks like a small cage, is to the right. All these moving parts are engine- powered, although the platforms have a manual backup." Terry showed her a picture on his phone.

"They're loud to operate, aren't they?"

"Well, the machine might not be noticeable over the street-level noise. On the other hand, it's a different kind of sound and Baker might be listening for it. He knows you're coming."

"But not exactly when or how," Sam said. "Isn't there a structure that secures these hoists to the building?" She pointed to the picture. "There. It looks like a tower or a ladder. Can't I climb that?"

"It's not made for climbing. It's also twelve floors."

"I'll pretend I'm back in basic training. I do wonder how Baker is going to manage?"

"We have to consider that he may already be here."

"Nightwatchman?"

"There'll be one and he'll be one of ours."

"Our killer is going to know I didn't come alone."

"He knows," Terry stated, his voice flat. "He doesn't care."

Seven hours later, Sam squeezed through the opening in the wire fence Fuentes had made for her. Rods, beams, and pipes were neatly stacked in piles, along with concrete slabs. A front-end loading truck stood idle. Twin cranes stretched over the structure, one at each end.

Sam tilted her head back. Not a tall building, not at fourteen stories, but from this angle, it looked daunting at night. She picked out the temporary scaffolding, somewhere between the sixth and seventh floor. It looked impossibly far away.

She made her way around to the side of the building, watching for the guard. He still had a part to play, and she wanted to avoid an encounter.

The personnel hoist sat at the base of the mount. At nine feet, it was just wide enough for two or three men. The elevator itself weighed maybe five or six thousand pounds, she guessed. The steel mount should be able to hold one moderately tall, moderately-muscled woman, even though it wasn't meant for climbing. Even though it was dark and cold. Even though the wind had picked up.

First, she hauled herself onto the roof of the hoist itself. She'd spotted the rolling safety ladder next to a pallet of masonry blocks. The ladder proved both heavy and awkward to move. She maneuvered it into position and locked it in place. That's when she realized that while the safety barriers reached the roof of the hoist, the ladder's topmost level stopped well below that.

Sam ran back down and found a plastic container to stand on. Not remotely safe, and the first among several regulations she would break this evening.

She stretched over the barriers, raised herself on her toes, grasped the side of the hoist frame, and pushed off. The ladder wobbled but stayed in place. Her foot caught the container, which toppled off the other side. With a groan, she heaved herself up to the roof of the little cage, her arms protesting.

Sam lay on the roof of the little cage, panting. Her watch said 10:40. And she still had to climb the side of the building.

"Buckle up, soldier," she said and pulled her scarf over her face.

Her experience with vertical climbing was limited to what she'd learned in the army. She didn't have the right equipment, and she was scaling the side of a building using a mast that, however sturdy, wasn't meant to be used as a ladder. She'd have to think before each movement. She couldn't rush the ascent, despite the ticking clock and the ticking time bomb who waited for her on twelve.

Nothing prepared her for the wind chill. Before she'd climbed to the third story, roughly thirty feet, she felt the cold cut through her padded gloves. The narrow crossbeams were spaced so far apart she had to bring her knee up almost to her chest. They were a lot less sturdy than the rungs on a conventional ladder and a lot more slippery, thanks to a thin coating of ice. Several times, she almost lost her grip.

Her lug-soled shoes didn't help. More than once, the slender metal beams caught in the deep indentations, and she had to pull her foot off and reposition it.

By the sixth story (only halfway!), her calves were burning, her arms were aching, her fingers were numb, and her jacket was in a losing battle with the precipitation that had begun to fall. She leaned against the mast, exhausted.

"You can do this," she heard in her ear. Terry.

"I'd like to see you try this," she rasped.

"No way. I'm in management now. I just give orders."

"Yes, sir."

The affectionate banter warmed her and she resumed the climb.

After what felt like hours, she arrived just below the designated floor. She could hear the music from the street fair below and see most of the festivities from her vantage point. Not that she could study the panorama since she didn't dare turn her head. She didn't envy the revelers, though. All she wanted was a hot bath, a shot of bourbon, and a warm bed.

"Looks like you made it," she heard Terry say when she stopped to catch her breath.

"Not quite," Sam said, her voice low. She hung from the mast, studying her destination. Unlike the other floors, this one had light. Not from a lamp but from votive candles that flickered in the breeze. The light was accompanied by a subtle roar. Baker was already there, perhaps running a generator. He could shoot her or wait until she tried to get a leg up before he pushed her off. But then he'd lose his audience.

She concentrated on how she might propel herself onto the concrete slab from her shaky perch. She imagined someone throwing a body onto railroad tracks, then ran the scenario in reverse. How could that even work?

She wasn't able to exit the mast unless she could heave herself off the left side. If she misjudged the angle, she'd end up splattered on the ground.

"You've gotten yourself into a little jam," came the unexpectedly light voice. Then Baker appeared, although half-hidden in shadow. Sam steeled herself against an expected shove. Instead, he reached down an arm. "Grab hold," he commanded and pulled her onto the floor.

Chapter 57

Sam fell onto her hands and knees, then pushed herself back and forced herself to stand, even though her body protested. Her arms and legs shook from the strain. She expected to see a gun pointed at her. Instead, Baker was kneeling beside a blanket in the center of the room, dressed in a down parka. Two large kerosene lanterns gave off a decent amount of heat. The sound Sam heard came from their burners.

Baker had set out a sort of picnic, complete with cheese, grapes, crackers, and a thermos.

She scanned the raw space. Bare bones, as Terry had said. The platform hung about six or eight inches off the front of the building, bobbing slightly like a canoe tied to the dock.

"Congratulations on a near-perfect landing, Lieutenant," he said. "May I offer you a hot toddy?" He pointed to the thermos. "Or do I need to search you for weapons or devices? I have a gun if that becomes necessary."

"It won't be." Sam opened her jacket, turned out her pockets, and handed him the decoy earpiece. Baker stomped on it, then swept the pieces under the blanket.

"Take off your boots, please."

She did so. Baker took his time, checking each seam and even the heel. He confiscated the weapons and pocketed them. "I appreciate your cooperation," he said. "And may I say, you look even lovelier than you did at the funeral."

He was slurring his words, Sam noted, and rocking on his heels. Sam couldn't tell if his unsteadiness was caused by alcohol or low blood sugar. Either way, she could use that.

Other than that, he appeared thin but not excessively so. His eyes, absent the glasses, were hazel, his chin soft, his sandy hair receding like an eroding beach. Altogether normal.

"Can I get you something?" he asked. "You must be famished. The hot toddies contain a generous amount of whiskey, I admit. Apologies for sampling it, but I've been up here a few hours. I even brought reading material." He held up a book, The Adventures of Sherlock Holmes.

"Why are we here, Derek?"

"To eat. To drink. To celebrate the new year. Or to come up with a plan to erase the hypocrisy of a culture that celebrates its failings when it comes to serial murder."

"Really?" she began. "I think we're here because you want to talk about your father. I suspect you'd like to right a wrong. The wrong done by your father. The wrong done to you when the authorities disbelieved your story."

Baker poured himself a generous cup of the hot alcoholic beverage and toasted her. "Dr. Sam Tate, psychologist extraordinaire."

"Your father hurt you."

"He never laid a hand on me. I mean that quite literally."

"Neglect is a form of emotional abuse, Derek."

"What would you know about emotional abuse?"

"I've had some experience," she ventured.

He scowled at her. "Have you, though? Allow me to explain. Emotional abuse is when your father regards you and your time-consuming, costly, messy disease as a threat that leaches the comfort, sympathy, and attention owed to him as a grieving widower. Emotional abuse is when he shares those feelings with his nine-year-old son struggling to understand why his body doesn't work. Emotional abuse," he continued, his voice rising, "is when he reminds his son almost every day that he'll never amount to anything."

"That sounds awful."

"Doesn't it? You've had trauma in your life, but you were always loved, always protected. A pampered princess, a child martyr, a resourceful detective. You have brains, looks, friends, health, and people who admire you. You've never lacked for attention. That's probably why you like hunting serial killers. All the glory, all the satisfaction, your skills put to good use, your accomplishments noted."

"You have skills, technical expertise."

"Tech people are a dime a dozen, lady. You know what I'm good at? Killing people. No, more than that. Staging murders, then executing them. Tell me, how exactly can you help?"

"I'm listening."

"I don't care. I'm done talking. I want to celebrate. I'm high in the sky on New Year's Eve with the infamous Sam Tate, catcher of serial killers." He sidled over to the platform, turned, and smiled. "Come look."

"No thanks, I'm good."

"Suit yourself." He looked away, then suddenly pivoted, strode over to Sam, grabbed her by the elbow, jerked her to the edge, and pushed her onto the platform. The movements, swift and almost choreographed, caught Sam off-guard. Then Baker stepped right behind her, pulled her into a choke hold, and pressed a gun to her ribs. Her gun.

"He's armed," came an unfamiliar voice in Sam's ear. "Do not attempt a shot. Repeat, don't shoot."

"What's he got in his other hand?" someone else asked.

"Nice view, isn't it?" Baker was saying. "Hope you're not afraid of heights. Sorry I got you out here so abruptly. I don't want to waste a minute."

"Derek, why don't we move back onto the concrete floor?" she pleaded. "It's cold and we're not wearing safety harnesses." As she talked, she worked out how she could disarm him. He'd pinned her shoulders in a one-armed bear hug. He hadn't left her enough room to turn or even move her head. She had to get him to relax, to move, even an inch.

"I thought you liked to live on the edge, Lieutenant. Maybe we need to make this more exciting for you." Without warning he slipped a noose around her neck and wound the rope around her upper body. So that's what he'd brought with him.

"You may think I want to kill you, Lieutenant," he murmured into her ear. "I don't, at least not at the moment. I simply require your acquiescence. Your attention, if you will. And some protection for myself."

She tried to speak.

"Relax. You can breathe if you don't struggle. Trust me, I practiced this. Oh, and I apologize if the implied intimacy makes you uncomfortable. I think it's probably best I keep a tight leash on you, so to speak, in case your friends have itchy trigger fingers."

His closeness made her queasy. Even outdoors she could smell his funk, a sweet and sour mix of honey, vinegar, and decay.

"I'm going to loosen my grip just a little. There. Much better, right?"

"Yes," she said. "Thank you."

"You're welcome. Now, let's get the party started."

Chapter 58

"This is Avenger," she heard in her earpiece. "Report. Reaper, anything from up there?"

"Close, but no cigar," another voice said.

"Shark, what about it?" the one called Avenger asked.

"The gun and the noose complicate things," came a third voice.

"So does the snow," chimed in a fourth.

"She knows what to do," she heard Terry say. "Sam, any wiggle room?"

Sam could move her arms below the elbows, enough to reach her neck. She managed to get two fingers between the binding and her throat. A start.

"I can't breathe," she gasped.

"Oops, sorry," Baker responded and loosened his hold just enough so she could swallow and squeeze in two more fingers. "Listen up, please. I need to explain my plan. You're an integral part of it."

"I think she's making a move," Reaper reported.

"Use your best judgment," Avenger ordered.

Baker was all smiles as he nodded to the streetscape below. "I'm afraid I can't let you turn your head, so you'll have to trust my description. There's a firetruck at one end of Main Street. Lots of people waiting for the firefighters to drop a ball from a 25-foot ladder. Big deal. I have something much better in mind. We're going to stage our very own ball drop, only we'll be the ball." He sounded giddy at the prospect.

"Derek," she sputtered.

"Oh, and in case you're worried no one will see anything," he continued, "I've got my phones all set up to live-stream us. One up here and one when we reach our destination. So exciting. Talk about attention!"

"Do you have the shot?" Avenger barked.

"Negative."

"Nope."

"Not yet."

"Maybe, if LT can give me a little room."

"I can—" Sam coughed, then went on—"only imagine." The pause between words was her way of responding to both her captor and her potential rescuers.

"I'll bet you can," Baker told her. "And I'll be with you all the way down." He grinned. "Until death do us part and beyond."

"Command, we can try to breach the rig," Reaper said.

"Hold on," Sam said.

"Stand down, team," Terry ordered. "Sam?"

Baker looked at her through narrowed eyes. "Are you addressing me?"

"I am. Listen to me, will you?" She kept her gloved hands at her neck.

"You have one minute," he said. "I want to sync with the countdown."

"How does any of this achieve your goals, Derek?"

He sighed as if dealing with a slow student. "I set up a website a few days ago, complete with a mission statement. A live feed is scheduled to begin in a couple of minutes. To be honest, I combined my message with your astute observations about getting the world to know my father's guilt. The audience will be bigger."

"You'd kill yourself for the notoriety?"

"Why not? And hey, you'll also be famous. Posthumously but spectacularly. Now, if you're finished, I need to make the magic happen."

Out of the corner of her eye, she saw two black-clad figures emerge from behind the pillars. She kept still, but Baker sensed a shift.

"We have visitors," he said and spun around. He crouched so the guard rail offered partial protection from behind and Sam served as his front cover. Imperfect, but it left her far more exposed than Baker. He still held the gun in one hand and the knotted rope in the other, but his focus was elsewhere.

Sam pulled forward, gaining a few crucial inches of give between her thorax and the noose. She clawed at Baker's face with one hand and got her elbow into his soft abdomen. He stood up and dropped the gun. A well-placed bullet between the eyes did the rest. Derek Baker tumbled over the guard rail, dead before his live stream began.

He still held on to the rope, and Sam couldn't free herself in time. She went over the side, head-first and too surprised to yell, tethered to the man whose life she'd tried to save.

Chapter 59

The lower scaffolding saved Sam's life. Or so she learned later. She wouldn't have guessed that at the time she crashed into it, just after she'd tugged the rope from Baker's lifeless hand. She bounced off the guardrail and managed to swing onto the floor as her assailant continued his plunge.

Even so, she had a rough landing. She hit the concrete hard and heard the crack of broken bones. Her body exploded in pain. She almost passed out.

Paramedics from the local hospital arrived within five minutes but needed another ten to get up using the bigger hoist. Stabilizing the patient took a little longer. Sam had managed to pull herself into a ball, which probably prevented her from seriously injuring her neck and back. Even so, she ended up breaking her wrist, her leg, her collarbone, and at least one or two ribs.

Of more immediate concern were the possibilities of internal bleeding and concussion. The EMTs kept up a steady stream of chatter in an effort to keep her awake. She wanted them to stop talking, but she was too exhausted to say so.

She wasn't aware of time, only selected sounds: an amplified voice counting backward from ten, sirens drawing ever closer, and the babble of voices. At one point, Terry was by her side, soothing her one minute and issuing directives the next.

"I don't give a crap about anyone's feelings," she might have heard him say, although not to her. "She's going to Hopkins." Fuentes (had he been there the entire time?) promised to handle something on the ground. Cleanup, processing, she couldn't remember the word.

Mostly, Sam tried not to move. She didn't want to disturb the blanket of relief her intravenous medical cocktail provided.

At some point, a familiar thump thump filled the sky and took her back to Afghanistan. She kept her eyes closed against the bright lights. She might have groaned. She felt someone squeeze her hand. Then she was lifted into a chopper, Terry by her side. More pain meds, more urging that she "stay with us." As if she could leave.

Sam couldn't recall much of the next thirty-six hours, although she got a complete rundown from Dakota Williams, who drove to Baltimore at 2 am to be at Johns Hopkins when the medevac arrived. First, Sam was rushed into surgery with a ruptured spleen which doctors were able to repair laparoscopically. Next, an orthopedic team set her bones. Finally, the neurosurgeon determined she hadn't suffered serious brain trauma.

Just before the New Year's Day sun rose at 7:23, Sam was returned to a private room and fell asleep for twenty-four hours.

* * *

Sam opened her eyes and took a moment to orient herself. She was in a pleasant-looking room. Sunlight streamed through gauze curtains. A plump couch sat opposite the bed.

Was she dreaming? Or dead? No, dead people didn't feel the pain that wasted no time making itself known.

Dead people weren't immobilized by bindings that ran down the length of one arm. They didn't wear casts on their left wrist and their right ankle, or bandages on their abdomen. They weren't receiving oxygen through a tube and fluids through an IV.

She was alive. She was hurt—oh, was she hurt—but still in the here and now. And not alone. She turned her head with an effort to see Terry slumped in a chair near her bed, clothes rumpled, face haggard, eyes closed. Only for a second; he'd been coasting on top of an approximation of sleep. He bolted upright, the fatigue hidden by a smile that lit his face.

He stood and walked over to the bed.

"Hey, there. I thought you were going to sleep the year away."

"Which year?" she croaked.

"I exaggerate. It's only been a couple of days."

"I fell."

"Not as far as Baker did," Terry replied. "I'll grant you, he didn't feel anything." He took her hand. "You did."

"No shit," she replied, and Terry roared with laughter.

"You're up!" came the cheerful voice. Dakota Williams pushed through the door, carrying two large coffees and sporting a wide grin. She looked as beautiful as ever.

"I'm trying," Sam replied. "I could use a little assistance."

Williams helped her adjust the hospital bed and the pillows. Sam sighed with relief, then grunted. It hurt to move.

"Assistant Director, how about you get some breakfast?" Williams said. "Or maybe you can catch a few winks in a real bed."

"Or a shower," Sam added. Williams snickered.

"Yes to that last suggestion. Then I have to head to work."

"No," the women said simultaneously. "I mean, with all due respect, sir," Williams continued, "you need to take care of yourself. The Bureau's PR machine is working overtime to feed the press while letting you and especially our woman of the hour recover. She's in good hands; you made sure of that."

"Maybe a couple of hours," Terry replied with a yawn. He grabbed his coat.

"Terry, wait," Sam called out. "What about Jax?"

"Jax is with the ever-dependable Detective McCready. I suspect he's getting all the love and treats he needs and then some."

Sam sank back with relief. "Thank you."

He gave her a thumbs up. "Agent Williams, make sure she rests."

Once he'd left, Williams treated Sam to details about the aftermath of her fall.

"Obviously I'm reporting second-hand, but Fuentes is a pretty reliable narrator."

"I still can't believe I survived," Sam said. "Or that Terry got me a medevac to get me to Johns Hopkins. That's a level-one trauma center. How did he work all that out? I'm not even a federal employee."

"I think he had help from Maryland Senator Sean Parker," Williams replied. "It does seem above and beyond, even for a resident. Or is there some sort of connection between you two I don't know about?"

Sam rolled her eyes. Even that hurt. "When I figure it out, I'll let you know," she said.

"Anyway, you're fully protected, although I don't think you're in danger from anything except an overzealous press," Williams laughed. Seeing Sam's expression, she added, "Don't worry. The hospital is very good at protecting its high-profile patients."

"It's the high-profile part I don't like. I didn't take Baker out, you know. That was all SWAT."

"But you're the brave and attractive face that will attach itself to the case."

"Just like Baker predicted," Sam grumbled.

The door swung open to admit a petite raven-haired nurse. "You're up," she observed. "Good. We'll get you turned and cleaned. I also need to take some vitals. How's the pain?"

"Just barely tolerable," Sam admitted.

"Understandable. I'm going to chase your friend out now."

Williams rose and tiptoed out the door with a wave.

"As for your pain," the nurse continued, "please remember you have a morphine pump so you can self-administer. You don't need to be a hero, Lieutenant. You already are."

Chapter 60

Sam slept on and off for a week. The doctors diagnosed a mild concussion and supported the now widely accepted approach of prescribing plenty of rest, although the pain didn't always cooperate.

After a couple of days, she eased herself off the morphine pump and switched to Tylenol. Her appetite increased and she was able to get through the night. She still couldn't read or watch television, but the nurses claimed her name came up a lot the first few days.

Sam didn't lack visitors. Terry came every day, Williams almost that often. The crew from Talbot County showed up, including Sheriff Tanner. McCready wanted to enroll Jax in an accelerated training course so he could be certified as a service dog. Terry persuaded him that rules might be bent at the hospital to allow for a visit here and there without taking such drastic action. Sam thanked her detective for his thoughtfulness and Terry for sparing poor Jax the ordeal of doggie boot camp.

In the middle of week two, an improved Sam was trying to lift her right arm when Suzanne Foster arrived with a single orchid. She wore her version of casual: pressed jeans, low heeled booties, and a cashmere turtleneck in royal blue.

"You seem more like yourself," Foster said. "I'm not certain you recognized me when I visited last week."

"I'm not sure I recognized anyone besides Terry and that's only because he slept here."

"I promise you'll get better." Foster took a seat and swept her gaze around the room. "Especially in five-star accommodations."

"Someone else is paying for this. I only found out recently."

"And accepting anything from Sean Parker makes you uncomfortable," Foster replied.

Sam studied her inscrutable new friend. "How did you know?"

"First, help me with what I don't know. How are you two connected?"

"We aren't. I thought we were related; he looks like he could be family, but a DNA test brought me back to earth. He also looks like someone I saw at my brother's wedding. I don't know if Terry told you—"

"He didn't," Foster cut in. "I read up on you before our first lunch. I'm sorry for your loss."

Sam swallowed the lump in her throat. "Most people would doubt the recall of a traumatized nine-year-old, but I saw what I saw. A friend identified him as a man named Quinn. Who I later learned worked as a hitman."

Foster blinked.

"What I don't know," Sam continued, "is why a hitman was at my brother's wedding. Or whether that hitman became Sean Parker, U.S. Senator. Or what I want to do about any of it. He's nothing to me."

"But you're someone to him, Sam. He's under the impression you're his daughter."

* * *

Sam relayed the information to Terry when he returned later that day.

"He's what?" Terry yelled loudly enough that an orderly stuck his head into Sam's hospital room.

"Everything all right in here?" he asked.

"Yes, sorry. Just reacting to some disturbing news."

"There's a lot of that going around," the young man said and closed the door.

"I know it sounds a little crazy," Sam admitted.

"It's not true, Sam. Maybe none of what the smooth-talking mob lawyer shared with Suzanne is true."

"The story explains a lot, Terry," Sam insisted. "Quinn could have been groomed by senior members of the Patriarca clan after he was adopted by the Parkers. They might have killed his fiancée because she didn't approve of his associates. She might not have known what he did in his off hours, but the family was afraid she might find out."

"Shades of every mob movie ever," Terry grumbled.

"It's how the mob operated back then. Nowadays, they'd probably do something more subtle, like plant stories about a senator's double life. Especially if that senator were targeting them publicly."

Terry considered her response. "I'll allow the possibility that the people behind Parker's rise may have been involved in his lover's death. I can see how he might have waited to take his revenge until he had his own kind of power. But baby snatching? I don't know. Besides, didn't Kingsley say the unborn baby died with her mother?"

"He did. But you know as well as I do that belief creates its own reality. Parker may have survived his loss only by believing he had something to live for, his daughter."

"Was he at the wedding because of you?"

"I can't be sure. My father ran a successful construction company. That kind of business used to be catnip to organized crime. He rebuffed their approaches, but they always came back. Maybe Quinn was sent to intimidate my father by hanging around the neighborhood and showing up at the wedding. Then he saw the green-eyed girl who would have been his daughter's age, a girl he couldn't find for twenty-five years until—" She stopped herself. "I'm speculating."

Terry offered a wan smile. "It's what good detectives do."

"Good detectives go where the evidence leads them. I don't have any."

"You have several credible witnesses who can corroborate parts of the story. That's enough for me." Terry bounced to his feet. "I need to make some calls. I can't have you in any more danger." He fished his phone out of his pocket.

Sam laid a hand on his arm. "Suzanne doesn't think Parker is going to be a threat."

"She's wrong. Parker is a predator."

"She said you'd say that."

"Oh really? What else did she say?"

"That predators can also be prey."

Chapter 61

Sam left the hospital a few days later, glad to be back on the Eastern Shore. More room, more friends in the area to look in on her while she recovered, and less of a press presence. An entire sheriff's department to run interference. A nurse twenty-four-seven for the first two weeks. Terry every weekend. Even a dog walker, courtesy of Pat McCready, who seemed to either know or be related to everyone in Easton.

She had a couple of debriefing sessions with Terry's boss and someone from DOJ. That wrapped up the case of the killer known as the Judge.

She still felt exposed, vulnerable. She flashed back to standing high above the ground with a rope around her neck. Sam was experiencing survivor's guilt. She was temporarily dependent on others for virtually everything. She was lonely. Both her therapist and her doctor assured her such feelings were normal.

Sean Parker vanished not long after Sam's release.

Simultaneously, Terry reported that DOJ's Public Integrity Section was conducting an investigation into the senator at the request of several fellow members of the Homeland Security Subcommittee.

"They claim to have received credible information that Parker was working with foreign assets in a way that might enrich him and undermine government functions. These days, that's usually code for 'Moscow.'"

"I wonder where the subcommittee got its information," Sam remarked.

"My contact at DOJ wouldn't say, but I have my suspicions." He reached across the table and took her hand. "This is good news, Tate."

"It is, Terry."

Over the next six weeks, the media remained occupied with the story of the missing senator. DOJ continued to put together its case. Members of Congress and even Parker's staff were heard to suggest the Maryland governor might need to appoint someone to fill the seat. Politics as usual.

Sam ignored the news and kept her focus on her rehabilitation. She'd broken several bones but she was strong and dedicated to her exercise. As her doctor told her, "Breaks will heal in someone of your age and stamina." The encouragement drove her forward but doubts persisted. She felt depleted at times, discouraged, and as physically fragile as she'd ever felt.

Six weeks out, she started to believe the doctor.

"How are you feeling?" Terry asked one night after the dinner Sam had prepared and proudly served.

"Better every day," she assured him. "Especially now that I can drive. I felt a little like I was under house arrest."

"As I recall, you suffered a couple of major traumas."

"All of which were resolved. And broken bones heal."

"Don't oversell it, Tate. I'll think you don't need me."

She touched his cheek. "Never in a million years. But you have to start taking care of yourself, okay? I worry. If you need to stay in the city, I'll be okay. I'll hate it, but I'll survive."

He put his arm around her. "We can do better than that."

Jax, ever alert for an opportunity to snuggle, bounced up from his bed and pushed his nose between them.

"Way to break in on a moment," Terry scolded, though he favored the dog with an ear scratch.

"Are we having a moment?" Sam asked. "I thought we were discussing my recovery."

"We were. We are. At the same time ..." He coughed.

"Terry?"

He brought his left hand up to reveal a small container he held just beyond her reach.

"First, a few words. You don't get to turn down what's in this box, Sam. Not just because it has a history in my family. Not because I love you, deeply and completely. Not because I think we make a great team in every way possible. Not even because I almost lost you. Because of all those things and more I'd share. Unfortunately, my mind is fogged by more panic than I ever felt facing the barrel of a gun or a congressional committee."

Jax was sitting on his haunches, eyes on the elevated box, tail wagging furiously.

"He thinks it's a treat," Sam said. She felt light, almost as if she floated outside herself. Was she dying? Having a panic attack? She ran a quick wellness check. No gut clutch, no headache or heaviness, only a sense that somehow by some miracle, she'd ended up in the right place at the right time.

Terry still held his hand in the air. Sam reached up and tugged his sleeve. "Hand it over, buddy," she whispered. "Whatever you have for me is what I want."

The small box held a ring whose unique qualities were immediately apparent. While Sam gaped at the piece, Terry shared details he'd taken the time to memorize.

"This was my great-grandmother's engagement ring; she designed it herself. Very cutting edge for the time. The emerald is 1.5 carats in a bezel set into a platinum band. My mom told me her Grandma Dot was fond of green. Dottie was also tall, self-reliant, and fond of outdoor activities. Not a ruffles and pearls kind of woman." He smiled at the recollection.

He nudged Sam, who remained fixated on the shiny object.

"Would you stop your ogling and try it on? I need to make sure it fits. It's not like I had your size handy."

She slipped the ring on her left hand and held it out. "It fits," she marveled.

"It does. And it matches your eyes perfectly. Which may be why my mother told me it would be perfect for you when she gave it to me four years ago."

Sam gaped at him. "You've had this for four years?"

Terry grinned. "I wanted to choose the right moment. How'd I do?"

She laughed, as full and as loud as she had in weeks. "So much better than a crowded restaurant or a hospital bed. But isn't there a question involved?"

Terry looked momentarily nonplussed. "I thought when you put on the ring ..." He snorted. "Oh, I get it." He slid off the couch onto the floor.

Sam sat up and so did Jax as Terry put his hand on hers.

"Sam Tate aka Sophia Russo aka the serial-killer-catching queen, will you marry me?"

"I absolutely will," Sam declared. She reached down to pull him to her, but the twinge in her shoulder stopped her.

"So much for grand gestures," she laughed.

"Maybe we can stick to small gestures." Terry came back to sit on the sofa. "How about we go to bed?"

"It's still early and I'm not sleepy."

"We won't be sleeping," Terry said. "We'll be celebrating. If you're up for it."

"I'm always up for a little partying."

Chapter 62

Sam's first engagement had been an understated affair by design. For one thing, she had nine months left on her tour of duty. For another, she still struggled with the idea of attracting too much attention, or maybe it was too much happiness. Which turned out to be prescient, as Jay died in a single-car accident before they'd even considered the specifics of where, when, and how they'd be married.

She'd long assumed that if the opportunity ever came around again, it would stay low-key, to the point of foregoing an announcement. Terry had no problem with that idea. The couple's colleagues, relatives, and friends had other ideas. Even the normally taciturn Dakota Williams latched on to the idea of a celebration.

"It's your first wedding, Tate," she said on a spring afternoon in early April. "It's a big deal." They sat in a shaft of sunlight at a trendy café near the FBI headquarters in downtown D.C. Black coffee, infinitely superior to what the Bureau served, and a piece of to-die-for apple pie they agreed to split.

"What if I don't want it to be a big deal?" Sam asked.

"That ship has sailed," Williams laughed. "You stopped the bad guy. Another bad guy in a series of them. You're a freaking hero, lady. You think that went away just because you had some broken bones? Nope. And let's not forget your hunky fiancé. Respected, admired, and climbing the career ladder. You are on track to become D.C.'s favorite newlyweds and that's saying something in this jaded town."

Sam put down her fork, her appetite stifled by a gut feeling that had nothing to do with instinct.

"It's a lot to handle, Dakota."

Her friend considered the observation. "Yeah, maybe. And I know you well enough to know you haven't wrestled all your demons to the ground. Here's the thing, though. You have more control than you think. Sure, you have people to placate, or Terry does. That doesn't mean you have to invite them to your celebration. Assistant Director Sloan can always explain he has to defer to the bride-to-be."

"Oh, stop!" Sam laughed. "That is so not me."

"No, but it might just fly. Seriously, though, here's my advice. Hire someone in public relations. Wait, hear me out. Isn't that what your friend Suzanne suggested last winter? Didn't she help you find someone who kept everyone out of your hair? By the way, I still think she's ex-CIA. I'm just waiting for you to confirm it."

Williams tossed her shimmering ebony hair behind her. Sam caught the covetous glances that came their way from both men and women. It was like drinking coffee with a super-model. One with a gun and a badge.

"Dakota, we don't talk about her past career, honestly."

"I don't believe you. But we're getting off-topic. Someone as well-known as you are needs someone else to manage public expectations, play up the happy ending while not promising a spectacle."

"No."

"Fine. You can have a tiny wedding. Don't elope, though. The public needs a little visual candy. Here comes the hero bride and all that. I, for one, want to see you in a wedding dress. Betcha Terry does, too."

This is what friends do, Sam reminded herself. They listen. They understand. They help you steer the boat. She felt a bubble of joy push away her doubts.

"You like my ideas, I can tell," Williams said.

"You sound like a PR flack."

"I'm not volunteering for the job," Williams assured her.

"Will I need a wedding planner?"

"Depends. If you keep it small, no. Ask your friends for help. Someone can be in charge of printing the invites, a service can mail them out. Someone else can field recommendations for venues. You and Terry can sample the cake. Your friends can sample the wine." She gave her familiar wink.

"Bridesmaids? Bachelorette parties?"

"Unnecessary. Your colleagues at work will throw you a party. Besides, how many girlfriends do you have?"

"Um, two? No, wait, three."

"Yeah, no. Besides, those kinds of parties are for kids, not people in their forties."

Sam crossed her arms and stuck out her lower lip. "Now you've hurt my feelings. You know my birthday is still five months away. And I'm getting married just before then." She peered at Williams. "You're awfully excited about all this for a hard-bitten, no-nonsense FBI agent."

"Living vicariously," Williams admitted.

"What's going on with Fuentes? I thought I saw sparks fly a while back."

"Cut it out, Tate," Williams protested. "He's my damned partner." Her suddenly rosy hue suggested more. She covered her embarrassment by looking at her watch. "I gotta get back to the salt mines. To be continued."

They paid the check and walked out into the bright sunshine. "Given any thought to the dress?" Williams queried.

Sam grinned. "I have. Someone I know back in Tennessee runs a store filled with beautiful vintage wedding dresses. And she ships anywhere in the world."

Chapter 63

"Senator Parker is still missing?" Dr. Putnam asked.

The therapist and her patient sat opposite each other in Putnam's Georgetown brownstone. Sam was pretending a calm she didn't feel. She noticed she was clenching the armrests on the doctor's nice leather chair and pulled her hands together in her lap.

"It depends on who you ask," she told Putnam. "As I mentioned to you, I received a watch in the mail last month, a Rolex. Parker's name was inscribed on it. The box included a note that read: 'It's done. 'No signature, no return address. Terry turned all of it over to DOJ. I guess I should be glad I didn't receive his liver or something." She rolled her eyes.

"You believe he's dead."

"I do. I think he was murdered by his former employers and they wanted me to know. Of course, no one can prove he's dead let alone who might have killed him. That means Sean Parker is officially missing for another six years and eight months, after which his estate can declare him legally dead."

"How does this make you feel?"

"What am I supposed to feel?"

"Given your complicated relationship with the senator—"

"I didn't have a relationship," Sam protested.

"No, but that's something you only recently discovered after several years of believing otherwise. And even though he wasn't a blood relative, you've had to process the disappearance of a man who held the key to your past. You must have a lot of questions, even if his fate isn't one of them."

"I did," Sam admitted. "Okay, I still do. But I doubt Sean Parker would have given me straight answers."

"You may never know what happened at your brother's wedding."

"I know as much as I ever did. The rest is history."

"It's your history, Sam."

"I realize that, but I'm learning to look ahead."

"Good. I hope this will relieve some of the pressure you've experienced."

"If only. I still have nightmares."

Putnam leaned over and patted Sam's arm. "That's to be expected. Six months ago, you almost died. A recipe for PTSD, even for someone who has faced plenty of danger. Then you found out the man you assumed was your relative was not, in fact, your relative but was a killer in a former life. A killer who convinced himself you were his long-lost daughter."

"The soap opera that is the life of Sam Tate."

"Let's not forget that while your wedding is a happier occasion, it represents a major upheaval that carries its own level of stress."

"Yeah, but it's good stress."

"I'm glad to hear it. Let's talk about that. You're planning to be married in the fall?"

"Mid-September. Terry is friends with a federal judge who's offered to both officiate and lend us the use of his beautiful home in Fairfax, Virginia. It's a big house with plenty of land. We're expecting maybe seventy-five people, we don't need a larger venue, which is such a relief. You're invited, which shouldn't be an issue since you're an old friend of Terry's, right? God, I'm yammering." Sam put a hand to her forehead.

"You're nervous, which is completely understandable."

"I am and I'm not," Sam admitted. "I mean, on one hand, it's Terry. On the other hand, it's me. And a wedding." She laughed. "I guess that's three hands."

"We can safely assume that Terry knows what he's getting into. As for the wedding, you have plenty of negative associations with the whole idea of marriage planning. You also have a chance to change that."

"True."

"It's to be expected," Putnam reassured her patient. "We can work to minimize the effects of so much upheaval. Speaking of which, are you house shopping?"

Sam smacked her head. "House shopping, not to mention cohabitation. The list of stressors is suddenly looking longer. At least we're not looking until a few months after the wedding, closer to when the new FBI campus opens and Terry moves over there. For now, I'm keeping my place in Easton. Seems like my relationship with Terry will continue as it is for a little while longer."

Putnam cocked her head. "Do you believe that? Or should I ask, do you want that?"

"I'm ready for change, Doctor. Truly I am. And this will be different from the other changes I've made. I'm not trying to escape anything. I'm not reluctantly returning to something. This is my choice."

"And you're not alone this time."

"No. I'm not alone."

They both smiled.

Chapter 64

The penultimate day of August promised to be as beastly as the rest of the month had been. Temperatures in D.C. were at ninety by 10 am, accompanied by suffocating humidity. Poor Terry was one of the few people working in the office. Sam pitied him.

They'd rented a dog-friendly cottage in St. Michaels over Labor Day weekend. Slightly lower temperatures and the twin benefits of bay and breezes.

The wedding was in just over three weeks. Terry suggested they should have planned for a pool party. "I don't suppose I can locate a sleeveless tuxedo anywhere," he jested.

"We could elope," she suggested.

"Not a chance. I need to see you in the gown Hattie says makes you look like Betty Grable. Or is it Myrna Loy?"

Hattie McCoy was the owner of a world-renowned bridal shop in Livingston, Tennessee. Her knowledge of vintage dresses had led then-Sheriff Sam Tate to the serial killer known as The Wedding Crasher. The day they met at the store, Hattie picked out a cream-colored forties-style dress. It was a white satin strapless gown, almost slinky, and it was breathtaking. So certain was she about her selection, Hattie put the dress "on hold" for five years, trusting Sam would need it someday.

"You could come out tonight and work from my house tomorrow," she told Terry. "Still hot here, but more bearable than downtown."

Terry arrived in time for a late dinner and a peaceful sleep.

Work was uneventful, although Sam predicted a spike in crime over the Labor Day Weekend. A third of the department was off this week and others planned to grab their vacations following the holiday, at least those whose children weren't starting school. Sam wondered if she'd ever fit into that latter category.

Let's find out what kind of wife you make before considering motherhood, she chided herself.

Gordy and his sister invited her out to lunch at 3rd & Ferry Fish Market, one of her favorite spots. "What's the occasion?" she asked as she debated whether to have the lobster roll or the crab cakes.

"We figured you're going to be pretty crazy the next couple of weeks," Gordy explained. "Once everyone gets back from vacation, the office will throw a proper party for you."

"God, I hope not," Sam laughed.

"Count on it," Carol Davidson said. "Anyway, we're not taking you out to lunch to celebrate your wedding. This is more like an early birthday lunch."

"Hey, I've got another month before I turn forty, people."

"You might need prep time," Gordy cracked. Davidson guffawed and Sam joined in.

The rest of the afternoon passed without incident. Sam got home at 5, giving thanks to both the light at the end of the day and the air conditioning inside the little house she called home.

Jax was waiting at the front door, as frantic as she'd ever seen him.

"Hey, buddy, did Daddy forget to take you out? Come on, then." She waved at the door. Jax ran outside, relieved himself, and came right back in, still agitated.

"Hungry, maybe?" she asked. "Okay. Let me say hello to our guy. Then we'll get you a treat."

Sam started down the hallway. Jax bounded ahead of her, whining. When she stopped to look into the den (empty, although the computer was open), he barked.

"What is with you?" she demanded. Abruptly, she froze, every sense on high alert. She backtracked to the den and opened the small safe that held her gun. She held a finger to her lips and whispered to the dog, "Show me."

Jax headed past the kitchen and the small sitting room to the sunroom. Sam had the porch enclosed and insulated when she first moved in. She had full-length windows installed with a view of the protected woodlands behind them. Terry enjoyed the room, and so did she. She loved everything about the house, from its updated kitchen to its old-fashioned façade. The first house she'd ever owned, it was small without being claustrophobic, secluded without being isolated. She could walk into town, about a mile away.

Terry sat in the old tweed recliner he preferred for reading or thinking. He must have heard her come in and noticed Jax's nervous bark. Yet he didn't turn around or say anything.

He's probably wearing his earbuds, she reassured herself.

She swung her weapon in a careful arc, her gaze sweeping the area, anticipating an ambush. She stopped and listened for the telltale squeak of a floorboard or a light footfall that she might hear. Nothing.

Still, she stood rooted in place, as if she could freeze this moment, preserve it as a memory of returning home after work to her faithful dog and her loving soon-to-be husband.

Jax nudged Terry with his nose, then backed away with a whine. Sam moved as if by rote, her approach born of experience and instinctive caution. She eased her way towards the chair, scanning for wires from an explosive device or bindings that might prevent movement or suggest captivity. She saw nothing.

"Terry," she said, her voice still low. "Honey?"

She clicked the safety on her gun, set it down on the table, and came around to squat in front of him.

He was tilted ever so slightly to one side, she now realized. His book was on the floor, next to his cell phone, which was open to the touch-tone pad. His left hand was clenched across his abdomen as if his stomach hurt. No blood, no visible wounds or marks, no signs of a struggle or evidence of poison that she could spot.

Sam forced herself to look him in the face. His eyes were open wide, almost as if in surprise. A thin milky film had begun to form over the corneas, dimming the vibrant amber to a muddy brown. She reached up for the pulse she knew she wouldn't find. She rested her hand on his cheek, which felt both cool and hard, like a stone carving. Rigor mortis began in the face, which meant he'd been gone for perhaps two hours.

Gone. Dead. Finished. She sat back on her haunches as the reality of his passing sank in. The pain began as a trickle and quickly transformed into a flood. For a moment, she thought about letting it wash her away.

Jax knew she'd just verified his worst fears. He issued a sound somewhere between his canine whine and an almost-human lament. She joined him, her keening intertwined with his caterwauling. The outpouring lasted a minute, maybe two, before she pushed her despair behind a temporary wall. She couldn't know how long the dam would hold, only that it had to for now.

The dog quieted and laid his head on her shoulder. She buried her face in his soft fur. "It's okay, boy," she said. "We're okay."

A necessary fiction she might have to maintain even though she knew better.

Chapter 65

"An aneurysm," Stein said. "Man, that's so random. At least he wasn't murdered." He reached for a canapé from a passing server.

Williams frowned. "Is that your takeaway, Rob? Dead is dead in case you haven't noticed." She tugged at her sleeveless black dress. "It's too hot for mid-September," she complained.

"You do know summer in D.C. now stretches into October," Fuentes replied. "Anyway, if they had to hold a memorial service anywhere, better out here in the country than in some old building with questionable air conditioning."

"It was nice of the judge to volunteer his house for the service instead of the wedding," Kinney said.

" It's a little scary," Stein continued. "To think that something like that could happen to a man in his early forties."

Molly Kinney put a hand up. "Can we not dwell on how Terry died? I'd rather think about all he did in his life."

"Sorry."

"Forget it." Fuentes clapped a hand on the analyst's shoulder. "It's a tough day."

"I think I'll go see how Sam is doing," Williams said. She walked away from the small table.

"Is she okay?" Stein asked.

"Are any of us?" Fuentes responded.

* * *

Between greeting and thanking well-wishers and supporting Terry's mother, Sam stayed busy. Fortunately, Helen Sloan had her new beau and a niece and nephew, each of whom brought a spouse. Their stories of childhood, of Terry's dedication to baseball and his willingness to make mischief, eased the weight of the ceremony.

Sam had her own support system. Her three loyal friends and colleagues came in from Easton. Her mother's cousin Karen flew down from Boston. Her friend from cybersecurity, Paula Norris. Williams and the other team members. Even her Aunt Rosa, too ill to travel, sent a beautiful note, along with a homemade apple cake.

Most of the guests were unfamiliar to Sam. She would have been lost without Millie Jefferson by her side to help with what the senior administrative assistant called, "the Washington meet-and-greet." Jefferson had been with the Bureau for twenty-five years. She seemed to know everyone.

Suzanne Foster was also on hand to make a few introductions, "although Millie has you well in hand," she told Sam. "My connections tend to be political."

At one point, Joanne Putnam, looking elegant in a two-piece black dress, came over.

"How are you doing?" the therapist asked Sam.

"Coping, all things considered." Sam looked into the warm brown eyes of the kind and thoroughly professional doctor who'd known Terry longer than Sam. "How are you?"

"Thank you for asking. It's a sad day. You have my number. Know that I will answer a call from you day or night."

Lena Small flew up from Atlanta. Although they'd never met in person, she greeted Sam like an old friend. They hit it off immediately. No surprise, given they were connected by a man they both knew and loved.

Small was one of several people who shared recollections at the outdoor service. Sam declined to speak. How could she deliver a eulogy when she should be exchanging her wedding vows? How could she even stand in front of a group of people in a scene reminiscent of a happier day that quickly turned tragic? If she tried to say anything, her accumulated grief would crash down on her like a great wave. She felt safer, if not better, in the back, flanked by friends.

Several hours in, Sam began to crash. She felt drained, as if she'd exerted herself physically as well as mentally. All she wanted to do was drive back to her house and lie down with Jax right next to her on the bed.

Gordy, who'd been hovering discreetly all afternoon, drove her back home. Williams offered to come and stay with her.

"I appreciate it, Dakota, I really do. I think I'm just going to get some rest."

Sam didn't say she was going to sleep because she knew she wouldn't. She pulled on sleeping shorts and a tank top, got into bed, and began to scribble in her notebook. Only once did she stop to think about the people who cared so much about her. She gripped her pen tightly and willed herself not to feel anything at all.

Epilogue

Every day she stepped out the front door of her small home, coffee in hand and two dogs at her heels. The animals would take off to relieve themselves in the grass. Then they'd explore "the meadow," a two-acre expanse she kept neat but not manicured.

She savored these moments before work. Perched on the massive uplift known as the Uncompahgre Plateau, she enjoyed the gift of clean air and magnificent vistas afforded by the Rocky Mountains. Cimarron Range lay straight ahead. Ninety degrees to her right, she could glimpse Mount Sneffels, one of the most photographed mountains in the state.

Six miles and 1000 feet down a winding mountain road sat the municipality of Ridgeway, population just shy of 2,000. The town boasted just one traffic light (the only one in Ouray County) and one doctor, but also about a dozen places to eat. Ridgeway was also home to a lively arts community.

Up in Loghill Village, where she'd located, life was insular in the ways that only money could buy. Construction never ceased, it seemed. The wild animals who lived there—the deer, bear, bobcats, wild turkeys, elk, and fox—were expected to share the wilderness with the intruders who would eventually replace them.

For now, the "village" was a nothing but a census-designated area containing a resort, a golf club, a dude ranch, and a few homes scattered here and there, all separated by plenty of land. People were friendly for the most part, but not nosey. That suited her.

She'd made a few acquaintances in town through one couple who, after a time, she came to think of as friends. Barry and Eve March lived one homestead over in a house he designed to take full advantage of the beauty that surrounded them. Unpretentious, intelligent, and talented, they shared a sensibility with the creative types in the town. She felt lucky to know them, especially since they got her through the first, unexpectedly rough winter.

They had dinner together several times a month, always at the March place. In the presence of their regal but aloof cat, they ate, drank, and laughed. The couple kept her up to date on the doings of the residents in the area. She entertained them with carefully culled stories from her past.

If they noticed she kept a part of herself walled off, they never let on. If they worried that she didn't appear to have any friends, they kept that to themselves. And if they wondered why a single, middle-aged woman would live up the mountain, they never asked her. She heard them speculating in the kitchen after dinner one night. Either an abusive relationship or a failed romance, they agreed. Nothing criminal, just heartbreaking.

She spent her first year healing herself mentally, physically, and emotionally. She adopted a young dog as a companion for her older one and saw how much less anxious he became. Seeing them play together lifted her spirits. Though she tried not to second-guess her decision to move, she had days when her spirits nevertheless needed lifting.

* * *

The temporary position in the Marshal's office interested her. Not because she needed the money, but because she needed to occupy herself after twelve months of so much self-care.

The job was for a deputy marshal to cover the late evening/early morning hours, which meant covering the phones, responding to the occasional drunk and disorderly or the rare break-in. Some foot patrols. Lots of quiet.

The inevitable background check raised an issue for her. She didn't have anything to hide, just a desire to remain hidden. Still, her curiosity drew her to visit the low-slung building that housed the small department. She pretended to inquire about the job for a friend. Marshal Wayland Colt, a seasoned cop with white hair and shrewd eyes, pretended to believe her.

"Does your friend have any law enforcement training or experience? That's a requirement. Not that there's much to the job at night. On the other hand, crimes do happen under cover of dark."

"That's fine."

Colt looked her over. "You sure you're not looking for yourself?"

"Me?" She made a dismissive sound. "I don't qualify."

"That so? You seem like someone who's worn a uniform. Ever serve in the military?"

"I'm not a candidate, Marshal."

"Damn shame." Colt squinted at her. "Something about you is awfully familiar."

Her hand went to the messy bun at the back of her head. She'd cut her hair and nature had added a sprinkling of silver. The lightly-tinted glasses weren't necessary but served as a kind of shield. "I guess I look like everyone else," she said.

"You don't look like anyone else," he came back. "Except maybe one person. Or her close relative."

She stood abruptly. "I've taken up enough of your time. Thanks for seeing me."

"Hold on, now." Colt rose, held out a piece of paper. "Why don't you take this application? Fill it out and drop it back here. Or use the online version. Since it's a temporary position, any background check is at the discretion of this office."

She took the form. An understanding passed between them.

"Let me know what your friend decides," he told her, his eyes twinkling.

Two weeks later, she was a deputy marshal working at the Ridgeway Marshal's Office.

* * *

The call came in at 9:15 pm. A disturbance at Steps Tavern and could she come over to help a couple of visitors in distress?

In the two years since she'd become a deputy marshal, she'd experienced a handful of calls, most of them related to domestics or break-ins. Some street-side drunken rowdiness, owing to bored young people for whom the outdoor magnificence wasn't enough.

She'd never been summoned to a bar, mainly because only Steps stayed open late. The bartender kept a rifle behind the bar and most of the regulars carried.

Anyone who brought a bad attitude into the bar could expect a bad reception. No one ever had.

She arrived on foot to find the music cranked, the clientele loud. No angry voices, no sounds of an altercation. More like whooping and hollering, accompanied by rolling laughter.

She pushed open the door and slid in. The bartender had joined a tightly-packed group. A fight, then, although maybe finished. No signs of danger, more like a sports event.

"Ridgeway Marshal's Office," she called out. "Please move aside."

Three men down, losers in a recent brawl. One cradled his arm. Another held a napkin to his bloody nose. A third rubbed the back of his head.

Two attractive women about thirty years apart in age stood over the men. They were dressed in shirts, jeans, boots, and canvas jackets. The taller brunette woman, mid-thirties, held a scrawny biker in one hand and a badge in her other. The smaller blond woman pointed an efficient-looking SIG at two burly men zip-tied to the bar.

"Thanks for coming, Deputy Marshal," the younger woman grinned. "Sorry for the dust-up. These gentlemen wouldn't take no for an answer."

"It's true," Dooby, the bartender, chimed in. "We all asked them to stop bothering the women, but they wouldn't listen. They got handsy and that was that." A chorus of assenting voices backed him up. "I tell you, if these gals ever want work as bouncers, they're hired."

"They're not paying for their drinks, that's for sure," declared a patron to a chorus of cheers.

Sam struggled to find her voice, dumbfounded. "Do either of you want to press charges?" she managed to ask.

"I think we're done here," said the older woman. "We'll leave it to you to handle these men however you see fit."

"Cut 'em loose with a warning, Dooby," she told the bartender. "Ladies, a word?"

The three women exited the bar and walked half a block before the deputy marshal whirled on her companions. "What the fuck are you two doing here? How the hell did you find me? And how do you even know each other?"

"First of all, hello to you, too," FBI agent Dakota Williams laughed. "Second, we had business in Denver. Third, how do you think we found you? We're investigators. And lastly, we bonded over your absence." Williams was no longer smiling.

"Hello, Sam," Suzanne Foster said. "May I call you Sam? Or do you prefer the name you're currently using, Ann Murphy? It doesn't really suit you, by the way, but it's close enough that you might remember to respond."

Sam kept quiet.

"Never mind. I get it. You didn't want to be found. We followed Dr. Putnam's advice and respected your space."

"Jesus, you talked with my shrink?"

"Who shared only that you were alive," Foster replied.

"Something we all needed to know," Williams added.

"All?"

"Yes, all," Foster said. "Your closest friends in Easton. Your aunt and your cousin. One or two colleagues in Manhattan and in Pickett County. The people who care about you, Sam. The people who've been grieving your absence."

For a moment, Sam allowed herself to acknowledge the regret she'd repressed. "I'm sorry I hurt anyone," she said. "And I'm glad Putnam let you know I was okay." More or less, she thought and suddenly felt defensive. "Are you here to check up on me?" she demanded.

"Actually, Sam, I'm here to make you an offer. First, though, Agent Williams has her own news."

"I'm going to be the new SSA for the Denver office," Williams blurted out. "I seem to check a couple of boxes for the Bureau and the job does that for me. I'll be out of Washington and closer to my aunt. If an office ever opens in Montana, I could be in line to run it."

"Wow. That's amazing. Congratulations, Dakota." She hugged the woman.

"Much better," Foster said.

"And you, Suzanne?" Sam asked. "Not retired?"

"Heavens, no. My son and I sold the firm for scads of money. He now happily works from home and co-parents. I'm starting a new venture out of Denver. Better climate, lower taxes, central location and all that."

"Sounds interesting. Look, I need to get back to the office," Sam said.

"You're not the least bit curious?" Williams asked.

Sam looked at her watch. "I've got two minutes."

"A firm, name to be determined," Foster began. "Two distinct missions. The corporate side will provide information, intelligence, risk-management, investigative, and cyber skills to a select group of high-asset non-criminal clients around the world. Income from that work —and it promises to be sizable—will fund the other side, which will focus on social justice issues and serve people who can't pay and won't need to."

"Sounds ambitious," Sam remarked.

"Not with the right connections, the right backing, and the right people. I have the first two. You could help me with the third."

"You want me to work for you?"

Foster touched Sam's arm. "Not for me, with me. I've been thinking about this for more than three years. You have a skill set and yes, you have name recognition which could be put to good use, especially for the philanthropic work. I can promise it won't be a desk job, not for you. Denver is larger than Ridgeway, but there are nice places just outside the city with a view to the mountains. And it's a very dog-friendly environment."

"A new beginning, Sam," Williams said. "With two friends already in place."

Sam stood on a street in Ridgeway, Colorado and marveled that two old friends had just suggested to her a future she'd never imagined possible. Her mind warned against opening herself up even a little. Possibility could bring pain, hope could open the way to sorrow.

She wrestled her emotions back into their cage and cleared her throat.

"I need to think about this."

"Take your time," Foster said, handing her a card with her name and number. "Goodbye, Sam." She and Williams walked on.

Sam stood where she was and let a decade's worth of living play out in about ten seconds. Then she called out to the retreating figures, "You weren't going to call it 'Foster and Tate,' were you?"

The two women slowed, then stopped. Foster turned. A small smile played across her face.

"I'm open to suggestions," she said.

—END—

From the Author

Thanks for reading *Judge Not*. I hope you'll take a moment to leave a review on Amazon, Goodreads, or any other social media you frequent. That way, I can connect to even more readers who are looking for books like mine.

This book is the fourth in the Sam Tate mystery series. It has been a joy to create, not only as a distinct stand-alone story but also as a part of a continuing narrative. Where we go from here is anyone's guess.

You can learn more about my various books and read posts and essays I've composed over the years at nikkistern.com. Type the address or scan the QR code.

I'm still on Facebook and Instagram, the last as @realnikkistern. I'm contemplating TikTok. I can always lead with my cute dog.

Also by Nikki Stern

Because I Say So
Hope in Small Doses
The Former Assassin
The Wedding Crasher
Bird in Hand
Freeze Before Burning